The MAID'S WAR

A KINGFOUNTAIN PREQUEL

BOOKS BY JEFF WHEELER

The Kingfountain Series

The Maid's War
The Queen's Poisoner
The Thief's Daughter
The King's Traitor
The Hollow Crown

The Covenant of Muirwood Trilogy

The Banished of Muirwood
The Ciphers of Muirwood
The Void of Muirwood

The Legends of Muirwood Trilogy

The Wretched of Muirwood
The Blight of Muirwood
The Scourge of Muirwood

Whispers from Mirrowen Trilogy

Fireblood
Dryad-Born
Poisonwell

Landmoor Series

Landmoor
Silverkin

The MAID'S WAR

A KINGFOUNTAIN PREQUEL

JEFF WHEELER

AMBERLIN

Text copyright © 2016 Jeff Wheeler

Published by Amberlin

ISBN-13: 978-1537798004

ISBN-10: 1537798006

Cover design by Shasti O'Leary-Soudant

Interior design by Steve R. Yeager

Printed in the United States of America

To Scott & Sierra

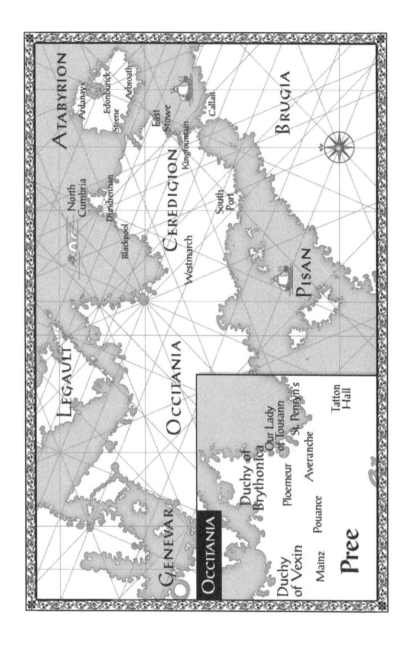

CHARACTERS

MONARCHIES

Ceredigion: Eredur (House of Argentine): after a brutal civil war, led by his father, resulted in his father's death and his family's exile to Brugia, Eredur wrested control of Ceredigion from King Henricus. Now in possession of the hollow crown, Eredur has consolidated his power and joined forces with Brugia to wage war on the King of Occitania, seeking to reclaim lands forfeited generations before. Eredur's banner, the Sun and Rose, has been unfurled, and the invasion of Occitania has begun.

Occitania: Lewis XI (House of Vertus): Lewis, known as the Spider King for his cunning, wants nothing more than to prevent another disastrous defeat such as the one his grandfather's army suffered at the Battle of Azinkeep a generation before. Lewis is the son of Chatriyon, who was the prince who defied Ceredigion and, with the help of the famous Maid of Donremy, secured his right to rule Occitania despite overwhelming odds. Lewis would rather bribe his way out of a conflict with his powerful neighbor than take the field against him.

Brugia: Philip (House of Temaire): succeeded his father as King of Brugia at age twenty-three after his father was murdered, purportedly by a poisoner hired by Chatriyon Vertus, Crown Prince of Occitania. The kingdoms of Brugia and Occitania have been enemies ever since. Philip has involved Eredur in his disputes with King Lewis, and the two kingdoms have joined forces to defeat and humble their ancient enemy.

LORDS OF CEREDIGION

Severn Argentine: Duke of Glosstyr

Dunsdworth Argentine: Duke of Clare

Lord Horwath: Duke of North Cumbria

Lord Kiskaddon: Duke of Westmarch

Lord Asilomar: Duke of East Stowe

Lord Hastings: Duke of Southport, king's chancellor

♦　　♦　　♦

The tree of Argentine kings has many branches and knots, the bark scarred with many usurpations and upheavals. But there is no disagreement that one of the greatest battles ever fought, by one of the greatest kings ever crowned, was the Battle of Azinkeep. Remember the Battle of Azinkeep. The King of Ceredigion defeated twenty thousand and only lost eighty of his own men. He became the ruler of Occitania when he married the princess and her father died. One simply cannot underestimate the depth of Occitanian hatred following such a humiliating defeat. But one must understand Azinkeep to understand the loamy soil that sprouted a Fountain-blessed girl. A girl who would change history. But I get ahead of myself. This girl would never have been permitted to meet an outcast prince in his outcast court had someone important not first believed in her. Her entire history blooms into vibrant color because of one young nobleman.

—Polidoro Urbino, Historia Ceredigica

♦　　♦　　♦

CHAPTER ONE

The Queen's Poisoner

The sound of laughter, conversation, and clinking goblets drifted in from the overcrowded ballroom down the corridor. Music bubbled over the din. The celebration seemed a little too exuberant considering the kingdom was facing yet another war with Ceredigion. Ankarette Tryneowy paused before a pillar, watching the light from the torch mirrored on the polished marble floor. She'd heard a sound, the clip of a boot, and wondered if she was being followed by a drunken Occitanian lord more interested in trying to steal a kiss than in returning to the rough camp of the army hunkering around the city of Pree.

The sound of shuffled steps in heavy boots came from behind, followed by a grunt and a slurred bit of Occitanian. She paused, adjusting her skirts, and then wobbled slightly and caught her hand on the pillar, giving the impression that she'd had too much to drink. As she pressed her stomach and breathed deeply, she dug her fingers into the folds of her dress, ready to seize the dagger hidden there to defend herself.

Ankarette's delicate beauty conveyed the impression of defenselessness, but she was his majesty's poisoner, the most dangerous woman in her realm. If she hadn't been, her king would never have sent her into the heart of the enemy's capital on the eve of war to seek a man who was one of the Occitanian crown's most notorious prisoners. The army of Ceredigion was encamped several leagues away on the other side of a river—the farthest they had marched into Occitania since the invasion that had led to their stunning victory at the Battle of Azinkeep. No cities had been taken as of yet, but the threat of conflict seethed in the air like smoke. Her instincts were taut and ready for battle.

The shuffling steps halted and then she heard the unmistakable sound of a man relieving himself against a stone wall. If he was that drunk, he posed no threat to her at all. Still, she did not lower her guard until the drunken lord staggered past her, oblivious to her presence even then. She thought for a moment that it might be a ruse, that this man was one of King Lewis's poisoners, come to kill her, but the man's bleary eyes, shuffling steps, and moans indicated liver infection. He must have been a man who frequently indulged in such nocturnal pleasures. Soon he was gone, and Ankarette let out a sigh of relief.

Moments later, a little palace drudge appeared with a bucket and rags and began mopping up the mess the nobleman had left reeking against the wall. The waif was a pretty little thing, but she could be no more than eight. She should not have been kept up so late. Ankarette had observed many such drudges in the palace, lurking in the shadows to earn their bread by serving the whims of the Occitanian nobility. They were invisible to most people and treated like dogs.

Turning from the column, she approached the girl and sank down onto her knees to be at her level. The waif blinked in surprise, taking in Ankarette's rich, fashionable gown and her delicately coiffed hair.

"Shouldn't you be abed?" Ankarette asked the child in a quiet, kind voice, reaching out and brushing some of the girl's hair away from her face. Her Occitanian was fluent, but she knew the capital Pree had its own flairs. Hopefully, her accent would suffice.

The girl seemed even more surprised by the show of compassion. "No, my lady. I napped earlier, but the fête is almost finished and we'll be cleaning till dawn."

It was only just after midnight. "That's a shame," Ankarette said, patting the girl's cheek. "It must be difficult cleaning up the messes of others."

The waif sniffed and shrugged. "You have a strange accent," the girl said offhandedly, dipping a rag into the bucket.

Children always noticed things that others passed over. Ankarette had made it a rule never to underestimate their usefulness.

"I'm not from Pree," Ankarette responded vaguely. "You have a different accent in the city."

The girl nodded, accepting her explanation. Another thing Ankarette had learned about children was their natural inclination to be trusting—most of them knew nothing of spies and the machinations of court. Ankarette continued speaking with her for several moments—the girl was chatty, and Ankarette soon had her revealing helpful information. The King of Occitania had been assembling all the princes of the blood in preparation for whatever conflict was to come.

And then the waif said something that made Ankarette blink in surprise. "All the princes save La Marche. The king will keep him trapped in that awful tower."

"The Duke of La Marche is here as well?" Ankarette asked. Her heart swelled with relief that the king's Espion had been correct. She had secretly dreaded that the duke was being held deep in the hinterlands in some faraway dungeon.

The girl shrugged as she squeezed the rag into the bucket once more. The floor was polished and gleaming now. "Of course. He's the king's prisoner," she said carelessly. "He's been captive here for years. I like him. He never scolds me."

Ankarette leaned forward eagerly, showing unfeigned interest. "The real duke of La Marche?" she pressed. "The one who fought alongside the Maid of Donremy?"

The waif nodded with sudden fire and delight. The story of the Maid was renowned throughout all the kingdoms. Even though the woman who had freed Occitania from Ceredigion's hegemony had died a traitor, she was now remembered as one of the most celebrated Fountain-blessed of all. "Oh yes! He's told me stories about her."

"Has he? You are a lucky young woman."

The girl blushed. "I'm not a woman yet. I'm only eight."

"I wish I could meet him," Ankarette sighed with disappointment. "I've always been fascinated by stories about the Maid. I've even visited Donremy. She led the king's army when she was nineteen, did she not?"

The girl shook her head deliberately. "Seventeen. She was Fountain-blessed." The last words were uttered like a prayer. Only the rarest of individuals could access the enormous power of the Fountain. They were each gifted in a different miraculous way, though the magic was not simply lavished on them—they had to develop unique habits to feed their power. Ankarette herself was Fountain-blessed, though only a few knew it.

The little girl looked hesitant. "I could show you . . . I could show you to the duke's room. If you would like."

"Is he not at the fête then? Are prisoners not allowed?"

The girl shook her head dramatically. "No, they are allowed. But he hates them," she whispered. "I can show you where the king keeps him. He is allowed visitors, but no one sees him anymore."

Could Ankarette's quest to discover what had become of the Maid's famous sword be resolved so easily?

"Thank you, yes!" Ankarette said with a kindly smile. The waif led her through the mazelike corridors of the palace, and the poisoner kept pace as she memorized all the twists and turns. The din of the party fell away behind them, and soon the only sounds were their steps and the hissing of torches. Occasionally they encountered other drudges, roused from their beds to prepare to scrub the ballroom clean before dawn.

They paused at the threshold of an ancient door with ornate iron hinges. "This is the one," the girl said, pointing. Then she clung to the bucket handle with both hands. "The duke is kept up there."

"There are no guards?" Ankarette asked, wrinkling her brow.

The girl shook her head. "He's old, my lady. The king wishes him to pass away in comfort. None of the palace guards would ever let him leave."

Ankarette nodded and then squeezed her shoulder. "Thank you. I'll see him in the morning."

The girl did a brief curtsy and then carried her bucket away.

Ankarette stood by the imposing door, taking a steadying breath as she stared at the nicks and gouges in the wood.

Did she dare wake him? If King Lewis or one of his many poisoners caught her, she would be executed, but not before they attempted to extract secrets from her. Of course, she carried a quick-acting poison in a ring to prevent that from happening.

This was her chance to speak with the old duke uninterrupted. She trusted her instincts, honed from years of duplicity and cunning. If she met the Duke of La Marche, she would discern whether he was a risk to her or not. The Espion had reliable reports that his role in several attempted insurrections against the Spider King and his predecessor would have earned him a traitor's death if not for his reputation among the people. If he did end up being a threat to her, she could dose him with a poisonous powder that would render him unconscious and wipe his memory clear of her. She could use another powder to get information from him even if he was unwilling to cooperate, but that was not her first choice. Either way, she needed answers; it alarmed her that King Lewis was celebrating in his palace while her king's army was camped near a major river in Pree. Neither king was a fool. It was like a Wizr board with the opposing pieces arranged such that it was near impossible to predict the outcome of the next move.

Reaching for the handle, she found it locked. That obstacle was overcome in a moment, and she found herself facing a black stairwell. She quietly shut the door behind her and waited there, letting her eyes adjust to the darkness. There were arrow slits in the tower that let in faint starlight. Keeping her back to the wall, she slowly and silently made her way up the steps, her senses alert once again for any sound that would betray a guard.

There was a door at the top of the stairs, and a faint light emanated from beneath it. Many people slept with a candle lit, but Ankarette assumed nothing and took nothing for granted. She tried the handle and found that it opened to the touch. Prodding it with the toe of her shoe, she pushed it ajar and smelled the wax of burning candles, the leftover gravy of a partially eaten meal, and the smell of an aging man.

The Duke of La Marche was awake.

From the thin crack in the door, she saw him sitting at the window. There were only a few streaks of buttery color left in his mostly white hair. Although there was a book in his hands, he was staring out the window at the night sky, lost in thought.

Ankarette had spent many a long evening in such a pose—sitting by a window, reading books of tales from the past. This was a man who had been convicted of treason twice, only for the sentence to be commuted—both times—because he was a prince of the blood. He had lived history, and she was a bit in awe of him.

After taking a moment to gather her courage, Ankarette pushed open the door gently and then shut it behind her.

The movement caught his sharp instincts, and he was out of the window seat in a moment—book down, dagger in hand. He had the stance of a soldier. Even though he was older, he'd not let his body go to waste. So much for the old and feeble man the waif had implied she'd find.

Then his posture changed. He stared at her, his blue eyes narrowing with scrutiny. "Oh, it's you," he said with a gravelly voice.

That took Ankarette off her guard. "Were you expecting someone?" she asked, standing by the door, preparing to flee.

She did not want to fight this man. She did not want to hurt him. Her heart had the deepest reverence for people who fought with conviction and honor.

"Of course I was!" he said with a bark and a laugh. "She told me years ago you'd come. 'Gentle duke,' she said." A tingle ran down Ankarette's spine. The Maid. His voice suddenly caught with emotion. " 'One night, when you are very old and a prisoner in the palace, you will meet a woman who is a poisoner. She will not come to kill you. She will come to listen to your story. You must tell her your story, gentle duke. And you must teach her about me.' " He stared down at the knife in his hand, turning it over once before he set it down on the window seat.

Ankarette felt a throb in her heart, followed by a sudden dizziness, and then she heard it. The gentle murmuring of the Fountain. It was so subtle that even the Fountain-blessed sometimes didn't notice its influence. But Ankarette had trained herself to listen for it, to be guided by it. And she realized it had guided her to this very tower, this very night.

Her magic told her that she could trust this man. He was a traitor to his king, but only because he served a higher cause. He served the Fountain.

All of her thoughts and plans and schemes melted away. She walked up to the grizzled duke and dropped down onto one knee in reverent respect. She looked up at him. "You are Alensson, Duke of La Marche? Your father was duke before you, and his father duke before him. Your mother is Marie of Brythonica?"

The duke looked down at her. "Get up, get up! None of that, girl. I'm the duke of nothing." He chuckled sardonically, his expression darkening. "La Marche has been in the hands of Ceredigion since the Battle of Azinkeep. They call it . . .

they call it Westmarch! Ugh. I do not like that tongue. You speak ours well enough, girl. I'm impressed. Come on, I said get up!"

Ankarette rose, almost too amazed to speak. "The Maid . . . she told you I was coming?" Her heart skipped faster at the thought.

The duke nodded sagely, folding his arms. Then he stepped back and seated himself on the window seat once again. "She did, lass. That was nearly forty years ago. Before she was captured. Before she was killed." His eyes turned hard as flint as he spoke the words. Even after so many years, the wound pained him. She could see it in his flesh, his cheeks.

"And I know why you're here," the duke said softly. "You're looking for her sword. The one drawn from the fountain at St. Kathryn of Firebos."

Ankarette's heart quickened at the revelation. "Yes. I was sent by my king to find it. Or to stop Lewis from using it against him."

The duke laughed—a brittle, gritty laugh. "Lewis doesn't have it," he said contemptuously. "And neither did his father. The one who betrayed her." Anger smoldered in his eyes. "Neither do I."

Ankarette was disappointed, but she had come too far to quit so easily. "Do you know where it is? The legends say it is King Andrew's sword. Whoever wields it will rule all the kingdoms."

The duke's eyes narrowed. "And that is what your king desires? Even more power?" He shook his head disdainfully. "That is all men ever want. There is no slaking the thirst of ambition. Don't I know. Don't I know." He hung his head sorrowfully. Then he clapped his hands on his knees. "What is your name, lass?"

karette Tryneowy," the poisoner answered without hesitation.

"Before we speak of the sword, Ankarette, we must first speak of her. Everyone calls her the Maid. But she had a name. She was a girl, like you. A peasant child from the village Donremy. She told me you would come, aye, and she commanded me in the name of the Fountain to tell you her story before I died." He leaned forward, resting his chin on his fist. "Sit down, Ankarette Tryneowy. Make yourself comfortable. It is a long story. But we have all night." He leaned forward. "To understand her, you must understand why the Fountain chose her. You see, the Fountain stopped protecting Occitania because we were unfaithful to it. When I was a young cub, my father died during the Battle of Azinkeep. You know of it, of course. My father sent a knight, Boquette, to safeguard me and my mother away from La Marche. Boquette trained me in war. He taught me about honor and Virtus, and all the things a father should. He believed the Fountain would choose me to save our people. And so I came to believe it too."

CHAPTER TWO

Vernay

Wars were not decided by battlefield tactics and the valor of half-drunken terrified soldiers. They were decided by trickery and deceit. It was an audacious plan. And Alensson was convinced it would work.

"There's the city," Boquette said under his breath, his voice husky with nerves. There was a slick feeling of fear in the air, but it was tempered by the thrill of the bet, the toss of the dice, the feeling of fortune hanging in the balance. "Have you been to Vernay, lad?"

Alensson bristled at the disparagement of his youth. He was fifteen years old, newly married to his best friend, a peer of the realm who was his own age, and he was wearing armor and riding a warhorse into battle. His mother and his wife's uncle had persuaded the prince to sanction his match to the heiress of the duchy of Lionn after Alensson's wardship to her uncle had proved more than amicable. Surely he wasn't a lad any longer, yet his father's old bodyguard still treated him like one.

"Aye, when I was a boy," he answered brusquely, letting the defensiveness show in his tone.

"You've never been bloodied in battle," Boquette said with a grunt. "You're a whelp."

"I've done nothing but train in war since my father died at Azinkeep," Alensson said between his teeth. "You've seen to that. There's not a man within a hundred leagues who can beat me with a sword—yourself included, Boquette."

Boquette chuckled to himself before replying, "A training yard is one thing, son. A very different thing."

"I will take back my duchy, town by town, castle by castle," Alensson said passionately. "We start in Vernay. Then we conquer Averanche. Then drive Deford out of Tatton Hall and send him back to Kingfountain with his tail cut off!"

"I like your energy, lad. But don't count coins until they're in your purse. Deford is lord protector. You're not just facing another duke, a man of your own rank. You're facing a man who can bring the might of the army of Ceredigion down on us."

"Let him then," Alensson sneered. "We won't be defeated like my father was. The Ceredigic king died of dysentery and left a newborn to inherit two crowns. Let's wrest one of them back before the brat gets his teeth."

Boquette chuckled sardonically again. "It wasn't dysentery, lad. A poisoner got to him." His scar looked white and puckered through the thicket of his unshaven whiskers.

"You think so?" Alensson hated the slight quaver in his voice.

Boquette nodded sagely. "I heard some men whispering about it over their cups. Deford is not the same man as his brother. He wasn't even at Azinkeep. This is our chance. If this ruse works, we'll take Vernay without a fight and have a means to support ourselves." He sighed. "But if it fails, you may get a chance yet to show off your, ahem, skills."

From their vantage point, disguised as guards and riding chargers, the situation looked strange and otherworldly. Their ruse was simple. Fifty men wearing the kilts and badges of Atabyrion were seated backward on their horses, their arms tied behind their backs, the customary position for defeated foes being marched as hostages after a battle. The dozen horsemen leading the prisoners wore hastily sewn uniforms bearing the badge of Deford, three white scallops on a field of black. Some peasant girls had sewn the liveries for them, and while they wouldn't withstand close scrutiny, they were convincing from atop a city wall. The Atabyrions' language was the closest to Ceredigion's, and the soldiers had been handpicked to be their spokesmen.

A horn sounded in the distance from the city of Vernay, sending a prickle of gooseflesh down Alensson's back. He loosened his sword in its scabbard. If the city guards didn't fall for the deception, then Alensson's troops would be hit with a hail of arrows from archers on the walls. Riders would chase down all who survived.

"I hope this works," Boquette grumbled.

"It will," Alensson said under his breath. "Now lift your head like you're a proud warrior of Ceredigion."

"I hope you know what you're doing."

"I've waited nine years for this," Alensson said. He changed his posture and bearing, throwing his shoulders back. Even though he was fifteen, he was fit and had often passed for a much older man. His thoughts wandered momentarily to the tearful kiss his young wife had given him before he left her three days earlier. It was her family's fortunes that were sustaining him, since his own lands had been settled on Deford, the new duke of Westmarch. The thought of the new title made him boil with anger. These were Alensson's lands! This was his city! He was confident he'd take Vernay and Averanche. Then he would set up his bride, Jianne, in the castle there while he fought for the rest of his lands.

Alensson had started in the training yard as a lad of eight. He'd been bludgeoned with wooden swords until he was ten. His nose had been broken once and his knuckles and fingers had been hammered mercilessly until he'd wept from pain. But the pain had never made him quit, for it was never as keen as the shame he'd felt over the loss of his land and title. Some even said Alensson's relentless determination to master the arts of war was an early sign the lad was Fountain-blessed. He'd never actually heard the whispers of the Fountain, but he religiously tossed coins into the chapel fountains wherever he went and listened to the lapping of the waters, seeking a sign that he had finally been chosen. These actions did nothing to discourage the rumors. And why would he want to discourage them? He hoped it would happen to him. Besides, building a reputation took time and success. Vernay would be his first.

Be careful, my love. Be very careful.

He could see her dark hair in his mind, hair that was naturally wavy and long. Her eyes were the color of cinnamon. She was worried about him, but Alensson was confident his plan would work.

As the 'prisoners' arrived outside the main gates of Vernay, the horses grew restless. The bound men were all holding the loose ends of their ropes in their clenched fists. They each had weapons concealed and ready to use. Their armor and faces were deliberately smeared with mud to give the impression they'd recently been in a battle. Their countenances were angry and sullen.

"Oy!" shouted his captain of the guard to the soldiers assembled atop the battlement. His cry rang out in the air. Many of the soldiers atop the wall wore the livery of Ceredigion. These were Deford's men. But most wore the colors of Occitania. This was a local garrison, provided by the Count of De Paul.

"Who are you?" shouted the officer atop the wall. "I don't recognize you!"

"It's me, Sir Sallust, you idiot!" the soldier said in a patronizing tone. They had chosen to impersonate him because of the man's widespread reputation for cruelty. Sallust balked at the merest hint of defiance or disobedience, so they were less likely to question him. "Deford crushed these Atabyrion knaves in a battle yesterday. He ordered me to hold them here while he chases down the men who fled the field like cowards. Open the bloody gate!"

A cheer went up from the soldiers on the wall and Alensson licked his lips. He trembled with anticipation, anxious for the matter to be ended. Movement along the wall was followed by the groans of timber, and the gate began to swing open to permit the hostages to be brought inside. Giddy triumph swelled in his breast. It was working, by the Fountain!

As the gate lumbered open, Alensson kicked his steed's flanks to get it moving and nodded for Boquette to join him as they rode forward. The garrison cheered them on as they entered, taunting the Atabyrion prisoners with contempt and rude remarks.

"When?" Boquette hissed under his breath.

"Hold," Alensson muttered back, holding up his hand and waving to the garrison soldiers as they came in. Someone thrust a bladder of wine up at him to celebrate, but he ignored the outstretched arm. He turned in his saddle, watching the horses come in. He outnumbered the garrison considerably. The cheers of victory would melt in their throats.

He rode up to the Atabyrion man pretending to be Sir Sallust, who was turned backward in the saddle, waving in the prisoners and jeering at them as they rode past. The chain hood helped conceal his face from the bystanders. The fellow had the best accent of them all. Alensson hadn't trusted his own abilities to mimic the brogue.

"When was battle, Sir Sallust?" the garrison captain said, walking up to the Atabyrion with a pleased look. "How many fell? We had no word there was an army even close to Averanche. Was it a surprise attack?"

"Oh, it was a surprise attack," the Atabyrion responded with a chuckle.

As soon as the young duke saw the last of the soldiers enter the city, he swung off the saddle in a practiced, easy move, and the garrison captain looked at him askance, his brow suddenly furrowed, as if he knew he should recognize Alensson's face but could not quite recall it.

"It was a short battle," Alensson said. "Because it was unexpected."

"You're Occitanian!" the garrison captain said in shock.

"It's the duke!" someone blurted.

"That's not Deford!" someone else countered.

"No, it's La Marche!"

Alensson drew his sword and bowed graciously to the garrison captain. "Good morning, Captain," he said. "The rightful duke has returned to Vernay. This is my city. Be so good as to surrender it back to me."

First, the sound of ropes sloughing off, then, complete pandemonium as the Atabyrion prisoners jumped off their horses with weapons in hand, ready to completely overcome the guards within the city.

The garrison captain was brave. Foolish, but brave. Alensson could have run the captain through before the man's sword was clear of its scabbard, but his training in Virtus would not permit him to kill a defenseless man who wanted to fight him. The two men crossed blades. The garrison captain was easily double Alensson's age, with a receding hairline and a few flecks of gray in his otherwise blond goatee. His eyes were wide with horror—he'd handed his garrison over to the enemy because of a trick, and Deford would doubtless be furious and vengeful.

Alensson parried the captain's panic-impaired attempts to kill him, then kicked him hard in the stomach and knocked him down on his back. The fight was over in seconds, Alensson standing above him with the sword pointed at his chest.

"Yield," Alensson said.

"I surrender," the captain gasped, for his sword had fallen out of his hand and was well beyond his reach. His face was white with terror. "Are you even a knight yet?" the captain said as he cowered.

"Not yet," Alensson answered brusquely. "Will someone ransom you?"

"My father will ransom me," the captain said in a quavering voice. "Sir Giles of Beestone castle."

"Then I accept your surrender and your ransom," Alensson answered. He lowered his sword and then extended his hand to help the captain to his feet. The Atabyrions had overcome the Ceredigion guards and were now stripping away the badges of Westmarch they had worn on their tunics. The derision they had faced upon entering the gates was now turned back on the guardsmen. The men had gone from being oppressors to prisoners in one fell swoop.

Alensson could not help but smile in pleasure. Not a single man had fallen. He gripped his sword hilt, savoring the joy of his triumph.

"I'll send word to my father at once," said the garrison captain. His tone was changing now that his life was no longer in jeopardy. Then a hard edge came to it. "But you won't be holding this city for long, boy. The duke is at Averanche with six thousand men."

Alensson turned and scowled. His blood boiled with fury. "I am the duke!" he roared.

CHAPTER THREE

Revenge

Alensson's heart fluttered with fear and excitement as he bounded up the steps to the battlement walls. The Atabyrion and Occitanian soldiers clustered together as they filled the rampart and shoved against one another for a view.

"Stand aside, it's the duke!" Boquette grumbled as Alensson finished climbing the steps, his hair suddenly tumbled by the breezy height. Soldiers shuffled past each other, trying to clear a space for him to look over the wall.

Then he saw it, a glimmering centipede of soldiers bristling with spears and pennants marching toward Vernay. The colorful flag of Deford's banner fluttered in the breeze.

"No hiding his approach," Alensson said to Boquette. His innards were seething with anticipation and eagerness.

"No, he's not hiding it at all," Boquette drawled.

"How many does he have?"

"The scouts say no more than seven thousand."

A thrill of confidence ignited inside the young duke. "We outnumber him then. We've drawn in nearly twenty thousand!" He laughed. "He's a proud fool. He should have sought reinforcements from Kingfountain. The rest of his men are stretched out across La Marche, trying to hold it. Seven thousand! I feared it would be fifteen."

Boquette rubbed his lip. "Remember his brother's army at Azin—"

"Don't say it, Boquette, don't even utter the words!" Alensson said, clenching his arm and squeezing it. "We will not be held hostage to memories of the past. We know their tactics. They'll use archers as they did before. They'll drive stakes into the ground to stop our horses. We know this! We've chosen the ground this time. We have a defensible position to fall back to." He shook his head angrily. "No, this is nothing like before. This is my chance to avenge my father."

Boquette did not look convinced. "Don't underestimate these foes, lad. I know the prince trusts you enough to have given you command of this army. But listen to the advice of the sergeants. Many of them fought in the battle of Azinkeep. They're still afraid."

Alensson shook his head. "That's our problem, Boquette. Fear. It saps a man's courage worse than a disease. I will not let it infect me or these men. This is our time. I want the soldiers called out to the field. Right now. We're going to fight them in an open battle. Let the enemy quail when they see our numbers. This is our first step in reclaiming Occitania. Prince Chatriyon is the rightful heir, not the dead king's brat."

Boquette grimaced. "That brat is a prince of the blood of Occitania!"

"But Deford isn't," Alensson said. "He may be the protector, but he holds no right on his own. He will bleed like other men do. Prepare for battle."

♦   ♦   ♦

Alensson sat stiffly on his war charger, heavily encumbered by armor. From his mount, he had a clear view of the field that lay ahead and the enemy soldiers arrayed opposite him. In addition to his usual sword, he was equipped with a battle axe—his father's preferred weapon. It was the same one his father had used in the Battle of Azinkeep, and the wood was still stained with blood. He brought his horse down the line of Atabyrion warriors who formed the front ranks of the army, nearly seven thousand in all. On each flank were Occitanian knights in their silver armor, pennants flapping as they anxiously tried to calm their mounts. Beyond them were thousands of paid Occitanian men-at-arms, men who clearly feared the fight ahead of them. That's why he'd put them in the rear. The Atabyrions were anxious for a brawl.

While Alensson rode in front of the lines, he could hear the clattering noises of the Ceredigions preparing for battle. His scouts reported that they were securing their baggage and horses behind the lines, that none of the knights were mounted. Hobbling the horses was a measure to embolden an army. It meant that none of the leaders would be able to ride away should the tide turn. It was the ultimate sign that they would conquer or perish. Well, let them perish if they so wished.

A blazing fire raged inside Alensson's heart. Was this what the Fountain felt like? He was fifteen years old and he was leading an army into battle. He felt confident that it was the Fountain's will that he drive the usurpers out of his ancient homeland and restore it to its former name and its former glory.

"Do not fear!" the young duke shouted to the men of his

army. "We will show these dogs from Ceredigion what men we are! Think of your homes. Think of your families. Think not on the shame of the past but on the glory we will achieve this day. I doubt not your courage. You are each one stronger than those camped yonder. They will fall before our steel! Courage, my brothers! Courage and strength!"

A cheer rose up from the soldiers, and battle cries rent the air. Alensson paused, straining to sense the Fountain. He longed for its reassurance that he was doing the right thing, that it would honor his efforts with success. If it did, he would be renowned in Occitania. He was the Fountain's willing servant, and it if it brought him victory, he would give credit where it was due. Still, he heard nothing in his mind except his own thudding heartbeat. He turned his horse around and rode down the line, repeating his speech, sending another roar across the camp. Then he raised his sword, pointed at the enemy lines, and started toward the Ceredigion forces.

The knights on horseback did not charge at once. No, Alensson would learn from the mistakes of the past. The Atabyrions marched in step with the horses, bringing the bulk of the army across the field like thunderheads. The smell of sweat and metal stung Alensson's nose. He was ready for this fight. This was the moment the tide would finally turn in his favor.

"Archers!"

The shouted command came from the throng of enemy ahead. The archers of Ceredigion marched a few steps forward, dropped to one knee, and then loosed the first volley of arrows at them. The swarm of black shafts hurtled into the sky and Alensson and his men raised their shields. The shafts came down like deadly rain. Some soldiers cried out and dropped to the ground, but the shields protected most of them. The bulk of the army moved closer, picking up speed, dodging the remains of the wounded and fallen.

Another storm of arrows came raining down. This was the basic tactic of the Ceredigion forces. Alensson knew if they could survive the deadly hail a bit longer, the arrows would no longer be effective. Shafts rained down on him, glancing off the sturdy armor of his mount, slamming against his shield but not piercing it. His arm grew weary from holding the shield in place but he dared not move it. The Atabyrions continued to march through the haze of pain and torture, faces twisted with grimaces of rage. They were not cowed yet.

"Charge!" Alensson shouted, kicking the flanks of his steed and closing the distance faster. The soldiers were jogging now, scrambling over their fallen comrades. The knights broke free of the men-at-arms, and the horses gained speed, filling the young duke's heart with the thrill of impending combat.

The front ranks of archers came forward and began hammering the pointed ends of sharpened stakes into the earth. The stakes were intended to impale the charging horses, preventing the knights from breaking through the ranks of lightly armed archers.

Alensson watched in surprise as the archers struggled to fix the stakes into the earth. Summer was nearly at an end, and the fields had been baked by the sun. The archers struggled to get them into position. The wall of spikes would not be ready in time!

"Onward!" he screamed, swinging his sword over his head. The euphoria of battle raged inside him as he realized the fatal flaw in their enemy's defenses. Whooping with glee,

Alensson let his charger plunge ahead. He and the other knights struck the front lines of archers like a scythe, slicing and trampling the men who stood in their way. The Ceredigions scattered like ants from a destroyed mound.

The explosion of noise and violence filled Alensson's eyes and ears. He was in the midst of the enemy, slashing on each side of his horse. The wall of archers had crumpled, and now the men-at-arms were rushing forward to save their weaker comrades. Alensson was ready for them. He met the enemy head-on, galloping into the ranks of the soldiers as he used the edge, hilt, and flat of his blade with every stroke. The battle cries of his men filled him with confidence. Exhaustion threatened to blunt his strength, but he would not succumb to it. No, he would set the example of courage for his men.

He and his men had plunged deep into the Ceredigic army. The sounds of battle raged around him, and he lost all sense of direction in the maelstrom of violence. Blood clung to his weapon; blood splattered across his armor. He drove forward, cutting and cleaving his way until suddenly there were no more soldiers left in front of him. He blinked rapidly, trying to see through the stinging sweat. It took him a moment to realize where he'd led his men—they'd completely crushed the right flank of the enemy and were now approaching the reserves and the baggage. The baggage was where they'd find all the treasure to pay the soldiers and where the food to feed them would be stored. There were horses hobbled there as well, defended by panicking men.

"Onward! Onward!" Alensson croaked with excitement. He had no idea what was happening in the field behind him, but he'd pushed all the way through to the rear of Deford's army. If they could encircle the army, they'd be able to attack from all sides. Alensson had hoped he'd be able to face Deford himself. Where was the false duke?

Then arrows began to fly at them from the baggage. One caught Alensson's horse in the leg and the beast screamed and went down. The weight of Alensson's armor started to pull at him, but he'd trained for this—he knew how to disengage from his armor before it crushed him. An arrow caught him in the breastplate, hitting him with enough force to spin him around. Where was his shield? Archers were now scuttling out of the baggage like cockroaches. The sight of them caused a shock of surprise and worry. Fear chased into him next. Where had the archers hidden? He began to jog toward the baggage, weaving in his steps to make himself a more difficult target. More arrows lanced at him. It was foolhardy for these men to shoot arrows so close to their own army's rear, but the archers kept up the withering fire and Alensson felt another bolt strike his helmet.

He spun and collapsed onto his back, the force of the landing knocking the wind out of him. His lungs heaved and twisted, struggling for air, but he couldn't breathe, and the terror of being strangled made him buck and twist. He rolled over onto his stomach, sweat streaking down his face. Someone hit him from behind with a bowstave.

Still unable to breathe, Alensson twisted his sword, maneuvering it up and out from his own armpit, and caught his attacker in the middle. Air began to squeeze back into his lungs and he coughed violently. The cockroach archers were now jumping away from the baggage and running toward his men, using daggers and hand axes as their weapons.

Alensson killed four of the archers, before another archer shot him at close range. This time the bolt did not simply spin him around—it actually penetrated his armor at his shoulder. The pain was white-hot and searing, and he flopped onto his back once more, groaning in agony. The crushed grass was hardly a cushion. His temples throbbed and his stomach threatened to turn loose his midday food. Cries of the dead and dying sounded all around him, but the world was spinning so fast he could not make sense of it.

"Alen!" Boquette shouted, suddenly standing over him. He knelt, his face turning white at the sight of the arrowhead embedded in his shoulder.

"Help me up!" Alensson grunted in pain.

"Lie still. You're wounded. Over here! Get a horse over here. It's the duke! Yes, he's alive!"

An arrow caught Boquette in the back and he stiffened, his sweaty face a rictus of agony, before slumping on top of Alensson's body, the older man's weight grinding him down.

The young duke tried to pry the body off himself, but his injured shoulder resisted any attempt to move. A boot kicked Alensson's head, stunning him, and then he realized the body was being lifted away.

"It's him! It's La Marche!"

The voices were thick with foreign accents and Alensson realized with dread that he was surrounded by his enemies.

"Is it fatal?" one of the archers asked.

"No, I shot him in the shoulder on purpose," said a gap-toothed man. "Why waste a ransom by killing him?"

Alensson wanted to scream at them. He tried to sit up and use his sword, but he suddenly realized he was no longer holding it.

"Down you go!" one of the archer's sneered, kicking him back down again. "There's Sir Carter. Oy! Sir Carter! Look who we captured!"

The knight who tromped up to Alensson wore battered and dented armor, but he looked hale and cheerful. "Who's this?"

"The Duke of La Marche!" one of the archers said proudly.

"Deford will love that," said the knight. "He's chasing down the rest of the army. We've got the Atabyrions boxed in. It'll be a slaughter. Get to the front."

"What about the ransom!"

"We caught him!"

The knight gave them an angry look. "You'll get your pay, lads. Come see me to claim it after the battle is done. The nobles belong to Deford." He looked down at Alensson grimly. "He'll want this one to himself."

The archers gave the knight black looks and then abandoned their prize. The knight knelt down by Alensson. "It's a bloody battle, my lord," he said, giving him a hard look. "You made us earn this one. Lots of dead to bury. But Deford won. Clear as day." He crinkled his brow. "Are those tears? The arrow must hurt like hornets. Here—have some wine to dull the pain."

But no amount of wine would ever be enough.

CHAPTER FOUR

A Duke's Ransom

A fragile silence shrouded the room, and Ankarette hardly breathed for fear she would disturb Alensson's story. These were the memories of a young man, hardly more than a boy, but they had left their mark on the old man standing before her.

The duke's craggy brows lowered and he turned back to face the poisoner, sitting on the small couch near the window, hands folded in her lap.

"And so I became a prisoner for the first time. By our enemies," he said, but it was obvious the old wound still festered.

"How long before you were ransomed?" Ankarette asked softly, coaxingly. The night was still impenetrable outside, the buildings and manors lost in shadows.

The duke's lips twitched. "Five years." Ankarette's eyes widened and the duke smiled at her show of emotion. "Remember, Ankarette, that I was newly married. I did not see my wife for the first five years of our marriage." He clenched his jaw and turned back to the window.

"Why so long?" Ankarette asked in astonishment. "Most ransoms only take months to negotiate."

"That is true," he answered softly. "But you see, Deford was determined to break me. He was occupying my duchy. He had claimed my title. He knew that my prospects were based on his downfall, so he was determined to squeeze until I broke. He demanded two hundred thousand crowns. A king's ransom. Not a duke's." He glowered at the window panes, the pain inside him throbbing visibly. "It took five years for my people to collect such a sum. Five years and all my bride's pleading with her father, who was a still a prisoner himself after falling at Azinkeep, and anyone else who would lend a single farthing. All of my lands, all of my manors, all of my curtains, all of my spoons. Every . . . single . . . thing." He chuckled softly. "And still it was not enough."

"What about the prince? Did Chatriyon lend any?"

Alensson shrugged. "Some. But he had to maintain his court at Shynom. Remember that this was all before the Maid. He relied on others for his own living just as I did. As long as men were willing to risk their coin that he would become King of Occitania someday, he could eke out his days and pay for soldiers he couldn't afford on his own. The battle of Vernay crippled Atabyrion."

Ankarette leaned forward. "I don't understand what happened, though. You broke through Deford's lines. That's usually a good thing."

He smiled at her. "You know military tactics, eh? You're more than a poisoner? I presume so. Yes, it is normally a good sign. We thought we were striking the main front of the army, but we had attacked on the flank where their lines were thin. The victory was a costly one for Deford's army, but while they lost several thousand men, we lost more. When my men saw they were surrounded, many tried to flee back to Vernay for protection. Deford cut them down in their retreat. Many commanders drowned in the moat. The counts of Omaul and Chevronne both died like that. Good men, princes of the blood. Once our main army was in retreat, Deford encircled the Atabyrions and slew them almost to the man, taking few for ransom. When the battle was over, Deford marched triumphantly back to Pree, the capital of Occitania, and was met with a celebration as if he were King Andrew himself." His lip quivered with disgust. "He took the victory as a sign that the Fountain was on the side of Ceredigion. It was a festive moment. And I was sent to Callait to rot for five years."

Ankarette looked at him compassionately. Her heart ached for the man, but even more for his young wife. "Such a fall must have been very difficult for you."

Alensson started pacing, stroking his chin and cheeks with a wrinkled hand. He was a such a riddle of a man, one that had fascinated her for years. Again she was struck by the enormous opportunity that was laid before her, to learn his history from his own mouth instead of a book.

"Of course it was!" he said with vehemence. "But I did not let the imprisonment shake me. Or shape me. The Fountain favors the bold. I was determined to be free, to repay every crown that had been borrowed on my behalf. I longed to see my wife. You cannot imagine what torture it was being parted from her. I thought she would hate me as the months rolled on. I could not see her, but we could write to each other. How her notes of encouragement comforted me. I grew to love her more in those years of privation than many husbands ever love their wives." He swung his arms wildly to emphasize his point. "Troubles are the furnaces, my dear. Troubles and heat, troubles and heat. Does not a baker need fire to stiffen the dough? For every kind of pie, there is the proper time in the ovens. The Fountain has a purpose—nay a recipe!—for each of us. If we endure the flames well, then we become more than the eggs, the flour, the spices, the drabs of honey!"

Ankarette smiled at his comparison. "I've never heard it put that way, but you are right. Even my own king, the man that I serve, was captured and held prisoner. It was his adversity that helped him establish a strong kingdom."

Alensson snapped his fingers and then wagged his pointer at her. "You see it, Ankarette Tryneowy. You understand it!" His eyes were big and eager. "In my five years as a prisoner in Callait, I did not rot . . . I cooked. Some men grow lazy in confinement. They grow cynical. I only grew more ambitious. I kept my body hard and firm by practicing with the guards. Through it all, I was a good-natured captive. Gall never attracts bees. You know this to be true! One year turned to two, then two turned to three. My wife, Jianne, helped bring it all together. She could have left me in the dust. Many women would have. Instead, she lived in a humble cottage. She kept a few fine gowns, of course, for when she needed to visit a countess or an earl, but she lived humbly, her only constant companion a single maid who never abandoned her, and she wrote to me, and slowly she assembled a vast fortune. Two hundred thousand crowns!" His voice throbbed with unquenched devotion. "She bought my release with sweat, and patience, and promises to repay that we dared not hope to be able to fulfill. When the sum was gathered, even Deford was surprised. He'd hoped to be able to keep me captive until he'd vanquished the rest of Occitania." A sly grin stole over his mouth. "But his ambitions had proven to be more of a challenge than he'd thought."

Ankarette felt a blossoming admiration for this woman she'd never met. "When were you reunited with your wife?"

He folded his arms and leaned back against the window abutment. "It was the summer, nearly five years after the failure of Vernay." He paused. "At the time, they said Vernay was a repeat of Azinkeep. But no one remembers it anymore."

Ankarette nodded. "I'd never heard of it either, and I've read many histories of Ceredigion."

"The reason is because what happened next will be remembered longer than even Azinkeep. It will be remembered for all time. You see, while I was in my cage, there was a young peasant girl growing up in the village of Donremy. She was special, Ankarette. I had always hoped that if I worked at it hard enough, the Fountain would speak to me. It did eventually. It did it through a girl—that stubborn, proud waif of a girl!" He pushed away from the wall and fetched a goblet, then took a single swill from it. "Let me tell you her story next, Ankarette Tryneowy. I knew it because I lived it. I was the poorest man in Occitania. I had nothing. Even my sword was borrowed! But when I met the Maid, she looked at me. She knew who I was even before I could announce it."

His eyes filled with tears. "She gave me my nickname that day. She called me her gentle duke until she died."

CHAPTER FIVE

Genette of Donremy

The Duke of La Marche was a free man. But everything he had, he owed to others. He had been given transport on a Genevese vessel bound for the Brythonican city of Ploemeur, and from there, he'd walked the uneven dusty roads on hot summer days for leagues and leagues wearing clothes belonging to another man, his feet shod in ill-fitting boots handed to him from one of his guards out of pity, equipped with a half-dull sword from a Ceredigion garrison.

His father-in-law, the Duke of Lionn, was still a prisoner in Kingfountain. He was an heir to the Occitanian dynasty, so no amount of ransom would be acceptable to the butcher kings of the East. Meanwhile, the man's main fortress at the capital city of Lionn had been under siege for years and was still holding desperately like an anvil against the hammer of the Ceredigion invasion. If Lionn fell, the rest of Occitania would tumble with it. But Alensson's wife was not in the war-ravaged lands of her father. She had taken refuge in the duchy of Vexins and was living in a small cottage in the village of Izzt.

This was Alensson's destination. He admired the lush fields of berries growing in the mild climate of Brythonica as he passed through them. The farmers and pickers he met treated him with courtesy once they knew his name, and gave him leave to snack on their berries. Yet none had a horse they were willing to lend the impoverished duke to hasten his return to his wife.

The Occitanian court had been relocated to Shynom, deep within the kingdom. Alensson needed to see the prince, to demand he take action about Lionn and to volunteer to help, so he very nearly stopped in court on his way to Izzt, but he was desperate to see his wife again. He continued onward until he reached the sleepy village. The castle that presided over it was situated in a lush valley amidst green vineyards. Even the castle was green, from the ivy clinging to the walls to the green mold coating the slate shingles. Small square turrets rose above tall walls of varying heights forming a square. The castle was so secluded it had not seen action in over a century.

Some of the groundskeepers hailed him and told him that the castellan was visiting court at Shynom that day. But Alensson's wife, Jianne, was waiting for him. They directed him to her cottage, which was connected to the outer wall of the castle, next to a porter door and a small hillock that defeated the purpose of the wall because someone could walk up the hill and jump over the wall at that back portion of the castle. Alensson shook his head in wonderment at the poor design.

The cottage was two levels high with a steep sloping roof, a single dormer window, and a few scraggly grapevines growing in the seams by the castle wall, only one of which was still alive and thick with leaves. Alensson paused at the door— even the brown wood was speckled with moss—overcome by emotion. His wife was the daughter of a duke. She should be living in luxury at the castle yonder, not in some moldering cottage that probably had a leaky roof.

When he heard the sound of humming on the other side of the door, he could hold back no longer. He rapped on the wood with his knuckles, shifting and fidgeting as he heard the humming cease and the sound of footsteps rushing to the door.

He anticipated it would be her maid, Alix. But it was his wife who answered the door. When he saw her, his heart surged up into his throat, and all the years of separation, all the years of longing, all the years of misery broke with the sunshine. Jianne was shorter than him, her wavy hair so dark it was nearly black. She was not wearing one of her court gowns, but she looked absolutely radiant in a peasant frock, her sunburned arms and cheeks a testament that she had labored out of doors.

"Alensson!" she breathed, a sleeper awakened from a nightmare. She flung herself into his arms, and he held her, burying his face in the mane of hair at her neck, hugging and squeezing her as the years of anxiety sloughed away like old bark.

"Where's your maid?" he asked with a grin, hugging her back fiercely.

"It's market day at Cienne. It's a long walk, so Alix won't be back until supper. But look at you! Come inside!"

Jianne showed Alensson the small kitchen, the warm oven, the well-swept stone floor, and the spacious loft where the bed had been assembled by a local carpenter friendly to

House La Marche. He drank in the sights, drank in everything about her. She seemed overjoyed that her husband was home, even if that home was borrowed. The small cottage had originally belonged to the porter who controlled the rear door. The old porter lived with his daughter now, and the place had sat empty until Jianne's arrival with her maid.

Later, as they sat across from each other at the small oak table, holding hands, Alensson stared into his wife's cinnamon eyes and said, "I swear to you, my love, I swear that I will make this up to you. This will not be your home for much longer."

She caressed his hand with her thumb. "I care not for castles, Alensson. I care not for rings or jewels. You are here, and I would be content to live out our lives in this cottage. I've fancied our children playing by the oven there. I've fancied you pruning orchards with your sword instead of spilling blood. Would that the Fountain had blessed us with a season of peace. This war, I fear, will never end." But from the look in her eye, he knew that she understood his restless soul, his determination to reclaim his lost inheritance. To pay back every crown she had borrowed on his behalf. "You must go to Shynom, my love." She squeezed his hand. "And I will go with you."

He smiled. "We will be welcomed there with great honor and respect. I heard your father's city is about to fall to the siege. Is that true?"

Jianne nodded, her countenance darkening. "I fear I shall never see him again. The people lose hope. The Fountain has forsaken us. Perhaps because we have forsaken *it*."

"We will go on the morrow then," Alensson said.

She shook her head no. "I beg one full day with you, my lord husband. Before you plunge back into the war, let me have a day of you to remember. A day just to ourselves."

And the look she gave him made him eager to honor her request.

♦   ♦   ♦

They had to walk most of the way to Shynom, and they did so hand in hand. Although his boots still hurt his feet, the journey was more enjoyable with his wife at his side. Alix was a dark-haired girl from the Felt family, a distant kinswoman who rarely spoke, but she seemed delighted that Alensson was back to relieve her mistress's worries.

There was something exhilarating about bedding down in the deep field grasses by the light of the stars. This was the life of a peasant. He folded his hands behind his head as he stared up at the sky, savoring the feel of his wife's hand resting on his chest. His head was full of thoughts, full of ideas. It was clear to him that relieving the siege of Lionn was the right strategy. Why was the prince still in Shynom and not traveling between cities and rousing a larger army to break the siege? When Alensson had last met him, he'd judged the prince to be an overly timid man. He was quick to laugh and drink and share a joke, but he rarely ventured outside the protection of the fortress of Shynom, one of the most ancient castles of western Occitania. His realm was being held hostage by a small toddler from Kingfountain. But the youth wasn't the enemy. It was the child's uncle. There was such a stark contrast between Chatriyon and Deford. They were opposites of each other in so many ways.

Chatriyon needed a bold commander. Someone who was decisive and would take action. Alensson had failed at Vernay, but not through cowardice or lack of ambition. But how was he to persuade the prince to give him command of an army again? All this dithering at court meant that Deford's army continued to hold and maintain the lands and cities he'd won years before. The Duke of Westmarch would fall. Alensson vowed it to the stars.

When he and Jianne reached the town crowded outside Shynom, they stopped at an inn to change for court. Alensson had carried their fanciest clothes in his pack. Jianne's gown was not of the latest court fashion, and she no longer had any jewelry. But she was determined to make an impression, and Alix helped braid her hair elegantly.

Alensson chafed in the common room, listening to the sound of rowdy drinkers. It was only midday, but many of the patrons were already drunk. He looked at them with disdain, his eyes darting from person to person. He was anxious to be on his way and hopefully get a command position, as well as a purse full of coins from his prince to reward him for his long imprisonment. He needed funds desperately. He needed a horse! He needed a decent sword.

What was taking Jianne so long?

There was a sudden commotion at the door of the inn. Alensson's head turned toward the bright outside light, which flashed across the crimson tunic of one of the prince's guardsman as he shoved a young man onto the floor inside the inn.

"If you come back to the gate again, I swear by the blood you'll get a thrashing next time! Now go back to whatever town it was you came from!"

The guardsman sneered and then slammed the door of the inn, rattling the windows with the violence of the action. Some of the patrons started to guffaw as they stared disdainfully at the youth.

"He still won't see you?" one of them jeered. "Should that

surprise you?"

"Give it a rest. It ain't no harm for trying."

"Oy," the landlord shouted, waving over the lad, who rose and rubbed his elbow. "I left a bit of bread at the table. But I told you they wouldn't let you in the palace. Right? Didn't I tell you? It's unnatural. Get a bit to eat. Maybe you should be on your way."

The youth gave him an angry look and then retreated to the table, sitting alone at the very end of it. Light from the window fell across its surface, reflecting white off the polished wood. A half-eaten loaf of trencher bread waited there on a plate.

She is a maid.

The whisper cut through the commotion of the room, striking the center of Alensson's heart. It startled him, because it was not a spoken voice so much as a feeling. His whole life he had longed for the Fountain to speak to him. That it should do so inside this squalid inn amidst drunken men, and not in a sanctuary, made him wonder. Squinting against the stabs of light, he rose and started toward the youth. As he studied her face, he realized his mistake. This was a girl, maybe sixteen years old, wearing a man's clothes. Her hair was shorn to her shoulders, but her face and hands were more delicate than a lad's. The look in her eyes spoke of pain and disappointment, and a tear trickled down her cheek as she stared out the window.

He felt an inexplicable pull toward her, as if a river current were tugging him along. He did not know her name, he knew nothing about her, and his *wife* was still changing upstairs, yet he found himself pulling aside a chair and sitting across from this stranger who had been humiliated, not for the first time, in front of the folk at the inn.

"Why do you weep?" he heard himself say to her, leaning forward. The words just came from his mouth.

She looked across the table at him and then stiffened in surprise, as if she recognized him. "*Gentle* duke," she said softly, "I weep because they will not let me see the prince."

She had called him by his title. His attire was fancier than hers, to be sure, but a stranger would have taken him for a knight, not a prince of the blood.

"Do you know who I am?" he asked her. His heart began to hammer at the strangeness of the experience, but beneath it there was a deep, soothing peace.

"You are the Duke of La Marche," she said as if that were the most obvious thing in the world. "Do you not know your own name?"

"Yes, but how did *you* know?" he asked her.

"The Fountain whispered it to me," she said, gazing back at the window a moment. Then she reached across the table and grabbed his arm. Her fingers were surprisingly strong. "Will *you* take me to the prince? I cannot get past the guards. They treat me very rudely and drag me from the doors. They mock me."

"Why must you see the prince?" he asked her in confusion.

Her dark brown eyes were piercing in their intensity. "Because I must obey the Fountain. It commands me to tell Prince Chatriyon that *he* is the true king of Occitania. He must be crowned at the sanctuary of Our Lady at Ranz. That is where the holy oil is. That is where he must be crowned to take his rightful place as regent. If he gives me an army, I will drive his enemies away."

Alensson stared at her in disbelief, his heart immediately torn between disappointment and something brighter, purer. He had wanted to be the chosen one. He had desired it more than anything. And yet . . . this girl seemed lit from within. He had never heard someone so passionate, so full of purpose and determination. Could she be Fountain-blessed? She had known who he was without any introduction. Trying to balance his emotions, he fumbled with his words.

"Who are you? Where are you from?"

"My name is Genette," she answered meekly. "My father's name is Jeannow. I am from Donremy."

"That's a peasant name," he said.

She let go of his arm. "I am!" she said proudly, almost defiantly. "Take me to the prince, *gentle* duke. I beg you. The Fountain has spoken to me. I swear this by all the saints. I swear this by the Deep Fathoms. I swear this as a *maid*. I am sent to bring the prince to Ranz and see him crowned," she repeated deliberately, firmly, passionately. "You must take me to see him! If Lionn falls, all is lost."

Her words throbbed in his skull and in his heart. She was not deluded. She was not some drunk babbler or pretender. He could see that in her eyes. And he felt as deep as his marrow that she was telling the truth.

He realized, with growing awareness and respect, that the girl sitting across from him was indeed Fountain-blessed.

"When did you—" he paused, nearly choking on the words. His words proceeded as a whisper. "When did you first hear it speaking to you?"

She blinked at him, looking at him boldly. "When I was but a child."

As he listened, a spear of jealousy stabbed inside him.

CHAPTER SIX

The Vertus Prince

The kings of Occitania had always ruled from the royal palace in Pree, a thronging city full of the splendors of trade and the majesty of a realm that was ancient in its customs and rites. But Pree was held by Ceredigion, and its peoples cheered for the Duke of Westmarch now. How much of the adulation was genuine, feigned, or driven by fear was inconsequential. So the Occitanian court had moved west, beyond the rivers, woods, and ravines that protected the hinterlands, to the ancient fortress of Shynom. It was a piece of irony that it had been the stronghold of the first Argentine king centuries before.

Alensson found the troubled prince there. Chatriyon was the lawful heir of Occitania, but he'd been driven into exile following the defeat of Azinkeep. At Shynom, he was protected by huge walls of thick stone, and his courtiers only granted a royal audience to people who shared their beliefs and allegiances. Thus it was no easy task to see the prince. Bribes helped pave the way, but while Alensson had no money, he was a prince of the blood himself, a cousin of the nobility, and a young man with a reputation for courage that preceded him. No one else had dared stand up to Deford so boldly after Alensson's defeat. He might have lost Vernay and brought trouble to the prince, but at least he had tried to do something. He was allowed inside the ballroom filled with lords and ladies dressed in bright silks and velvets. The ladies' hair was coiffed with intricate headdresses, a fashion that was copied by their Atabyrion allies. The odor of strong wine hung in the air, and the clamor of loud laughter and debate battled against the musicians for dominance. The polished floor was made of white and black marble like a Wizr board.

The young duke worked his way through the throng, accosted every few steps by a butler offering him a goblet, which he refused, as he searched for his sworn lord.

Chatriyon was found in halfhearted conversation with two lords and a deconeus. He had dark hair that was combed forward, barely seen under a puffy, wide-brimmed velvet hat. He wore a red tunic with a fur collar that billowed out at the shoulders in a V shape, giving the illusion that he was a muscular man. His gaze darted to and fro above his pear-shaped nose as he listened to his companions. It was obvious he longed for an escape. His eyes widened with sudden interest when he noticed Alensson's approach.

"And here's the man himself, my noble cousin!" Chatriyon said good-naturedly, a genuine smile spreading across his face.

One of the lords, an older man with an earring dangling from his lobe, turned a dark look on Alensson. "He's the one who brought her inside the castle!"

The deconeus pawed at the prince's sleeve. "You must not

speak to her, my lord!"

"A moment, a moment," the prince said, batting away the man's hand. "Cousin!" He reached out and took Alensson by the shoulders, gazing at him fondly. The prince was only half a dozen years his elder, but he had the haggard, harried look of a man nearly forty. "The Fountain delivered you! I heard about your release and had hoped you'd come to Shynom straightaway. Is Jianne with you?" He craned his neck, his eyes searching the hall.

"No, my prince," Alensson said, grateful for the warm welcome. "She's anxious to greet you again, but she is waiting outside with someone who has not been permitted to enter."

The scowling lord stepped forward. "My lord prince, if you admit a peasant into your court, you will be a laughingstock! Send the girl home!"

Alensson flashed a glare at the older man. He recognized him as the Earl of Doone, though the man had aged quite a bit since he'd seen him last.

"You've seen her?" Chatriyon asked eagerly, looking at Alensson. "What is she like? They say she is dressed like a page boy. Isn't that rather peculiar?"

Alensson shook his head. "Not at all, my lord. She did it for protection. The road from Donremy brought her past hostile forces. She was escorted here by two soldiers from a garrison along the way."

The deconeus, an older man with a limp and a sneer, butted in. "She's probably just a camp follower, my prince," he said contemptuously. "Seeking to increase her fortunes among those of more noble blood. Like the Earl of Doone, I suggest you send her away."

"What do *you* think, Cousin?" Chatriyon asked Alensson, his expression alive with curiosity. He was not a weak-willed man, Alensson knew, but the prince tended to listen to advice endlessly before making a decision. He was very cautious. His inheritance had been reduced to cinders and ash, leaving only a few smoking coals behind. He breathed lightly on them, not wanting the flames to extinguish utterly.

Alensson turned to the deconeus. "Have you tested her, Deconeus?"

The man looked affronted. "What? You think I'd waste my time on a mere peasant girl? I'm no fool, my lord duke."

"You act like one," Alensson said, a little hotly. Then he turned to the prince. "I spoke to the girl in a tavern this morning—"

"A tavern!" Doone scoffed.

"Where else would she be welcome if not there?" Alensson said. "My lord, listen to her. I tell you, the girl is Fountain-blessed. The Fountain *speaks* to her."

The look the prince gave him had changed. There was a slow budding of hope, but it was clouded over with heavy doubts. "Cousin . . ." he said, shaking his head.

Alensson pressed his cause. "Just meet her, my lord. You will know, as I did. The Fountain has sent her to save Occitania. To save *you.*"

Perhaps they were just the words a drowning man needed to hear.

Doone would not give ground easily. "How many drinks did you have before you spoke to her, Alensson? How deep in your cups are you already?"

"Not a one," Alensson said, offended. "How many have *you* had?" he asked, nodding to the goblet in the earl's hand. The prince smirked at the gesture.

The deconeus shook his head. "I've had none myself either, my prince, so I hope you'll heed my counsel. There are many who parade themselves as Fountain-blessed to dupe believers into giving them money. They come and stand on the edge of the fountains and prophesy some doom or another. Then people come and toss their coins into the water. Before you know it, rogues harvest the coins in the night and make off with the wealth. This girl wants money. And so does this young duke. He's a pauper himself. Be wary, my lord. Be wary!"

If the man weren't a deconeus, Alensson would have struck him for that. He had impoverished himself to the dust to win his freedom, and he'd not be addressed in such a way by a man living in splendor in a sanctuary he'd not built himself. A threat blossomed on his lips, but before he could utter it, the prince abruptly put his arm around his shoulder and directed him away from the other two.

"You can see my dilemma, can't you, Cousin?" the prince said. "Word of this girl reached me months ago. I've not sent for her, yet she continues to beg for an audience. Should a peasant—a girl, no less!—be on the same footing as a prince? What if she's deceived you? Don't be offended. I'm not saying that she has, but after all I've lost, after all *you've* lost, don't you think caution would be the more prudent course? I'm grateful you've met her, Alensson. That is helpful to me. You think she's Fountain-blessed. What convinced you? You know I value your judgment more than those old fools."

Alensson turned to face the prince. "I don't know how to describe it, my lord. Her words ring true, like . . . like a bell in your heart. The conviction in her eyes. She's not mad. She's an innocent who's been called to greatness. I know about camp followers, my lord. I've been in war. She's not like those haughty girls. Just meet her. That is all I ask of you."

The prince's wince was telling. "But if I do, then I risk

offending men like Jerson and the deconeus. Men whose money I need to keep court at Shynom. I can't risk offending them, Cousin. Can't you see that?"

He saw it all too well. "Yes, my prince. They've given you enough to keep you under their thumb. But not enough to relieve the siege at Lionn. What happens when Deford breaks through it? He'll flood this valley with soldiers, and then you'll find yourself defending Shynom. Or will you flee *again*?"

He'd meant to provoke his cousin and it worked. The prince's eyes darkened. "Lionn has held firm for several years, Cousin. You've been in prison too long to understand—"

Alensson shook his head. "What surprised me, my lord, was how *little* has changed since Vernay. My wife's father is the Duke of Lionn. She has given me as much information about the siege as one can get from those still loyal to her family."

"I'm sure her father's plight is very concerning to her," Chatriyon said. The prince was always trying to soothe the feelings of others without committing himself. He was wonderful at empathy. He was terrible at action.

"I'm not here because of the duke. I have nothing left except the will to fight, and I came here to fight for *you*, my prince. The siege at Lionn needs to be broken. Surely you do not dispute that! Just see the girl, my lord. Just for a moment. It can be in private, if you prefer."

The prince shook his head. "No, no—not in private."

The Earl of Doone and the deconeus were creeping forward like rats, trailing them. "My prince, listen to me," Doone said.

The prince turned with practiced patience. "Yes?"

"Send the girl away for good. She'll bring you nothing but

trouble."

The prince gave Alensson a look.

"The Fountain sent her here," Alensson said sternly. "Let her be tested then. In front of us all."

The prince thought a moment and then tapped his chin thoughtfully. "I have an idea. A little game, actually. A test. Bring her in, but not to me. Let her find me."

"But your red tunic shows you're the prince!" the earl complained. "It's the royal color of House Vertus!"

"I know, I know!" the prince said glibly. "As would she. So, my lord earl, we will exchange tunics before she comes. Alensson, you'll wait over there where you can see and hear us. But you won't be able to direct her to me. If she hears the Fountain, as you said, then she will know she's being deceived. If not, what a little joke it will be! No one will be able to criticize me then for having allowed her in. Either way," he said smugly, "I do not lose."

The deconeus and the earl exchanged a look.

"Don't bother arguing with me," the prince said. He snapped his fingers and his herald approached. "Bring in the maid."

◆   ◆   ◆

Alensson watched furtively by one of the massive hearths. He did not like the prince's plan—his heart told him the trick was beneath them—but it did make sense. Besides, it would soothe the various egos involved. Staring across the crowded hall, he watched for her eagerly. At first, he was unable to hear anything over the commotion of talking, but then a sense of quiet came across the room, spreading like liquid from a spilled cup. The lords and ladies in their finery began to whisper as the peasant girl in men's clothes slowly made her way through the assembly. Genette walked by herself, no one guiding her, her mouth a little open as she took in the decadence of Shynom.

Jianne appeared at his side, her hands closing around his arm. "What is going on, Alensson?" she whispered to him. "When they let her in, I was told I couldn't accompany her. Someone told me where you were. Why isn't the prince wearing red?"

"Sshhh," Alensson said to her. "It's a test."

"A test of what?" his wife asked worriedly.

"To see if she *is* Fountain-blessed," he answered. "The prince doesn't wish to be taken for a fool."

"Look how they're sneering at her," Jianne said, her tone filled with concern. "This isn't right, Alensson. They're making a mockery of the poor girl. You told the prince we met her? He didn't believe you, his own cousin?"

"He must show the counsel of his court due consideration," Alensson answered. Genette was getting closer to them. She noticed them both standing to the side, but she did not come to them. Walking cautiously through the crowd, she looked from side to side until she spied the red tunic.

"This is unfair," Jianne whispered sadly as Genette marched deliberately forward. "They'll make a sport of her."

Alensson felt a frown of disappointment on his lips. Could he have been wrong? The Earl of Doone had his back to the girl, and he was in quiet conversation with the deconeus and the disguised prince. The prince watched Genette's approach from behind his goblet, his eyes narrowing as the unkempt, shorn creature approached them. The eyes of everyone in the hall followed her, the nobles' expressions mirroring the disgust they felt. Some had even grown bored with the ruse and were talking lightly amongst themselves.

Genette walked directly up to Chatriyon, ignoring Doone completely, and then knelt before the prince, bowing her head. "My prince, thank you for permitting me to see you."

Alensson felt a throb of victory and his frown turned into a triumphant smile. His wife squeezed his arm, gasping in surprise. She was what they'd both sensed her to be.

There was a startled look on Chatriyon's face as he lowered the cup. "You mistake me, my dear," he said with a joking tone. "This is the prince." He motioned toward Doone.

The girl looked up but not away. "*You* are my prince," she said boldly amidst the hush of the room, without any hesitation or even a hint of doubt. "The Fountain has sent me to you, to see you crowned at the sanctuary of Our Lady at Ranz. You are the true king, my lord. And the Fountain has given me a sign to prove myself to you."

The prince's eyes bulged with astonishment. "A sign? What sign?"

"I must show you in private, my lord. The Fountain does not wish it to be seen by so many unbelievers. There is a chapel yonder with a fountain. May we speak there, my prince? It is there that I must show you the sign."

"My lord, no!" Doone warned, his cheeks flushed. "She could be a poisoner! This is a ruse!"

The maid turned to the earl. "Who are you to challenge my mission?" she demanded. "I am from the village of Donremy. I bring no poison. I bring no weapons." She turned back to the prince. "Please, my lord. I am a simple maid. But through me, the Fountain will give you the kingdom of your fathers. *Believe.*"

The prince glanced across the room at Alensson, stuck between courage and fear. Alensson met his eyes and nodded.

This was a moment that couldn't be ignored. The duke had hoped to be the one chosen by the Fountain to save his people, but it had chosen an obscure maid instead. So be it then. He would support her, and by doing so, support the Fountain.

"Take my arm," the prince said, offering his elbow to the maid. And he escorted her, to the wonderment of the entire hall, to the chapel.

CHAPTER SEVEN

Signs

The atmosphere of the great hall had changed in an instant. Gone were the mocking sneers and the incredulity. A mood of excitement and intensity had settled over the nobles, who began discussing the scene that had just unfolded in their midst. Who was this peasant girl? Where did she come from again? Donremy? Wasn't that near the borders?

Jianne glanced furtively at the archway as she stroked Alensson's arm. "This means another battle, doesn't it?" she whispered.

"I hope so," Alensson answered truthfully. He instantly knew he'd chosen the wrong words, and a glance at Jianne confirmed it. There were already tears quivering on her dark lashes.

"My love, my love!" he soothed, pulling her into an embrace. He stroked her hair. "We both knew this would happen! I am a beggar. I am worse than a beggar. If I'm to repay all who lent money for my release, I *must* do this!"

She cried quietly into his chest and he continued to soothe her, wishing they were not in such a public place.

"I know it, I know," she answered, shaking her head. She looked up at him through her tearstained eyes. "But I've been without you for so long, my husband, and I had *hoped* that we wouldn't part so soon." She traced her fingers along his shoulders. "How are we even going to afford a suit of armor? It is costly going to war, and we owe so much."

"The prince will provide," Alensson said.

She looked doubtful. "I pray he does. Did it take much convincing before he'd see her?"

"This court is full of vipers," he said, growling. "Look how they've changed in such a short time. They were ready to claw her for presuming to be here. Now they'll fawn over her." He seized her hands. "This is the moment Occitania has needed. You felt it in her as well. After you and Alix came down, you heard her stories about how the Fountain speaks to her. We both listened to her tale before bringing her here. Can you imagine what it must be like? She hears its voice every day, like music audible only to her. The music of the Deep Fathoms."

Jianne wiped her nose. She stood up straighter, putting on a brave face for him, and said, "So strange that it spoke to one so young."

"How I wish it were *me*," Alensson breathed, trying to wrestle down the wriggle of jealousy in his heart. The thought flared for a moment, but he struck it down violently with his mind.

"I will return to the cottage," Jianne said, looking up into his eyes.

"Nay, stay at Shynom!" he insisted. "If the prince summons an army, it will take time to gather them. It will take time to drill and train."

"Do you think the prince will do it?"

He nodded. "He will not miss this opportunity. Look at the hunger in their eyes. They have an appetite for hope. We all do. You must stay with me, Jianne."

She winced. "An army isn't a suitable place ... for a woman. There's so much swearing, so much lewdness. I ..." She blushed furiously. "I wouldn't want to be taken for a camp follower, Husband." She looked away.

Her browned skin, her callused hands, were a symbol of all she'd suffered in their marriage. She was right. While the nobles knew that her father was the Duke of Lionn, the rough soldiers would likely treat her with impertinence. Neither of them could bear that.

"I will return to Izzt with Alix," she said firmly, seeing the look in his eyes. "Before you go to battle, come and see us. I will wait for you, my husband. I will always wait for you." She reached up and smoothed a lock of hair from his brow.

He wrestled with his feelings, with the conflict of wanting her to be near yet knowing he'd worry about her if she stayed. His focus would need to be on training soldiers anyway. In his mind, he recalled that quaint, idyllic cottage overlooking a lazy river, fields of vines, and a stubborn old castle that was all squares and bent angles. It was a peaceful, quiet place. He would like to imagine her being safe there while he fought the prince's war.

Cradling her face in his hands, he kissed her mouth. All the chatter suddenly fell away. At first Alensson was puzzled—were the others watching them?—but then he realized the prince had returned.

Chatriyon's countenance had completely transformed. All

the calculation, defensiveness, and pride had been scoured away. He looked like a man stricken mute with wonder. The Maid was on his arm.

"This girl has spoken true," the prince finally said, his voice quavering slightly. There was no other noise in the hall—all eyes were on him, all ears pricked to listen. Chatriyon swallowed, trying to bolster his courage. "I have seen a sign of the Fountain's will. She is truly called to bless us. Be it known throughout my realm that the Fountain has chosen a maid as its instrument."

The prince paused, glancing around the hall, surveying the courtiers who stood transfixed before him. Alensson did the same. Many of them looked doubtful, and some were shaking their heads. "I know that some of you doubt her," the prince continued. "I know that many of you suspect her. My word will not be enough to satisfy you, so you will test her, Deconeus. In this hall, in front of these witnesses. Test her knowledge of the Fountain. Test her worthiness. Ask her whatever question you wish answered. Then she will be tested by a woman to prove she is a maid." His eyes searched the hall before settling on Alensson and his wife. "The Duchess of La Marche will do it. Then the Maid will give us another sign that what she has said is true. You are all witnesses this day. You will all bear witness to the Fountain's will. Occitania belongs to us, and we are intended to win her back with the sword. This maid has been chosen to lead us into battle against our enemies. Deconeus!"

Alensson squeezed his wife's hand hard enough that she pulled it away and rubbed the soreness from it. He glanced at her apologetically and then watched as the deconeus shuffled forward.

"My lord prince," the aging man said worriedly, pressing his wrinkled mouth and making his finger rings glitter. "I've had no time to prepare! Give me a moment to gather my thoughts." Beads of sweat popped onto his brow amidst curls of graying hair.

The prince shook his head. "It must be done now, Deconeus. Test her knowledge! Use the rite of purging. Make her swear an oath by the Fountain."

The deconeus wrung his hands. He had clearly not expected such a spectacle, especially after being so vocal in his warning about her. But he gathered himself together and approached the prince and the Maid.

Even though Genette was dressed plainly, and in men's clothes, her presence was as forceful, as stiff and formal, as if she were a knight come to report to her ruler. She bowed respectfully to the old man.

"Tell me, child," the deconeus said with a shaking voice, "what are the first words of scripture about the Deep Fathoms?"

It was highly unlikely that the peasant girl could read or had the means to procure a book to learn. But she met the deconeus's gaze without flinching. "In the beginning was the word of power," she recited. "And the earth was formless. It was void. Darkness lay over the Deep Fathoms. The water spirits moved upon the face of the waters. And the first word was spoken."

The deconeus blanched. "Where did you learn that catechism, child?"

"The Fountain whispered it to me," Genette replied. "It has taught me words of power."

His brow crinkled with concern and fear. "Are you a Wizr?"

She shook her head. "I am not. The last true Wizr was

imprisoned in a mound of boulders. I am not a Wizr. I am a Knight of the Fountain."

"You are a knight?" he asked, perplexed. "Is it not forbidden for a woman to be a knight? Is it not written in the scriptures that only men are called to war?"

"Was not Diborra called to lead her people in ancient times?" the Maid answered sharply. "Was she not also a woman? I *am* called to deliver our people from their bondage to Ceredigion. Use the rite on me, Deconeus. I do not fear it. I am no water sprite. You will see."

The deconeus nodded gravely. He whispered something to one of his underlings, who disappeared and quickly returned with a bowl of water from the fountain in the chapel. The lad handed the bowl to the deconeus and then melted back into the crowd. The girl knelt in front of the deconeus and bowed her head.

"If you are a water sprite, I abjure thee!" he said in a loud voice. He tipped the small bowl of water over her head and the water came splashing out, soaking her hair and her tunic and her clothes. None of the water reached the marble floor. A collective sigh came from the crowd.

The deconeus blinked with relief. "She is not waterborn," he said to the prince, nodding with pleasure. "She is mortal, not a Siren—a water sprite—bent on leading us to destruction like in the tales from the past."

Genette lifted her smiling face as the water streaked down her cheeks. A servant came with a towel and helped her mop up the damp.

The prince turned to Jianne and gestured for her to approach. When she and Alensson did, he said, "Take her and examine her, my dear. You are a princess of the blood. By your word, we will trust that this girl is truly the maid she claims to be."

Jianne nodded obediently.

Genette turned to Alensson. "Make ready, Gentle Duke. You must teach me how to fight. The Fountain wishes you to train me."

Alensson blinked with surprise and before he could stop himself, the words came gushing out of his mouth, put there by the Fountain. "But you do not have a sword," he said, feeling awed and a little confused at the words which tumbled out.

The maid looked at him and then lifted her voice. "The Fountain commands you to fetch me my sword, Gentle Duke. On my journey here, I passed the sanctuary of St. Kathryn in Firebos. Kneel before the fountain there. Inside the water, you will find a heap of coins. Do not take the coins. Beneath them, you will find a sword. That is my blade. And that is my sign to all of you that the Fountain has indeed sent me. Take the sword, but nothing else." She looked into Alensson's eyes and lowered her voice. "Hasten! Before someone unworthy tries to steal it."

As their eyes met, he felt something dark pass through his heart. What sort of blade was this? Did it possess powers imbued by the Fountain? The desire to keep it struck him forcefully—maybe he could still be the hero Occitania needed —but he wrestled the feelings down.

In a sharp voice, the prince suddenly commanded, "Doone, take your men and go with him. Under pain of death, no one must enter that sanctuary until the Duke of La Marche comes! Go at once!"

CHAPTER EIGHT

Firebos

The old duke's expression changed to one of amusement as he regarded Ankarette, who had been sitting spellbound by his tale. "If you could only see your face, lass. I mentioned the blade and you leaned forward, keen to know more. Where is it now? Where is it hidden? That is the secret you want to know most." He gave her a cunning look, and the poisoner realized the answer would not soon be forthcoming. "But what you should be asking is this. What sign did the Maid show the prince to convince him to trust her? That is what you should be asking." She had to admit that his tale had completely reeled her in, that she was drawn to his words like a starving man craving a feast.

"And what was it?" Ankarette asked, hoping not to be distracted from her goal.

"She showed him a vision of something in the waters of the fountain. He refused to speak about it, even to me. I only know that he could not touch it. It is a great secret, I should think. But now to your purpose. You seek the sword. I already told you that the King of Occitania doesn't have it," Alensson said. "Nor do I. The sword is not part of the contest at the moment."

Ankarette felt so close to her goal, but it was like trapping smoke. "You said you'd tell me about it. After you spoke of the Maid."

"I did," the duke said with a nod. He chafed his arms, and Ankarette suddenly became aware of the chill of the room. Her fascination with his tale had made her oblivious.

Alensson knelt by the brazier, grunting as he lowered himself down. After adding fresh coals from the bucket, the duke stirred up the flames and rubbed his hands together over the fire, warming himself.

"What does the blade look like?" Ankarette asked, hoping to learn something beyond the meager scraps gleaned from the trial records.

"It's a fair-sized blade," Alensson said, staring down at the smoldering coals. He held his hands apart. "About this long. The blade is tempered, has a wood-grain texture, if you will. There are stars on the blade itself. It is an ancient sword, but it bears no stains."

Ankarette frowned. "I heard there was rust on it when it was drawn from the fountain at St. Kathryn's in Firebos."

"That isn't true," Alensson said, shaking his head. "People said that, but *I* was there. The blade had been buried in water, but it remained pristine. The coins were rusty." He gave her a smile and a wink. "Perhaps that is what they meant." He chafed his hands vigorously a moment longer and then returned to her. "Five of us who rode from Shynom arrived at the sanctuary together. Some of the knights couldn't keep up.

It was just as the Maid had predicted. Doone thought it was some sort of Wizr magic. He didn't trust the girl." He shook his head firmly. "He was always doubtful. He actually suggest- ed the girl had hidden the blade in the fountain before she came to Shynom. Bah! Such nonsense. She was a penniless peasant, almost as poor as me! The blade would have cost more than a peasant's wages." He snorted with disgust. "Still many wouldn't believe. Even after the signs. But others did."

Ankarette glanced out the window, grateful there was no sign of the approaching dawn yet. She was not tired in the least, but she did need to return to her king's army the next day.

"It went against their pride," Ankarette said in a coaxing tone. "You had no pride left, my lord. It had been taken from you coin by coin."

He nodded approvingly. "You see the truth, lass. It's not luck that calls down the Fountain's blessings; the Fountain-blessed are *chosen*. Everyone who is Fountain-blessed has a certain power or set of powers, but those powers must be summoned through disciplined action." He put his foot on the window seat. "What would you say the Maid's skill was, Ankarette? Her way of replenishing her magic?"

Ankarette gave him a curious look. "It was said she was exceptional with the blade. Uncannily so for a girl."

He grinned. "The source of her power came from needle-work. Sewing."

Ankarette was startled. "Truly?" It was especially curious since it was also *her* method for replenishing her Fountain magic. It made the Maid feel more real—less like a story, and more like a girl from the village of Donremy.

He nodded emphatically. "So few know anything about her at all." He cocked his thumb and jabbed it into his chest. "She earned her skill with the blade from me. I taught her to fight. She was a natural, there can be no doubt of that. The Fountain had endowed her with multiple gifts, but she needed to sew to fuel them. Repairing shirts and clothes would work, but she loved to embroider the banner she carried into battle. She worked on it *constantly*, adding little embellishments. What? I've startled you again. I see it in your eyes. You weren't just surprised it was sewing."

"You read people too well, my lord," Ankarette said. She had let down her defenses, something she rarely did. "I flinched because that is my . . . my favorite thing. I love to sit and think and do needlework. I always have. Whenever I have a thorny problem, I reach for my needles."

Alensson smiled approvingly. "As did she. As did our little Genette." He sighed, lost in a memory. "When we returned with her blade, it was further evidence the Fountain had chosen her as its champion. The prince commanded that a suit of armor be fashioned especially for her. A woman's set of armor. The blacksmith was agog at the request! The steel was so well polished it was practically white, and the suit was measured and fitted for her. There was a design on the breastplate, a little embellishment like ivy and thorns. The blacksmith was inspired by her, I think. I was given a suit of armor myself. Lord Doone was to command the army to be sure nothing foolhardy was attempted, but I was given orders to train the Maid in the arts of war—to teach her to fight, to ride, to understand the supply wagons and such. It took time for the armor to be done and for the army to muster together."

Ankarette saw the faraway look in his eyes. "Did your wife return to the cottage with Alix?" she asked delicately.

Alensson looked chagrined. "I sent her away too quickly.

She feared being a woman in a soldiers' camp, as I mentioned." He put his foot down and then went for his goblet. After taking a healthy sip, he started to laugh. "She shouldn't have worried about *that*."

The poisoner gave him a puzzled look. "And why not? Armies do tend to be rowdy and vulgar. I speak from experience, my lord," she added.

"As do I, of course," the duke said with a meaningful look. "I've never fought in an army that wasn't. Except for one. Hers. Genette was different. She was . . . how can I put this? She demanded us to be better. She was intolerant of vice and as outspoken as a deconeus. She never tried to persuade or influence, mind you." He chopped the edge of his hand against his palm. "She was Fountain-blessed and that was authority enough. So she *demanded* the army to behave. Yes, there were camp followers there at first, but the Maid ordered them out." He grinned at her. "At the point of her own sword too!"

Ankarette stifled a laugh. "I wish I had seen that."

He nodded appreciatively. "It was a sight to behold! Imagine it: a girl of seventeen railing on brazen women of twenty and five, some even older! I remember the night she drove them away from the camp. That was before we marched to Lionn." His eyes took on that deep feeling again, as if he were reliving memories that were sacred to him. "Who can forget the siege of Lionn? What feats we accomplished." His lips were quivering with emotion. Then he straightened. "You recall, Ankarette, that Lionn had been under siege for years. The city and duchy belonged to my father-in-law, who was a prisoner in Kingfountain. The city held for him, but they were losing hope."

"How did the city hold out so long?" she asked him.

He nodded, pursing his lips. "A good question. People rarely ask good questions anymore. But you do. I like that about you." He set the goblet down on the table. "I'll tell you about Lionn and how Genette finally broke the siege. But first, let me help you understand who the Maid was. She led us to victory through the force of her personality. She was so certain the Fountain was with her. And it was."

CHAPTER NINE

Resurgence

Spectators flocked to the training fields in Shynom to watch the impoverished duke of La Marche teach an unskilled peasant girl how to fight. Bawdy jokes were only half hidden behind hands. Bets were passed from purse to palm. There was the perception that it would take more than a few weeks to train such a peasant, Fountain-blessed or not, in the arts of war.

Then, on the third day, stunned silence fell on the onlookers as Genette disarmed him. Twice.

It was the sword, they said. The blade that had been drawn from the fountain at Firebos was enchanted. In defiance of such talk, Genette exchanged weapons with Alensson and repeated the maneuver that had disarmed him. Within moments, she sent Firebos flinging out of his hand and thudding onto the packed earth.

Alensson stopped wondering *how* she did it. And he began

teaching her in earnest. Soon he was also defending himself in earnest.

He'd learned some tricks from the soldiers of Ceredigion during his long confinement in Callait. Alensson deflected a blow that made his elbow ring with pain, then stepped in and hooked his foot around Genette's ankle. He was taller and more muscular, and he levered her backward as their sword guards locked, trying to trip her. Her hand reached up to grab his belt as the momentum between them shifted. Alensson realized he'd fall right on top of her; he hesitated. Anger flashed through her eyes, and she twirled away and rounded on him.

"*Gentle* duke, you are *too* gentle!" she scolded. Her dark cropped hair stuck to her face and she was breathing heavily, nearly as heavily as he was.

He paused to catch his breath. "Are you chiding me?"

"I am," she replied, shaking her head. "You should have let me fall!"

"I didn't want to crush you," he countered.

Her eyes flashed with anger again. "What do you think I am made of? Glass? When we fight against Ceredigion, do you think our foes will treat me with delicacy?"

He stared at her curiously. "You are planning to *fight* at Lionn?"

"Do you think the men will fight as hard if I'm not fighting with them? Of course I will fight. Which is why you must *train* me!" She shoved him hard and then lowered into a battle stance, her eyes narrowing.

Alensson followed suit, preparing again to wage war on this peasant girl who had somehow already learned to beat him. She had a sense about her that was eerily akin to magic. It was as if she could sense his weaknesses, sense where he was going to attack and when. But perhaps these too were gifts from the Fountain.

He did a feinting thrust and then whirled around. She deflected the blow, whirled around as he had, and then suddenly her blade was at his throat, pausing just before his quivering skin. He stared at it in shock, realizing that she could have taken off his head.

"I won't fool with you, Gentle Duke," she said. "Harder! Fight harder!"

They went at it again, and then again. Most duels between knights lasted for a brief time, but it took Alensson nearly twice the normal time to subdue her. He still came out ahead five times out of seven, but each day that ratio leaned more in her favor.

"Rest, Gentle Duke," she finally said, mopping her forehead with her arm. She was breathing heavy and fast as well.

He let slip an oath of amazement and saw her wince.

"Do not swear against the Fountain," she chided, but this time she looked more injured than infuriated. "It is my friend."

The words had slipped out of his mouth unintentionally. "Forgive me."

She nodded to him in response. They went to the water bucket, and he let her fetch the ladle first. She was thirsty and sweating and looked like a soldier in her men's clothes. But there was a feminine quality to her face, to the arch of her brows. He felt for the girl as a brother does for a cherished sister, protective and caring. There was something too sacred about her for baser feelings. None of the men in the camp had dared harass her.

She handed him the ladle and he scooped up some of the fresh water, drinking it heartily before he scooped some more and dumped it on his head to soothe his burning scalp. He was battered by their training, but teaching such a prodigy had also made him better.

"You're really going to fight?" he asked her, feeling a certain protectiveness well up inside him.

"The Fountain sent me to free our people," she said calmly. "Our enemies will not give up unless we force them."

"Have you ever seen a battlefield, Genette?" He frowned at his own memories of a field of corpses filled with crimson puddles.

She looked at him. "Yes."

He was surprised. "Where? Was there a skirmish fought near Donremy?"

She shook her head. "There was a small one nearby, but I didn't see it."

"Then which one did you see?"

"I shouldn't tell you." Her expression had turned wary.

He put his hands on his hips. "Why not?"

A small smile quirked on her mouth. "You are already half frightened of me. I don't wish to make it any worse."

"I'm not scared of you," he said with a chuckle, but her accusation had some truth to it. He had always wished to be an instrument of the Fountain, yet it was daunting to see the girl imbued with its power so dramatically. "Tell me."

She yanked off her gauntlets, then hung them from her belt and soothed her battered knuckles. "I've seen battles we will yet fight."

His eyes widened.

She nodded, keeping her voice low. "The Fountain shows me things. I've seen Lionn, even though I've never been there. There's a river and a bridge. And two sets of towers."

"That is true," Alensson answered in amazement. "The

Fountain has sent you, Genette. I believed it when I first met you in the tavern."

Her smile was gratifying. "I know you did, Alen. That is why I tell you these things. Because you believed in me before anyone else did. We will fight against Ceredigion at Lionn. They will not give up easily, but if we are persistent, if we *fight*, then we will win and drive them out of the smaller towers." She gave him a steady look. "You must not fear for me. I will be wounded in the battle. Right here." She pointed to her collarbone above her left breast. "I am not afraid of pain. I *know* it will be all right."

Her words sent a shudder through him. It was as if the wind were speaking with her voice. He wanted to ask her a dozen questions. If the lass could see the future, what did it mean? What else had she seen?

"You want to ask me something, but you dare not," she said with a small laugh. "I told you that I frighten you." She reached out and put her hand on his arm. "Hold your questions for now. Just believe in me, Alen. Follow my commands. Then I will explain the rest."

There was power in her touch, in her voice. He sensed it like a vast, rippling lake full of boats and wriggling trout and summer breezes. And yet there was also a sense of peace radiating from her.

"Who are you?" he asked in a whisper. If he hadn't witnessed the deconeus performing the rite, he would have suspected she was a water sprite in mortal form.

"I am a maid," she answered him simply, letting go of his arm. "The Fountain can work wonders from the lowliest of creatures. I have power because I believe in it. Maybe you will too someday." She smiled at him, but her words cut him to his core. For years he had fostered doubts in the Fountain because he had never felt its power himself, despite his many efforts. Perhaps those tiny seeds of doubt had always stood in his way.

It had grown late and they walked side by side back to the army encamped outside the fortress of Shynom. Soldiers had built small cookfires and were starting to prepare skewers of meat. A few were already drunk, their boisterous voices filling the air with commotion. Genette scowled as they passed, her eyes brooding and dark with anger. Inside the camp, all the grass had been crushed by dirty boots and filth. The air was filled with the buzzing of flies, the stamping of horses, and the braying of mules. There were tents everywhere—some small, some larger—their size representing the relative importance of their inhabitants. Chatriyon had summoned an army at last, but it was a rowdy group numbering only a few thousand. Some of the soldiers had been drawn to the miracles they had heard about. Some had only come because of the pay.

"This is no army," Genette muttered under her breath. "Tomorrow I will start them cleaning. We cannot live like this."

"It gets worse, you know," he told her. "Wait until it rains. The smell . . ." He shook his head.

Genette looked at him askance. "You are one of the leaders, yet you permit this disorder?"

"This is the nature of men and war," he answered with a shrug. "I may as well frown at a mountain and expect it to change."

"Men are not like stone," she answered, staring into his eyes. "They are more like clay. There is a potter in my village. I loved watching him coax his clay into shapes. You are a potter of men, Alen. Do not let things shape you."

Genette knew none of the subtleties and social graces of court. But she was uncommonly wise for a peasant—even more so for one so young.

They reached her small tent, marked by a white pennant hanging from the center pole. She usually worked on her needlework in the evenings. "How is your banner coming along?"

"It's not ready yet, but it will be finished in time for Lionn," she answered. There was a boy of twelve at the door of the tent, her page assigned to her by the prince's own household. He was a tawny-haired lad who brought her meals and helped run errands for her. His name was Brendin.

"I will see you tomorrow," Alensson said, nodding first to the boy and then to Genette. "I think I'm too tired to eat." He started toward his tent, which had been pitched within sight of hers. He noticed a woman lurking in the shadows next to his tent. A suspicion began to form in his mind when he heard Genette's voice calling him.

"*Gentle* duke."

He stopped and looked back at her. She was staring at his tent, not at him, and a frown had stolen across her face. Motioning for the page to follow her, she walked fiercely toward Alensson's tent.

"What is it?" he asked, but she brushed past him. Hands on his hips, he stared at her in confusion.

But Genette did not even pause—she walked right up to the woman loitering by the tent and seized her arm. He had never seen her before, but it was clear she was a camp follower.

"Out! Get out of this camp! Be gone!" Genette shouted.

The woman's gaze blazed with hatred as she glared at Genette, struggling to remain in the shadows as she tried to back away from the tent. The commotion brought attention from all corners as the soldiers fixing their meals stopped mid-action and began to gawk.

Alensson's eyes bulged as the Maid unsheathed the sword Firebos. The woman began to cower and free herself from Genette's firm grasp.

There was fire in the Maid's eyes. Suddenly, she swung the flat of the blade against the girl's rump, causing her to yelp and squeal. "Out! All of you! Out! I will go tent to tent. If I find one of you here in the morning, I will thrash her in front of the rest of you! This is the Fountain's army! It bids me purge it! Be gone! Seek your coin doing more honest work. Out!" She whacked the woman again as she scrambled to flee.

It caused an uproar throughout the camp, for the Maid began searching tent after tent, fulfilling her promise. Within the hour, all of the camp followers had packed up and fled, much to the chagrin and consternation of most of the soldiers. But no one dared bring a girl back that night, not even the nobles.

Word spread that the Fountain had spoken to the Maid again, whispering which tents the girls would be in, and no one wanted to be the one caught in the act of defying her, even if they didn't believe she was sent from the Fountain.

It was dark when Genette finally returned to her tent with Brendin, who carried the garments and articles left behind by the strumpets. Alensson, holding a bowl of camp stew, looked at her in admiration. She paused before going into her tent.

"No one will take your wife's place at your side," she told him, glancing at him. "I will watch over you, Alen. Until she returns to you."

CHAPTER TEN

The Maid's Fury

A change came over the royal army that night. It was noticeable the next day as the soldiers rose from their sleeping mats and tents. There was normally a commotion of grumbling and jibes, but the camp was unusually quiet. It became even more so as the Maid turned her will toward her next mission: tackling the cursing in the camp. Whenever she passed a man who let out an oath or swore because of pain or pretense, she quickly rebuked him—even if the man in question was older than her father—and admonished him to cease profaning. And the men obeyed her—some grudgingly, some shamefully, but they still obeyed her.

The soldiers drilled. They marched. They mended armor, fixed the nicks in their swords, battle axes, and spears. All the while, Genette the Maid, as they began to call her, sewed her banner with fleurs-de-lis, flowers shaped like decorated fountains.

It had taken the prince several weeks after her miraculous demonstration in court to gather the army together in one place. One afternoon, a few days into the army's transformation, Alensson inspected the supply wagons and consulted with the local captain about the food provisions they'd need, to relieve the siege at Lionn. The captain thought it would take another month, perhaps two, to break the will of the Ceredigion defenders. A two-month siege would require nearly double the rations they had, so Alensson went to the command pavilion of Earl Doone to seek the counsel of the lord. He was surprised to find Genette there, in her armor, dictating a letter.

"Withdraw, or I will compel you to. I am the Maid and thus the Fountain bids me."

"What is this?" Alensson whispered to her young squire.

The squire was gawking at his mistress, her hair freshly washed, her cheeks slightly flushed from her excited manner of speaking. In the days that had followed the incident at Alensson's tent, her demeanor had shifted from peasant to nobility, as if she had commanded servants all her life.

"Read it back to me," she demanded of the scribe, Doone's man, who looked at her as if she were some madwoman.

"Do it," Doone said, giving Alensson a nod that spoke of his bewilderment.

The scribe cleared this throat and pushed his spectacles higher up his nose. "Ahem. 'To the Duke of Deford. To Lord Scales and Lord Tenby. To Lord Ashe. Greetings to you, lords of Ceredigion. In the name of the Fountain and the true king of Occitania, I—Genette the Maid—order you to abandon the cities you unrighteously hold.'" He paused, tapping his cheek with the quill. "That is not a *proper* word . . ." he added sheepishly.

"Keep reading!" Genette snapped.

"Very well, ahem, 'I implore you, on fear for your life and lands, on the lives and duties which you hold to your wives and your children, that you withdraw immediately from Lionn and all the towns up to the river Argent. If you do not, I will attack you and drive you out, and much blood will be shed. You have usurped the rights of Occitania, which displeases the Fountain. Withdraw, or I will compel you to. I am the Maid and thus the Fountain bids me.' "

The scribe lowered his head, looking at her from above his spectacles. "Is that all?"

"Send a herald to Lionn and have this delivered to the garrison captain, Lord Tenby."

Earl Doone stared at her agape. "You're going to warn them we're coming?"

"Of course," Genette said, full of confidence. "We must give them a chance to leave before we attack."

"But telling them defeats the advantage of surprise. No doubt their spies have watched our army growing. They know we're going to attack, but they do not yet know *where*." He looked at Alensson for support, gesturing for him to speak up.

Alensson looked into Doone's eyes. "I see no harm in her strategy."

"You too?" Doone's tone was full of accusation. "After what you did at Vernay, I was expecting something more subtle!"

Alensson raised his eyebrows. "Do you think they will believe we are coming to attack them when we say we are? Might they not consider it a ruse?"

Genette stamped her foot. "I intend no trickery. Why are we debating this? We should be at Lionn already. Did I not tell you the power of the Fountain is with us?"

"You did," Doone said with a grimace. "But surely it expects us to use wisdom and judgment. We're gathering supplies for the army. Men can't eat promises, girl. They need to be paid. How much longer will the supply wagons take, Alensson?"

"We almost have enough for the first month, but the captain of the supply wagons thinks the siege might take months, so—"

"Enough of this!" Genette interrupted. "We must go. We must go at once. We will break the siege in days, my lords, not months."

Alensson stared at her in surprise. Had she seen this in the visions she'd told him about?

She nodded vigorously and pounded her fist into her palm. "Believe in my mission, lords of Occitania. Believe I am what I declared myself to be, or believe me not at all. We must ride today. The people of Lionn have suffered this siege for too long. Lord Tenby will not surrender the city to us easily. He will fight. But we will win. Send this letter ahead of us. Send a copy to Deford himself in Pree. No matter how much they try to prepare, they will fail. They may as well try and stop a flood." Her words had an ominous sound to them.

Doone threw up his hands. "I'll notify the prince that we are leaving *now*. We'll see if *he* supports this risk."

Genette smiled triumphantly. She turned to her squire. "Fetch my banner at once."

◆　　◆　　◆

Alensson had thought he'd have time to see Jianne before they departed for Lionn. The suddenness of their decampment prevented that, and he knew she'd worry about him, so he hastily wrote another letter to her to inform her of his departure and to seek her forgiveness for not coming, but he added that he hoped they would next meet in her liberated city. He rode astride a borrowed warhorse, next to Genette and her squire, down the dusty road toward the city of Lionn. There would be no disguising the army's approach, and the letter had been sent ahead. Surely their enemies would await them.

Despite Genette's confidence, which he had pretended to share while in Doone's tent, Alensson was wary and had dispatched scouts to warn them of any ambushes along the way. There were none. It took the army four days to reach the town of Blais, but their progress was halted there when word arrived that the prince had changed his mind and commanded the army to halt.

The Maid was incensed by the sudden delay, but Doone refused to countermand the prince's orders. The army camped outside the city, the men restless and eager to continue. Genette ordered them to continue drilling and training, but she chafed at the prince's sudden change of heart, which she saw as a show of cowardice.

"Why must we stop here?" she complained to Alensson. "Lionn is only two leagues away!"

"The prince has ordered us to send scouts ahead to test the city's loyalty. He fears we may be riding into a trap." Alensson was equally impatient with the delay, but he understood the prince's precaution. It was a sign of Genette's utter conviction in the Fountain and her cause that she could not.

She gripped the hilt of her blade and scowled at him. "There is no trap! The city is weak and disheartened. But they are faithful to His Grace!"

Alensson put his hand on her armored shoulder. The sheen

wasn't as radiant after being buffeted by the dust of the journey, but it was still new. She was like a caged bear, full of pent-up fury. Looking into her eyes, he said, "You know that. *I* know that. The king is more cautious. We were defeated at Azinkeep. We were defeated at Vernay. The risk of another loss weighs heavily on him."

Genette took a deep steadying breath and slowly released it. "You speak wise counsel, Alen. I will try to be patient."

♦ ♦ ♦

Her squire approached quickly. "My lady, Earl Doone requests that you both ride with his contingent and a small force to Lionn. Our scouts have returned. The city is loyal to us. The rest of the army will stay here until the prince approves."

"Progress, at last," Genette muttered under her breath. The delay had been for several days already.

Although they left the bulk of the army in Blais, they rode ahead with an escort of seventy knights—the primary nobles of the camp. No one wanted to miss the upcoming confrontation. As they crested the last wooded hill before reaching Lionn, Alensson pulled up his reins to gaze on it. He'd not been there for years, but it was a familiar and welcome sight.

The fortress of Lionn bore similarities to the city of Pree in that a river cut through it. Also as in Pree, the city had expanded in ever growing circles around both sides of the river, creating layer upon layer of defenses as the city swelled. It made defeating cities like this very difficult because penetrating one series of walls required piercing further obstacles. The Maid had said it would take a matter of days to liberate Lionn. Though he understood Doone's doubts—he did not understand how such a thing could be possible—Alensson had confidence in the girl after seeing so many demonstrations of her powers.

Unlike Pree, where the two halves of the city were connected by many bridges, Lionn had only one bridge. The Ceredigic army had first successfully captured the smaller, western half—the part that lay before them—and it was manned by a garrison of enemy knights. Although smaller than the city on the other side of the river, it was very defensible, with a tower fortress butting up to the bridgehead. The wooden planks of the bridge had been dismantled by the city's carpenters during the siege to prevent the soldiers from using it to cross. Only the stone arch supports were left. The river flowed swiftly, far too wide for an army to cross without boats. The rest of the Ceredigic army was encamped on the opposite side of the river, where they hacked away at the remaining defenses of the city. If they succeeded in taking Lionn, it would give them a huge stronghold from which to launch an attack on Shynom itself. The people of the city were hungry and frightened, but the progress of the siege had been slow. Alensson could see why. So many walls had yet to be claimed, allowing the inhabitants to hunker within them and ride out the storm. The Maid's army would have the same trouble trying to drive the army of Ceredigion out of their portion of the city. There were fewer walls, but they were high, allowing the enemies an opportunity to shoot crossbows and rain stones down on those attempting to climb up. Alensson shook his head as he saw the smoke stains over the beleaguered city.

"Have courage, Gentle Duke," the Maid said as she rode past him.

There were small camps of Ceredigic soldiers outside the

walls of the conquered part of the city, but not nearly enough to threaten seventy knights, and they withdrew back behind the fortifications as the Occitanians approached.

The inhabitants had made preparations for the arriving troops and several ferries issued out from the besieged part of the city, upstream from them. Their horses were blindfolded and led to the ferries, and oarsmen steered them into the waters as the current brought them swiftly toward the unoccupied half of Lionn.

"The towers there," Alensson said to her as they gazed up at the fortifications, "they are called the Turrels. We can't get too close or their archers will rain arrows down on us."

Genette frowned. "Will they try with boats? I'd welcome a fight."

He smiled at her enthusiasm. "The river is just as dangerous for them to cross as it is for us. See how our portion of Lionn is so much larger?" he said, pointing across the river. "They have a strong foothold in the city. But we hold the stronger part by far."

She nodded and then stumbled into him as the skiff shook on the water. The water was rough, but he somehow managed to keep them both upright. In short order, they reached the safe side of Lionn, where they were greeted on the dock by the mayor, the nobles, and a screaming crowd. Genette carried her banner with her, and the people went wild when they saw it. Her message had been delivered to the townspeople. Rumors of her had spread like fire, and here she was in flesh and armor, looking like a soldier and a woman and a true champion of the Fountain. She smiled at those assembled, waving her banner triumphantly, and Alensson felt a thrill as he watched her ride forward through the crowd that parted to make room. This, he knew, was a moment the world would remember.

There was an equivalent set of towers on their side of the bridge, facing the Turrels. It was the most fortified portion of the city, and the Maid and her leaders were taken there through streets that were filled with well-wishers. When they arrived in the main gallery of the palace, they found Earl Doone had already arrived and was speaking to the garrison captain, a weather-beaten man in dented armor. He had fiery-red hair and a scar that split his lip by his nostril, giving him a fierce look. A huge sword was strapped to his back.

"I thought an army was coming with you," the red-haired giant growled. "This is all? Seventy knights?"

Doone looked defensive. "Don't be harsh, Aspen. The prince ordered the army to halt at Blais for a while. He wasn't sure how ready the city was to receive us."

The Maid looked to Alensson curiously, nodding toward the giant of a man.

Alensson lowered his voice and whispered in her ear. "That's Lord Hext, my wife's uncle. He's been defending the city. His nickname is 'Aspen' because of the coloring of the leaves in the autumn."

Genette nodded knowingly and then strode forward. The giant looked down at her, unimpressed. "You're a little wisp of a thing, aren't you, lass?"

She did not cower before his size. "My letter was given to Lord Tenby?" she demanded.

Aspen Hext chuckled sardonically. "Aye, lass. And they put the herald in chains afterward and barraged us with arrows for the insult."

Alensson watched her nostrils flare white. "Did they? To a herald?"

"They weren't of a mind to heed your threat, lass. I gladly

accept the help. I don't care if the Fountain sent a crowing rooster to liberate us. This is war, and war is a messy thing. I have a room waiting for you to take a nap, little girl. Leave the men to plan this thing."

"But he answered my letter," she said stiffly, eyes blazing hot. "Didn't he?"

Lord Hext gave her a second look, this one more guarded. "Aye, lass."

"What did it say?"

"I'd rather not repeat the insults. Especially in the presence of a *maid*."

"What did he say?" Genette asked, her voice dangerously close to a growl.

Alensson saw that Hext was goading her. But it was obvious the big man didn't want to repeat the words. They were probably unseemly.

Aspen Hext shrugged. He was a soldier. Rough language didn't concern him. "In part, he asked me to tell the little *whore* from Donremy to ply her trade in another city." He gave her a stern look as he said it.

Putting her hand on her hilt, Genette marched right past him, causing a ruckus of confusion. Infuriated by the insult, Alensson followed her, as did many of the men, Hext and Doone included. She strode confidently, as if she had been in the castle a hundred times, and headed directly to the tower stairwell leading to the roof. The clang of armor spurs on the stone steps rang through the tower like a bell as the group ascended.

When they reached the roof of the turret, Alensson watched as Genette strode to the edge of the barricade, the sun glinting dazzlingly off her armor. She stood facing the Turrels, the wind sweeping her cropped hair back from her brow.

She leaned forward, planting one hand on the stone, and cupped the other hand by her mouth. "Lord Tenby! I am the Maid! Surrender the Turrels before I take them from you! This is your final warning before you drink from the Deep Fathoms!"

Could they even hear her words across the river? She had shouted them with all the emotion and rage in her heart.

They did hear her, for Alensson heard a building roar of riotous laughter from the other side of the river. Instead of launching arrows, the men began to mock Genette in the most vile language he'd ever heard soldiers utter.

Her face went dark with danger while her mouth turned down into a stern frown. She listened and did nothing for a while. Then she said darkly, almost to herself, but loud enough that they could hear it over the noise. "Beware of pride, sirs. It is always the stone that causes the stumble."

CHAPTER ELEVEN

The Siege of Lionn

Word finally reached them the following afternoon that the prince had ordered them to mount the attack. Alensson was relieved, for Genette had taken to pacing like a caged lioness, her temper short and easily provoked. At least the time they'd spent with the besieged half of Lionn had given them time to plan. Genette had impressed Aspen Hext, who'd expected she would cower from the enemy's threats and insults. Together, the leaders of the group had discussed strategy, but Genette refused to trick or decoy their enemies or consider any strategy besides breaching the walls with scaling ladders. If the soldiers bore the abuse with determination, they would drive the defenders from the walls. The certain way she said it made Alensson wonder what she knew, what she had seen.

When the army decamped from Blais and arrived in Lionn after nightfall, they were greeted by the Ceredigic defenders. The enemy was outnumbered and quickly withdrew back into the city gates, barring the doors and lowering the portcullis. The battle for Lionn began almost at once, during the night, and soon Alensson was in the thick of it. He knew Genette was sleeping in the city across the river and she'd be angry no one had awakened her. But he also realized that the cover of darkness would help them mount the attack. The defenders were scrambling to cover the entire breadth of the wall, spreading their numbers thin in their effort to keep it protected. Alensson and Hext had agreed that it was too risky to send someone across the river in the dark to fetch Genette and that her presence would be more inspiring after sunrise when the troops could see her and her banner. She would get one more night of sleep before the images of war gave her nightmares.

As he moved amongst his men, trying to rally them, he heard shouts announcing the arrival of the Maid. Alensson was thunderstruck that she had crossed the river at night to join them. He pushed his way through the crowd until he found her. She sat there astride her horse, full armored and carrying her banner, her eyes filled with scolding anger.

"How did you cross the river?" he demanded, looking at the disheveled hair coming loose from the mail hood covering her head.

"I rode across," she answered stiffly, and he stared at her in shock. The feat was impossible because of the depth of the river, and besides, the horse was not wet and neither was she.

"I don't understand," Alensson said gruffly.

"No, you don't," she answered. "But my words are true. Remember that the Fountain has power over all water. It awoke me in the night to tell me the battle had started. You should have sent for me."

"It was too dangerous!" he said. "They attacked us when

the rest of our men arrived, and we drove them off. Lord Hext thought it better to press our advantage under the cover of darkness."

Genette nodded firmly. "It's a good plan. You should have summoned me."

He looked up at her on the horse. "It's dangerous. We won't breach the walls tonight. There will be chance to fight tomorrow, when everyone can see you. Come to the command pavilion. We can discuss it there."

She shook her head stubbornly. "I said I would drive them out. And I will fulfill my vow." She jerked the reins of her horse and headed toward the walls of the embattled city.

"Fountain help me," Alensson muttered, then yelled for his horse and joined her.

◆　　◆　　◆

Alensson followed the Maid all the way to the walls, where it rained arrows instead of water. Feathered shafts poked out of the grass and dirt of a field covered in fallen soldiers, many writhing in pain, many more dead. The men were shouting at each other, calls of challenge and rage that were not quite words. There was hatred between these two sides, and one could feel it in the air like a choking smoke. Every attempt to put a scaling ladder against the wall had been repelled, and men fell from great heights to lie crumpled on the ground with broken limbs. Archers from the walls continued to rain death down on them, but the archers on the Occitanian side found their marks as well. The cries of injury came from both sides.

The memories of Vernay were assaultive. Alensson's heart was in his throat; his pulse was pounding in his skull. The longer they stayed, the more men would die. A crew of soldiers equipped with shields and a battering ram hammered at the main door. Each grunt and charge rocked the doors, but every few moments one of their numbers dropped, felled by archers. Alensson kept Genette in sight at all times, watching her cry courage to her men as she waved her banner before them. If a stripling girl had the courage to make herself a target for her enemies, none of the men would dare break and run.

Another attempt was made to put a scaling ladder against the wall. Several men held it down while others began to climb. Genette planted her banner in the destroyed ground and rushed forward to help the attempt.

Alensson remembered her warning the instant before it happened.

An arrow pierced Genette's chest, right near the neck, a blow that would have killed any man. Genette toppled backward from the force of the impact and the men around her watched, momentarily stunned. A cheer went up from the wall of defenders as Alensson raced over to her. She had warned him of this, but it was one thing to hear her tell it and another to see it happen. His heart breaking with sadness, he grabbed her beneath her arms and began pulling her away. Another man joined him, hoisting her legs so that they didn't have to drag her. She groaned with pain from the movement, and cries of anguish rose in the air as the men watched the Maid be carried off the field, her banner rustling listlessly near where she had fallen.

"Fetch a surgeon!" Alensson shouted to a soldier with a panic-stricken face.

"Set me down!" Genette said through a grimace.

They had put some distance between themselves and the combat, and although arrows continued to fall nearby, they were stray ones. Alensson nodded to his fellow, and they carefully set her down. The arrow was embedded deep inside her. The wound would cripple her arm, he could see that at once—and that was only if she managed to survive the bleeding. The armor was stanching the wound somewhat, though, and he was surprised there was not as much blood as he'd feared. Of course, there was only moonlight and starlight to see by, no torches.

"Pull it out," Genette said with a gasp, looking at his face.

"It may do more damage that way," Alensson said, shaking his head. "Sometimes it's better to push it all the way through. I sent for a surgeon." His hands were shaking. The bitter taste of defeat was in his mouth—familiar and acrid. Could he survive another Vernay? He wasn't sure he could bear it.

"Pull it out!" she insisted, grabbing his hand and trying to lift it.

He jerked away from her, recoiling. "I dare not! It could kill you!"

Genette's face was pale. Several other soldiers had gathered around them. Suddenly, Aspen Hext pushed his way into the circle, shoving aside a bystander so hard the man went down.

"She fell?" Hext growled. The look of respect in his eyes was immense as he stared down at her writhing body. She had proved she was no figurehead of the army. She had struggled on the front lines alongside the bravest of them. "The men started to flee when they heard!"

Alensson looked back and saw the soldiers slinking away from the battle.

"Pull—it—out!" the Maid growled, her eyes finding Alensson's. "It's a bee sting. I need to get back there. They cannot flee. We must take the outer wall tonight!"

"Lass," Lord Hext said. "You need a surgeon. It will take

hours to get that out." The huge red-bearded man turned to face Alensson. "I'll carry her to the tent. Try to rally the men. No, girl, stop!"

Alensson had been looking at Lord Hext, so he hadn't seen Genette reach for the arrow herself. With a cry of pain, she wrenched it from her shoulder and flung it aside.

"Get me up! Get me up!" she said viciously, grabbing the front of Alensson's tunic to hoist herself up. Somehow the girl made it to her feet. Somehow, he didn't know how, she stayed on her feet, though she wobbled.

"Back to the wall!" she said. "They need to see me! Back to my banner."

She grabbed Alensson's arm and started back the way they'd come. At first Alensson's feet wouldn't heed him—how could she be walking? How could she even be standing? He'd seen how deeply the shaft had penetrated her. She should be gushing blood; she should be *dying*. Though he genuinely believed she was the Fountain's champion, this . . . well, he'd never seen the likes of this. Her stride grew stronger as they walked together, one of her hands clutching his arm, her other hand on the pommel of her sword. He noticed the raven symbol on the scabbard. It caught his eye, though he couldn't explain why. Was she drawing strength from the blade Firebos? Was the Fountain itself pouring life back in to her?

"I told you this would happen, Gentle Duke," she said, noticing his bafflement. "Why didn't you believe me? The wound isn't serious. I'll be fine."

When they reached her discarded banner, it was still upright, though there were several arrow holes in the fabric. Releasing her grip on him, Genette walked forward with calm strength and hoisted the banner again, crying out to her countrymen, "Courage! Courage! The Fountain is on our side! Take courage!"

A battle cry swelled from the ranks when the men saw her waving the banner again after having fallen to a mortal wound. The Fountain was on their side, and they could not lose. The soldiers had been peeling away from the wall, but they flooded back triumphantly. Three ladders started up again, but this time two of them held, and soldiers managed to clear the wall. Fighting broke out on the ramparts above, and bodies began to topple over, but it wasn't clear which side they belonged to. Shouts of victory began to surge from the prince's army.

Genette was quick to follow. Gripping the banner in one hand, she started scaling the ladder, using the arm that should have been permanently disabled to haul herself up the rungs. Alensson came up behind her, amazed at her endurance but determined to protect her. As soon as they cleared the rampart, several soldiers from Ceredigion charged at her with their swords. Alensson leaped in front of the Maid, his sword ringing from his sheath. He skewered one man and blocked the attacks of the others. Paying no attention to the danger she was in, Genette swung her banner over her head from atop the wall, and a roar of cheers sounded from below.

More and more soldiers from the Maid's army arrived, and Alensson saw with satisfaction that the enemy was fleeing, abandoning the outer fortifications to try to reach the Turrels in time. There was more than one wall defending their position, and the tower would be even more difficult to breach. But somehow they had succeeded. He didn't know the cost in life at this point, but it was worth it. In one night, they had begun to overturn the defenses of Lionn. By dawn, they would have shelter from the arrows of their enemies. They would have more supplies. They would win; finally, Alensson would be part of a victory.

"Watch, Gentle Duke," the Maid said in his ear after he'd dispatched another soldier, killing him. He swiveled and looked, saw her arm pointing to the tower where their enemy had fled.

Men with torches stood atop it, overseeing the disaster unfolding below. He couldn't see their faces, but their tunics bore the enemy's standard.

One of the men was running down the narrow stairwell that wrapped around the outside of the tower wall, leading down to the battlements below. And he watched in horror as the man with the torch stumbled and then plunged off the tower wall, landing in the massive river with a splash that could be heard over the noise of the fighting.

"By the Veil!" Alensson gasped. "He was wearing armor too!"

He saw the corners of Genette's lips start to curve. "He was indeed. That was Lord Tenby."

"The commander? How do you ... ?" Then he caught himself.

"I did warn him," she said with a knowing smile.

CHAPTER TWELVE

Triumph

The mood in the army had changed overnight. By morning, the defeat Alensson had once seen in the eyes of the Occitanian soldiers had blossomed into hope. There were no shouted taunts and bravado from the defenders; all was stony silence. The outer walls of the defenses had been breached, and now the fighting was happening in the streets beyond.

Alensson hadn't slept in almost two days and he felt weary and beleaguered, but the air was electric with energy. It was the same as the crackle of wood before a tree falls down. They were winning—they were finally winning! Deford's army was still in Pree, it was said. He had neither believed the Maid's threat nor considered her a true danger. Now his captain in Lionn had drowned in the river and the defenders were leaderless and frightened.

But to finish what they started, they needed the Maid. Alensson walked through the makeshift camp outside the walls, making his way to Genette's tent. He had sent a surgeon to attend to her wound. To his surprise, she was sitting up when he entered. Her breastplate and gauntlets had been removed, but she was still armored from the waist down. Her sweat-stained tunic was begrimed, and there was a huge tear in it from where the arrow had penetrated.

"How deep was the wound?" Alensson asked the surgeon.

"It was nothing," Genette insisted.

The surgeon put his hands on his hips, shaking his head. "I don't know how she pulled it out without bleeding to death. The wound seemed to ... close on its own. I used no stitches." He spoke the words in an undertone, as if even he did not totally believe them.

"I told you I wouldn't need any," Genette groused. "You've made me undress in front of all these men. Now let me put my armor back on so we can take the Turrels!"

Alensson sighed. "We had to be sure you were all right, Genette," he said patiently. Her squire was already girding her again for battle. The surgeon shrugged in bafflement and then hurried from the tent to tend to the other wounded.

"That arrow should have killed you," Alensson insisted.

As she shrugged on the breastplate, his eyes found the place where the arrow had pierced the metal. It was much more pronounced in the daylight. She frowned when she saw him looking at it. Then she sighed and looked him in the eye. "I am truly unhurt now," she said, her voice dropping lower. "Would I be standing like this if I were pained? Thank you for your concern, Alen. One of the smiths can fix this in a trice." Her voice became more urgent. "But later! We must go! How is the attack going? We must hammer at the towers until they fall. If they try to escape by boat in the river, we must stop them."

Alensson folded his arms. "The orders have been given. Lord Hext is leading the attack. The mayor is watching the dock to make sure no one tries to flee. But it may be too difficult to spot them under cover of darkness."

She shook her head as her squire fixed the shoulder blades onto her armor. "It will fall today."

He didn't bother asking how she knew that. After spending so much time with her, he'd come to learn that the Fountain spoke to her daily. She was unlike any Fountain-blessed in their records. She didn't demonstrate just one or two powers, but several—and they seemed to sprout whenever she needed them. Her knowledge of warfare and sieges was that of a seasoned battle commander.

A herald stormed in to the tent, then caught himself when he realized he had entered a woman's tent without announcing himself. He stammered an apology, but Genette had lived among men for several months now and did not require one.

"What news, Herald?" she demanded.

"I bring word from the lord mayor," he said. He bowed to Alensson. "The city's carpenters have joined the battle. Remember the bridge connecting the rest of Lionn to the Turrels? The stone is still standing, but all the planks were removed when the siege began. The carpenters are repairing it —and quickly. Soldiers are out there with shields, providing them cover from the archers. The lord mayor will commence attacking the Turrels by the bridgehead within the next few hours. They'll have to defend both sides at once!" The herald beamed.

It was welcome news. "That is impressive!" Alensson said, relieved. He smiled encouragingly at Genette.

"The people were inspired by the Maid," the herald said, giving Genette a respectful nod. "Everyone is helping. I've never seen Lionn so hopeful before. This is the first time we've had any hope since . . . since Azinkeep."

"Then go, Herald," Genette said calmly. "Tell the mayor that I thank him. We will meet in the tower. Tell him to bring a yellow flower. A lily, if he can find one."

The herald looked at her in surprise and so did Alensson. That flower was his wife Jianne's favorite. The Maid gave him a secretive smile as she finished dressing for battle. The scabbard and sword were still belted to her waist, and Alensson's eyes found the raven's head badge.

"That symbol is from Brythonica," he said, finally placing it.

"It is indeed," she replied, brushing her hands together. She turned to her squire. "Bring me my banner. We will make short work of our foes."

◆　　◆　　◆

From the heights of the Turrels, the soldiers were pelted with stones, crossbow bolts, buckets, and dozens of other makeshift weapons. The men were weary with exhaustion, but they continued to shove a battering ram against the tower doors with concerted grunts and pure brute strength. The freckled Aspen Hext led the charge, roaring his oaths as he gripped the front end of the ram with another man. Soldiers kept falling away wounded behind him, but he did not falter.

"Onward! We have almost won! Courage now! Stand fast!" Genette's voice could be heard over the cacophony of violence. The sound lent steel to the soldiers, who rushed forward to fill the gaps when men fell. Her cheeks were smudged with smoke, her voice was raw from screaming, but her eyes blazed with valor. Her expression wilted just slightly when a soldier standing nearby succumbed to blows, but she gritted her teeth and waved the banner even more vigorously.

Alensson ordered men to fire arrows up at the defenders, keeping up the pressure to make it more difficult for them to hobble the efforts below. Sweat stung his eyes, but he clenched his jaw and muscled through the fatigue and discomfort. Genette's courage made him all the more determined to win the day.

A splintering sound filled the air and then the pulverized door blew apart. A battered portcullis waited beyond, full of teeming soldiers armed with spears and lances. But even at this distance, Alensson could see the fear in their eyes. They already knew defeat lay ahead.

"Open the gate! Open the gate!" Alensson screamed. Soldiers flooded forward, and the men in the first row, Hext included, pulled at the heavy portcullis while soldiers tried to stab them through the slats. Many fell, their cries piercing the air. But others quickly replaced them, and they stacked pieces of timber under the gate to keep it up. Aspen Hext drove the defenders back from the gate with his two-handed broadsword. There was a flutter of white, and Alensson watched as Genette joined the fray, one hand on her banner, the other on the sword taken from the fountain at Firebos. She seemed oblivious to the death screams raging around her. Her eyes were fierce, her mouth fixed with courage. Arrows fell all around her like hailstones. The enemies were targeting her, but none of the archers found his target.

Sensing the danger to her—the Ceredigions all recognized Genette's importance by now, and they would all surely charge her—he pushed his way into the press of men crowded at the gate. But the Maid was surrounded by enemies before he could get to her. He howled in frustration, then watched in surprise as she defended herself using the principles he had taught her. She swung the flat of her blade around and hit a man in the side, but it was as if she were a reaper of wheat: Her one blow scattered four men instead of one. Her opponents exploded away from her, and then no other man dared face her, this maiden holding the sword of a long-dead king.

Alensson's eyes darted to the weapon, lingering on the rippled pattern in the metal, the five stars engraved on the blade inside the fuller. A part of him awakened at the sight of it—his ambition—and it howled like a wolf. If he could get his hands on that weapon, if *he* could use it instead of her, then he could become the next king of Occitania.

It was an ambition it had never before occurred to him to have.

In the sludge-like mire of his thoughts, amidst the shouts and screams of mortal combat, even in the act of slicing one of his enemies who confronted him, Alensson felt a desire for that sword that overswept even the love he had for his wife. He had seen Genette use it before and it had not roused such feelings in him. But those feelings were so strong now, they threatened to change him from the inside.

Half-formed thoughts, grievances, and fears swirled around inside him. Who was Chatriyon Vertus but a sniveling coward? Did he deserve to be king? Did he deserve the loyalty that had been shown him by those who had risked everything?

Someone brought a battle axe down on Alensson, and he spun around and gutted the man with a savage stroke. He kicked him next, and then he was fighting beside Genette, in awe of her power, in awe of the sword she held, and for the briefest flicker of a moment, he was tempted to shove her down in the confusion and yank the blade out of her hand.

But no. *No.*

He shook his head as if to rouse himself from an intense, lurid dream. After all he had given up. After all he had sacrificed, after all the years he had spent in Ceredigic confinement, he would not sell his honor so cheaply. His integrity was the only possession he truly owned; he could not bear to lose it.

Alensson took up a position behind her, defending her back as the battle raged inside the tower. There were so many people that Alensson found himself fighting friend as well as foe in the confusion. He kept glancing back at Genette, making sure she was still within sight amidst the flood of men-at-arms.

"Stay near me, Gentle Duke," he heard her say. "It is almost over."

But the fighting grew more savage and desperate before it ended. These were the last defenders, a brave and mighty foe who would neither yield nor ransom themselves. They expected no mercy after all they had boasted, all the ills they had done while ravaging Occitania. Alensson was jostled by one man just as another lunged toward the Maid with a spear —he elbowed the one in the face and then chopped down at the spearhead, knocking it aside before it reached her.

There was a groan of wood, followed by the rending sound of metal. The other gate of the Turrels was being breached by the city soldiers. Another wall of soldiers came flooding into the courtyard. Everything seemed to slow down, and Alensson turned to watch the newcomers join the fray. They devastated the remaining defenders, many of whom finally flung down their weapons in despair and sank to their knees in humiliation and defeat. They had the hollowed, anguished look of men who didn't know if they would live or die—and who didn't seem to care. He recognized it because he had felt that way before.

In the viscous haze of battle, he saw a hummingbird flit through the melee, an incongruous sight. He could almost hear the frantic buzz of its wings. Genette was standing still, her banner arm drooping as she stood, eyes closed, as if listening to a voice no one else could hear. The storm of chaos meant nothing to her. There was a peaceful air about her, and when she finally opened her eyes and looked at him, they were filled with joy.

"We have won the battle, Alen," she said with triumph, speaking above the noise. "But the war is not over."

The fight ended like a spilled cask, all the energy draining out of one side as the other began to whoop and cheer. The pride of victory swelled within them, stronger because of how long they had been oppressed. The soldiers mingled with their brothers who had come across the bridge. Aspen Hext pushed through the crowd. His armor was stained with blood and grime, but tears of joy trickled down his ruddy cheeks and mingled with the grit sticking in his beard. Then he started laughing—big bellowing laughs like a bear—and he went and hugged Genette, pulling her off her feet and kissing her cheek. She smiled with embarrassment, unable to do anything with her arms pinned to her sides. The soldiers were jumbling to crowd around her, chanting over and over, "The Maid! The Maid! The Maid!"

Alensson felt a surge of pride in Genette as he watched Hext set her down. She patted the lord's arm in an awkward gesture, her smile making her look very young and inexperienced. Sometimes it was easy to forget that both were true. Hext then led a cheer that could be heard all the way across the river. Alensson joined in until his throat was raw. The

Maid looked discomfited, but she patted Hext's arm again, trying to signal for him to stop even though she could not be heard. He was proud of her and ashamed at himself for the feelings that had momentarily insinuated themselves in him. He was a prince of the blood. But he was not the heir to the crown of Occitania. His duty as the Duke of La Marche was to fight for the man who was—not to decide if he deserved it. And he would play the role he'd been assigned, just as Genette had played her role as the redeemer of Lionn.

The surviving soldiers from Ceredigion were herded away and brought to the dungeons below the towers they had once claimed. Alensson felt sympathy for them, but he was grateful it was no longer his turn to play the captive. Lionn had been liberated in days, a feat that no one in Shynom would have imagined possible a fortnight ago. What miracle would happen next?

He saw Genette approach, the mayor of Lionn at her side. He saw the yellow lily in her gloved hand. The mayor was weeping with joy.

"This is for Jianne," the Maid said, offering him the flower. "She will be arriving soon. I have seen her coming. Her father may still be imprisoned in Kingfountain, but this is his city, after all."

"Thank you," he said, taking the delicate flower from her. Like the hummingbird he'd seen, it was incongruous in this bloody place, yet all the more beautiful for it.

"Thank *you*," Genette whispered, her voice falling low. "For not betraying me."

And in that moment of candor, in that moment of forgiveness, he realized she had seen inside his soul and knew he had been tempted.

CHAPTER THIRTEEN

Poisoner

Ankarette watched Alensson's face as he seated himself in silence at the window seat. The blush of dawn on the horizon was a reminder that their time together was growing short. The kitchen staff would be rising soon to pound loaves of bread with their fists. There would be chamberlains and squires to coax life back into the spent brazier coals.

But while the poisoner was starting to feel anxious—she had perhaps stayed too long—she did not rush him. It was clear he'd experienced the siege of Lionn anew in the telling of his story, and she could feel the residue of shame that still lingered in his soul.

"You didn't have to tell me the part about how the sword tempted you," she said in a comforting voice. "Perhaps you were too honest."

A little twitch on his lip almost blossomed into a smile. He stroked his mouth, his shoulders hunched, his elbows close to his sides.

"There is a certain power that comes from confession," he whispered gravely. "Speaking to you tonight has helped, in a small way, unlock some chains that I'd bound myself with over the years. Yes, I was tempted by the sword. It is the nature of magic, I think, to invoke such feelings. It is the nature of men to be ambitious." He cocked his head. "Your own king is proof of that."

Ankarette smiled knowingly. "He shares that quality, to be sure. But he's had his own portion of troubles. He's lost his kingdom twice. Won it thrice. It's almost as if it were a game."

He gave her a look that was wise and cunning and full of secrets. She hungered to learn everything he knew—not only because it would help her king, but also because she derived pleasure from knowing secrets.

"War *is* a game," he said after a lengthy pause. "We won that round at Lionn."

"What about the other soldiers from Ceredigion, the ones who were besieging the larger part of the city? You took the Turrels, but what happened to the rest of the army?"

Another smile quirked his mouth. "Another good question, Ankarette. The balance had shifted. They knew they were falling, yet our foes were courageous. The Ceredigions knew Deford would come with a larger army, and he was not a forgiving man. If they had fled without a fight, he would have punished them severely."

"It's also not wise to turn your back on an army seeking revenge," she added thoughtfully.

"Precisely. No, the surviving enemy forces had gathered into an army outside of Lionn, along the road leading back to Pree. They thought we were going to attack them, you see, which"—he tapped his chin and then wagged his finger at her—"was precisely what any reasonable battle commander would have suggested. But the Maid was no ordinary battle commander. The army was hers, by this time, surely you realize that. Doone and I may have held rank. Lord Hext may have been taller and stronger. But everyone looked to the Maid for direction, including those I just mentioned."

Ankarette waited a moment, watching his eyes narrow slightly. "What did her voices tell her to do? What was the Fountain's will?"

He gazed at her. "It was the feast day of St. Kathryn. I don't think any of us remembered it. But the Maid did. She said we would not fight a battle on a feast day."

She looked at him with startled surprise. "But surely the Ceredigic army—"

He waved her quiet. "We arrayed our troops across from theirs. Most of their archers had been killed at the towers, so they had few left. There was perhaps a stone's throw between our camps, and both were bristling with spears and swords, waiting for the order to attack. Genette said that if they attacked us, we could destroy them. But she would not order an attack on a feast day. Instead, she summoned the deconeus from the sanctuary inside Lionn, and he heard confessions and accepted prayers. He walked down the line of soldiers, going from man to man, including Genette herself. All the while, our enemies looked on in surprise. They saw that we weren't going to attack them, so they were poised to attack us. If one dirk had been hurled, it would have been a bloodbath. There were no taunts this time. Both sides were edgy, unsettled, keening for a fight. Genette was there with her sword and banner, waiting for them to make the first move. Preposterous! No one starts a battle that way! It was one of the most amazing sights I'd ever seen. And then . . . poof!"

Ankarette blinked. "What?"

"They left," he said with a laugh. "Their army crumpled. They lowered their swords and spears and began to retreat. The back ranks first, then the middle, and then finally the front. They turned and departed."

"And then you chased them?" she asked with a quizzical look.

"Then we chased them," he answered. "Nothing serious. Mostly to stop their siege engines from being used elsewhere. We raided their baggage, took their treasure." His eyes glittered at the word.

"And you got a share of it?"

He nodded. "Finally. You must understand, Ankarette. All of Prince Chatriyon's support came from rich nobles who wanted to keep him on a short leash. He said he couldn't afford to reward me, but I think . . . I think that in time he grew to hate being on a leash himself, so he liked to strand others who were in that situation. I used part of the treasure I earned at Lionn to repay some of the debts my wife had incurred to achieve my release. It wasn't enough . . . not hardly! But it helped me take my first few breaths of freedom. The Maid had conquered Lionn in four days and not a single Ceredigion soldier was left. In fact, we wreaked havoc on them all the way back to Pree."

He paused again, listening intently.

She heard it too. The sound of steps coming up the stairwell outside the tower. Ankarette's heart began to pound and she cursed herself. She was so absorbed by his story that she'd allowed herself to forget that she was a poisoner inside an enemy castle in the heart of the enemy court, while her king's army was a league away, getting ready to continue the war the Maid had ended decades before.

"The bed," Alensson said, pointing to it, but she was already on her way there. If she hid behind the tall mattress, she could slip under it if she needed to and give herself more time to hide. The footfalls in the stairwell were too soft to be from a man's boots. It was probably a servant.

She reached the hiding place just as a knock sounded at the door.

"Enter!" Alensson said gruffly.

A maid entered the room with a tray of bread and cheese. Ankarette knelt by the bed, positioning a pillow in front of her face. It concealed her, but she had left a gap so she could watch. The girl's hair was a little disheveled, and the lacings at the front of her servant's gown had been hastily tied. Her hands were shaking, making the tray rattle slightly.

"For you, my lord," the girl stammered, walking in. "Where would you like the tray?"

"I don't recognize you," Alensson said. "Where is Katalina?"

"She's . . . sick," the girl apologized. Ankarette could hear the lie. The girl's face was pale. Her eyes were lowered, but she kept starting to turn and then stopping. Ankarette deduced that she hadn't come alone and the person who had come with her was skilled at moving quietly.

"Right over there, if you please," Alensson said, motioning to the small table where the remains of his dinner still sat. "Take the other tray with you, girl."

"Yes, my lord. Anything else, my lord?" The girl was absolutely frantic to leave. She hastily went to the table, then set down the new tray and began cleaning up the other one.

"Yes, one thing."

The girl paused, her shoulders quivering. "Yes?"

"Tell the man who poisoned my food that I'm not very hungry."

Ankarette closed her fingers over the pillow. Her heart was pounding, but her nerves were taut. She saw someone move in the shadows of the doorway. The man took one step forward and threw a dagger at Alensson.

Ankarette had expected it after hearing Alensson's pronouncement about the meal. She flung the pillow at exactly the right moment, and it blocked the dagger from meeting its mark. The old duke was quick and was already leaning to one side. The blade would have sailed past him and crashed into the window if Ankarette hadn't changed its course. The serving girl shrieked and cowered, gibbering with fear as Ankarette rushed after the murderer.

He was already fleeing back down the steps when she reached the doorway. Her aim with a dagger was better than his.

She had poisoned the tip, naturally, and its venom worked quickly. By the time she reached his trembling body, his eyes had rolled back in his head and his lips had turned blue. She found the poisoner's supplies and quickly confiscated them. His fall may have been heard lower down the stairs, so she needed to act quickly. She pulled his body back up into the room.

"Garderobe?" she asked, panting with the exertion. All the muck from the privies in castles was sent down garderobe holes, which dumped into the moat around the yard. This palace was built alongside a river, which would make it even easier to hide the body.

Alensson was kneeling next to the girl, comforting her, but he pointed toward the closet.

With a heave, Ankarette tilted the body of the poisoner

into the garderobe shaft and listened to the sickening scraping noise it made it as it slid and then plummeted into the abyss.

She was sweating from the work, but she'd dragged bodies before.

By the time she finished, Alensson had gotten the serving girl talking. The poisoner had killed her friend, who'd refused to assist in the murder attempt, and he'd grabbed her next. She was so grateful to be alive, she'd do anything they asked of her.

Alensson patted the serving girl's shoulder. "Now, you tell the butler, Geoffre, what happened. Do you understand me, lass? Tell him that a man tried to kill me tonight. But you tell him that the old duke won't be beaten so easily. Don't tell him about her," he said, pointing to Ankarette. "Would you do that for me?"

She was sniffling and wiped her nose. "I swear it, my lord. I swear it."

"Good girl. Now be on your way." He gave her a kindly smile, and she took the dirty tray and the poisoned tray away.

After she left, Alensson turned to Ankarette. "We worked well together, Ankarette. Would I could persuade you to rescue me from this dungeon. That's the third time Chatriyon's son has tried to murder me."

Ankarette felt bile rise in her throat. "The third time?"

Alensson nodded. "I'm a popular choice for executioners. Yes, I've committed treason. Who wouldn't when you have such a *black king*." He enunciated the last two words slowly and deliberately and quite differently, his eyes watching Ankarette's for a reaction, but he saw only befuddlement. He seemed disappointed.

"King Lewis has an inordinate number of poisoners working for him," Ankarette said. "They call him the Spider King in the poisoner school in Pisan."

Alensson chuckled. "A fitting name for a cunning king. His father, my king, had a different title. Chatriyon Le Victorieux. Chatriyon the Victorious." His face crumpled with resentment.

"I take it you do not agree with the nickname," Ankarette mused.

Alensson's frown was fierce. "He never fought in a single battle," he said tightly, his voice throbbing with anger. "He was a coward, though he justified his cowardice through the claim that his son was too young. If Chatriyon died, it would have been easy for his enemies to fetch and destroy his heir. The Ceredigics are butchers, you know. For them, defeating a man isn't enough—they also try to wipe out his heirs. They want to end the game, you see," he added darkly in a half whisper.

"You've mentioned that several times," Ankarette said curiously. "What game?"

He smirked, but Ankarette could see he regretted his choice of words. "The game of war, of course," he said, covering for himself poorly. "It's always been played." That was not what he had meant, and she knew it. There was something more, something deeper that she was beginning to gain awareness of.

"Why did you rebel against your king?" she asked him pointedly.

He folded his arms imperiously. "Let me tell you the rest of her story. We don't have much time before the guards arrive. You need to be gone unless I can persuade you to take me with you."

"Tell me the story before I decide," Ankarette said. It would be difficult smuggling Alensson out of the palace. But she was fascinated by his story and wanted to know more. She knew what had happened to the Maid. That story was famous. But what about Alensson's wife, Jianne? Had they had any children? Was she still alive?

"I will be brief then," he said, taking his seat again at the window. "When Lionn fell, my wife came immediately with the court. The Maid had prophesied that she herself would lift the siege and she had. It was absolutely evident that she was truly Fountain-blessed. Word of the victory spread and the Maid insisted that she fulfill the Fountain's will by bringing Chatriyon to the sanctuary at Ranz and crowning him king. Well, Ranz was inside enemy territory. There were several garrisons of Ceredigic forces occupying defensive positions along the route. The Maid insisted that the army march and clear the way for the prince to attend his coronation. All our enemies would fall." He laughed and shook his head. "The audacity! She was a spirited girl, Ankarette. I admired her and respected her. And yes, I was envious as well. Why hadn't the Fountain chosen *me* to save our people? Why had it entrusted its will to a slip of a girl who should have been carding wool in Donremy? Instead of shearing sheep, she'd shorn her hair, donned a suit of armor, and carried a banner into war. She was extraordinary!" He sighed at the memory. "But my wife was worried about the danger after seeing the battlefield. She grew fearful that something was going to happen to me. She was so worried that I would die."

His voice became tender as he said the words. "I miss her so."

"What happened?" Ankarette asked. "Obviously you did survive."

He grinned at her. "I nearly did not."

CHAPTER FOURTEEN

A New Heart

Alensson was in a war council with Aspen Hext, Earl Doone, and Genette when word arrived that the prince's court had been spotted approaching Lionn and would soon arrive. They hovered around the bulky parchment map spread across the circular table where they had been poring over the rivers, cities, and towns of Occitania. Their attention was narrowed on the road from Lionn to Ranz—and its proximity to where Deford's army from Westmarch was gathering in Pree.

Lord Hext jabbed his finger on the map. "Chatriyon is almost here and we still haven't agreed on a course of action. Why not attack Pree?"

"Because the Fountain wills that the prince be crowned at Ranz," Genette insisted. "We will take Pree in proper order, my lord. But first he must be crowned. It is imperative."

"But I don't understand why," Hext argued. "Look here. The road to Pree is the most direct road to Ranz."

"We could go this way, through Troye," Doone suggested, tapping another city midway between them but farther south.

"Yes," Genette said. "That is the way."

"Once a boulder starts tumbling down a hill, it gains speed and power," Hext said. "The men are feeling triumphant after our victory here. Let's test them against the gates of Pree!"

"And we will," Genette said, looking up at him. "But first, we must crown the king. Our safety depends on it."

Alensson felt there was some deeper meaning beneath his words, but he couldn't comprehend it. "And you feel it is the Fountain's will, Genette?"

"I don't feel it, Gentle Duke, I know it."

Alensson looked at Hext. "Why are we arguing against her idea?"

"Because it goes against the principles of military strategy," Hext said, exasperated. "Don't give your enemy time to recover. Hit them again, while they are off balance. They are more likely to topple as word of our victories spread through the kingdom. You don't think that the people are *happy* having a usurper as king?"

Alensson folded his arms. "The usurper is a child, Lord Hext. His father defeated us at Azinkeep. Deford is merely doing his duty. I agree that we must reclaim our land. But if we lost Azinkeep because we ceased heeding the Fountain in the past, this is our opportunity to mend things. We must present a united front to Chatriyon. No doubt the gossips and double dealers at Shynom have been whispering in his ear, persuading him this is folly. If Genette says our destination is Ranz, then we go there." He glanced at her and saw the grateful smile on her mouth.

"We must go to Ranz, my lords," she said. "The prince will not argue about the route we take."

Hext sniffed in through his nose. Alensson could tell it galled him that they were taking advice from an inexperienced girl. It went against his feelings, against his nature, against his better judgment. Lord Hext had hailed her victory as a miracle after the siege of Lionn had broken. But now that the deed was done, its magnificence and wonder were beginning to fade. One feat could not make him forget the habits and beliefs of a lifetime.

"So be it," Hext said, sniffing again. He looked at Doone, who nodded to him in agreement, and then they dispersed from the war council to wait in the courtyard for the entourage to arrive.

It was a long wait.

When Chatriyon Vertus finally arrived at Lionn, the city took up a cheer that was impressive in its volume and clamor. Alensson rocked impatiently on his heels, his hand gripping his wrist behind his back. Jianne had sent word that she was coming with the entourage, just as Genette had foreseen, and he was anxious for her to arrive.

"Patience, Gentle Duke," the Maid advised him with a wry smile.

"So says the doctor who does not have to endure the medicine himself," he quipped back. Her smile broadened. "Did you leave a beau back in Donremy, Genette?" he asked, suddenly curious. "Is there some young shepherd pining for your return?"

That easy smile quickly vanished and a strange, almost guilty look crept into her eyes. "No one, my lord," she stammered. Her cheeks began to flush.

"I'm surprised. Or maybe I shouldn't be," he said jokingly. "You are rather outspoken."

The flushing deepened to a rosy blush. She had feelings for

someone, that much was clear. But her reticence implied her affections were not returned. "Ahh, I see." He leaned closer. "Your secret is safe with me, Genette. I'll tease you no further."

All her self-confidence and bravado had vanished, and she looked very much like a young woman in that moment, even encased in polished armor—a bit dented, although the gash had been repaired by the blacksmith—and holding her war-ravaged banner. She might look like a soldier, like some knight-errant—but she was still a young woman with a woman's tender feelings. She gave him a grateful look, a short nod, and then stared fixedly at the gates.

Chatriyon arrived in splendor, wearing the crimson jeweled tunic that he had doffed several months ago to impersonate someone else. Off came his hat, its sweeping plumes flutter-ing in the breeze as he swung it low as a token of respect to the Maid, who had won her first battle.

Genette quickly fell to one knee. "My lord," she said with a hint of anxiety in her voice. "Welcome to Lionn. Your city greets you."

"Thanks to you," Chatriyon said in a pleasant, respectful tone. His horse was restless, and several royal grooms rushed forward to help him dismount, an act which made Alensson sneer inwardly. A pampered man who ate the best foods, wore the best clothing, supported by the richest nobles.

As well as the poorest one, he thought blackly to himself.

And then he saw Jianne amongst the crowd, his eye drawn to her like an arrow to its mark. He bowed to the king re-spectfully and then hurried to her side. She had a fearful look in her eyes, as if uncertain of how to dismount amidst such a crowd. She had no servants to look after her or tend to her needs. Alensson was only too grateful to oblige.

"Let me help you, my lady," he offered, seizing the reins. He whistled softly, soothing the mare.

"Alensson!" Jianne gasped with emotion, her eyes suddenly swimming with tears. He reached up, fixing his hands around her waist, and helped bring her down gracefully. Her hair was windswept, her hood hiding the mane that he longed to see. Her cheeks were a pleasant pink despite her dusky skin. He enveloped her in his arms in front of everyone and kissed her soundly on the mouth, the act bringing a chorus of cheers from a group of soldiers who happened to be nearby.

She returned the kiss in an almost greedy way, not caring if the world saw them. Then she pulled back and stroked his cheek. "You need to shave, my lord husband," she said, running her fingers through his shaggy hair.

"I'm too poor to afford a barber," he said with a smile, "but if you'd do the honors?"

She nodded eagerly and then hugged him close, pressing her cheek against his chest and squeezing him so hard he felt little tremors in her arms. He held her like that for a long while, stroking her hair.

♦　　♦　　♦

"Now I can kiss you properly," Jianne said, wiping the last bit of lather away with a towel. With all the commotion going on in the castle, they had been interrupted at least a dozen times by knocks and servants asking when the duke would be able to join his lord down in the war room. He was hungry to see her again, hungry to be alone with her again, anxious for the noise to fade and the night to fall and for the blissful silence that would eventually come.

He kissed her again, feeling his heart burning with unquenchable love. Soon he would leave again. Too soon. After a lingering kiss, he pulled away. "I must go."

"Before you do," she said, catching his sleeve.

He looked at her curiously. They were sitting side by side on a small sofa. He took her hands and gave her a probing look. "What is it?"

She looked down nervously before looking back up to meet his eyes. "Alensson, I think I'm with child." The words were spoken almost fearfully, as if she wasn't sure how he would react.

He was unprepared for the news, which made him feel as if a lance had struck his shield in the perfect spot, hurling him from the saddle and down on his backside in the dust. He was speechless, shocked, and then his insides roiled with delight and feelings he had never experienced before, feelings so pure and tender and bright it was like staring too long at the sun.

"Are you, dearest?" he asked breathlessly, cupping her cheek. Was it a dream? Would he suddenly awaken back in his tent amidst a war camp? "I could not imagine . . . I dared not hope so soon!" He felt a fiery intensity inside his chest and he pulled her close to him, kissing her neck, kissing her cheek.

"I'm not . . . absolutely certain," she said with worry in her voice. "I could be wrong."

"But you *think* it's true," he said, shaking his head, smoothing hair from her brow. "I'll not second-guess you. A woman should know these things better than a man! My love, I cannot tell you how happy I am. My heart is fit to burst!"

She winced at his words. "But you are going *away*," she said, taking his hands into her lap and squeezing them hard. "You must go. I'm not trying to stop you. But I know so little about childbirth. There is no midwife we know or trust. There may be troubles. And I'll worry about you." Her eyes filled with tears and several streaked down from her lashes. "I'm grateful, so very grateful to have you."

And it was at that exact moment a knock sounded on the door. Alensson gritted his teeth, preparing to curse at whoever was disturbing this moment. If it was the prince himself, he'd earn a scolding that would blister his ears.

"Be patient, they don't know," Jianne said worriedly, seeing the frustration in his eyes.

Alensson marched over to the door and yanked it hard by the handle, ready to spew out oaths that would make the intruder shrink and cringe.

Genette was standing at the doorway, no longer in her full armor, but wearing a chain hauberk beneath a royal tunic the prince had brought for her.

His mouth was open, the words ready to tumble out, but he slowly shut his jaw.

"*Gentle* duke," the Maid chided softly. "The prince commands you to attend to him." Then she looked at Jianne and a tender, sympathetic look rippled across her face. "Greetings, sweet duchess. I congratulate you on the news."

Jianne looked momentarily surprised, but she had been an ardent believer in the Maid from the beginning and her look shifted to gratitude. "Thank you, Genette," his wife said, rising from the couch. She reached over and squeezed her husband's hand. "You have a duty to the prince," she said.

"My first duty is to you," he reminded her, pinching her chin. She nodded, her eyes filling again with tears, and she hugged him, though not as fiercely as she had before. This embrace was full of resignation.

Genette stared at them awkwardly, waiting.

"I'll return later tonight," Alensson promised.

"I know," Jianne answered, stepping aside.

Genette stared at them. Then she approached Jianne and took her hand, giving her a tender look. "I promise you, sweet duchess, that he will return safely to you. Take courage. He will be there when the child comes."

Jianne's eyes widened with surprise at the words. The worry and fretting melted away from her in an instant. It melted from them both. Alensson knew she had visions of the future. It gave him solace to hear the promise. He believed it.

"Thank you," Jianne said, taking the Maid's hand and kissing her knuckles. She started weeping with joy.

There was a knowing look in the Maid's eyes. She smiled at Jianne, patting her hands, and then turned to leave, glancing at Alensson to see if he would follow her.

After kissing his wife once more, this time in relief, Alensson followed Genette back down the corridor full of servants rushing to and fro to meet the various needs of their noble guests.

"You truly love her," Genette said to him as they walked through the frenzied hallway.

"She waited for me faithfully," he answered, not looking at her for fear of running into someone. "Indeed, I love her well."

"That is noble, Alen. Not all husbands are so devoted. Especially not at Shynom."

The anger simmering in her voice was unmistakable, and he could only wonder what she had seen. Genette was driven by unflinching principles. She even had shamed soldiers away from cursing. Her sense of right and wrong was like the checkered design of a Wizr board.

They reached the main hall, which was bursting with noise, music, and a raucous crowd that had only grown as the day progressed. It was common gossip at court that the prince's political marriage was a loveless one. They had sired an heir and no other children had followed. Chatriyon and his wife were rarely seen side by side, and it was common for him to be found talking amidst the men while his wife socialized with the women.

The court thrived on such gossip, so it should have come as no surprise that he and Genette were greeted by plenty of raised eyebrows when they walked in together. No matter. Alensson cared little for gossip and intrigue. He was going to be a father. His wife would give him a child. A boy? A girl? He didn't know and didn't care. He would love either. Since hearing the news, he felt as if he'd grown a new heart.

CHAPTER FIFTEEN

The Maid's Vow

There were similarities between the battlefield and court. Both required strategy, quick wits, and an unflagging constitution. But Alensson despised politics. He much preferred the disarray and mayhem of a siege. The Occitanian army had followed Genette's plan, and now they were facing the last enemy bastion on the road to Ranz: the city of Foucaulx. Shouts from the warriors attempting to breach the city walls mixed with the grunts and groans of men squirming in their death throes. Arrows and crossbow bolts whizzed down from the ramparts, and every few minutes the catapults inside the city sent boulders flinging over the wall, smashing anyone in the way. It was a grim death, and many had died already. Those closest to the walls were the least affected by the threat, but there were horrors to face still.

With smoke stinging his eyes, Alensson stood in the shadow of the wall, shield up, watching Genette as she waved her stained banner, shouting for the men to advance, to breach the walls that penned in their enemies. She had demanded, once again, that the city surrender and open its gates, but they had remained defiant, expecting support from Deford's army, which was still hunkered down in Pree. It was said the Duke of Westmarch had summoned an enormous force from Ceredigion and it was marching at breakneck speed. The canny duke would not be tricked into committing his Occitanian legions without reinforcements. A mighty host was on its way to punish the Maid. And so Foucaulx held firm and Chatriyon's army hammered relentlessly at its walls.

An arrow struck Alensson's upraised shield, the blow battering his arm and making him stagger back. There were arrows sticking in the dried earth all around Genette. Her voice rang out amidst the cries and blasts of horns.

"Onward! Courage! Let's drive these foes back to the ice caves! Take heart! We will win!"

Alensson admired her courage and tenacity. She had shown equal strength when dealing with the politics of court. Many nobles had gathered around the prince, whispering in his ears to distrust her counsel, warning him that she was leading his forces to their deaths. But the prince had hearkened to Alensson. Lionn had been the test, and had she not passed it? Was not the Fountain truly blessing them with victory?

Chatriyon and his inner council had ridden with them, but the prince was staying in a town less than a league away, surrounded by knights who could carry him away if needed. His army was cutting their way to the sanctuary of Ranz—and he was following a few steps behind it. Alensson felt his heart blacken with thoughts of the man's cowardice. But perhaps he and the Occitanian prince were both fighting the battles to which they were best suited. Alensson would have sent the schemers away bleeding.

It was a pivotal moment. After Foucaulx fell, there would be a clear path to Ranz. Even if Deford decamped from Pree to face them, he would not reach the sanctuary in time. If the fortress held for weeks, the momentum would be lost. But there was victory in the air. The men were energized, and they flung themselves into danger without cowering. He watched the battering rams slam against the gates, his mind focused on the path ahead.

"Alen!"

He turned his head sharply. It was the Maid, looking back at him, her face pale. He realized she'd been calling to him for a while—he had been too lost in his thoughts, too distracted by the melee to notice until she shouted his name.

"What?" he asked, glancing around to see if there was some imminent danger.

"Move. Over there!" She pointed with her finger.

"What?" he repeated.

"I said move! Over there!" She gestured impatiently, shaking her head at him as if he was being a fool.

Alensson took several steps backward, gesturing with his sword to the spot. She nodded and then turned her gaze back to the siege.

"Climb the ladders! Get up there! Climb!" she called to the soldiers nearby.

Every attempt at fixing the scaling ladders had ended in disappointment; the defenders were quick to repulse them and send them crashing back down. Arrows felled the soldiers who attempted to bring them back up. Alensson frowned and scowled. If they didn't succeed in breaching the gate or climbing the wall, it would drag on forever! How many men had they lost that day? He felt another arrow slam into his shield.

"My lord duke," said a squire, rushing to his side. "Earl Doone is suggesting we fall back and regroup. We're losing too many men."

Alensson glanced at the squire over his shoulder. "She will say no. And I agree. We must keep at it. No one said it would be easy."

"My lord, he swore he would send a courier to the prince seeking orders to retreat. How many have died already?"

"You tell the earl," Alensson said angrily, baring his teeth, "that if he's so worried, he should leave the safety of his tent and help! It'll be dark soon and the night will help cover our movements."

"A blind archer could hit one of us easily enough," the squire said disdainfully.

"You tell the earl we'll not have it," Alensson snapped back. "If the Maid says it will fall, it will fall! How can he lose faith so quickly?" He raised his voice. "Genette! Doone wants to retreat."

The Maid turned her head and gave him an annoyed look. "No, we fight on!"

"I will tell him, but he won't like it," the squire said with a shrug.

There was the sound of machinery, followed by the ominous thump of the taut timbers jerking down, and then a huge segment of castle stone came vaulting over the wall directly at them. Alensson stared at the hulking mass, saw it looming in the sky like a moon and then plummeting right for him. He tried to move, tried to get away, but his legs felt as if they were running through water. The huge projectile slammed into the ground next to him, shaking the earth. Alensson's teeth rattled with shock as he fell to his knees. The squire had vanished beneath the enormous boulder. Alensson gaped and then turned to face Genette with an open mouth.

It had landed right where he had been standing moments before she'd warned him.

A small, tight smile appeared on her mouth and she nodded to him. "I promised your wife, Gentle Duke," she said. "I promised her you'd make it through."

He was still too startled and shaken to speak. His life could have been snuffed out. It would have been if she hadn't warned him. The poor squire! Was it a trade then? A life for a life? Had the Fountain claimed its due?

"Up the walls!" Genette shouted again. She muttered something under her breath and ran toward the earth-filled part of the moat, where the soldiers were struggling with the siege ladders. She jammed her battle standard into the ground, then grabbed one of the ladders and helped the men lift it back up. Did she intend to attack the fortress herself? Alensson raced after her.

"What are you doing?" he demanded, grabbing her arm.

"I'm going up," she replied angrily. Drawing her sword with one arm, she gripped the first rung of the ladder with the other. Before he could say another word, she was scampering up the ladder like a sailor on the rigging.

"Hold it steady!" Alensson barked at the two men who were watching her dumbfounded. They grabbed the ladder and pressed their full body weight against it. Alensson's heart hammered fearfully in his chest as he watched her scale the wall toward the ramparts. She was nimble, even in the armor, but despite his belief in her—in the Fountain—he was worried she'd fall and injure herself. Worried she would make it to the top and get captured by the enemy. He stared at her, amazed at her courage and self-confidence.

The defenders were ready. They used hooked poles to shove the ladder away from the walls. Alensson and the two men struggled to keep the ladder upright, but Genette's body weight and armor sent it careening backward. Horror-stricken, Alensson saw her dangle from the ladder by one arm as it toppled and then fell.

He let go of the ladder and tried to get under her, but she landed on her back right in front of him, a look of surprise on her face that quickly transformed into one of pain.

"Genette!" he gasped, sinking to his knees, shielding her limp body with his own bulk. Any moment he expected an arrow to strike his back. She had fallen from a considerable height, and it was likely she had broken her back, perhaps her legs and arms too.

"Don't stand there gaping like a fish," she scolded him. "Help me up!"

He suddenly became aware of the soldiers who had crowded around them, providing an extra wall of armor to protect the fallen girl. And when he looked up, he saw the rage in their eyes, the determination for revenge. The Maid was their sister in arms. There was a howl, a shout, and suddenly men were scrabbling toward the walls as if they planned to scale them without ladders. More ladders started to be thrust upward and multiple men began to climb simultaneously. The greater weight helped hold the ladders steady, and the men on the ground used spears to help counter the use of the hooked poles.

"Help me," Genette said, reaching out and gripping Alensson's arm. She started to pull herself up, her face wincing with pain. Her back should have been broken, and from the look in her face, she was in agony.

"Lie still," he urged her. "I think your back is broken."

"It *is* broken," she said through a mask of pain. "But it will not be for long. Help me up!"

He was amazed at her words, but even if she managed another miraculous recovery—he knew after Lionn that she could do it, though he did not know how—surely she would need time to recover. "Let me carry you back to a tent to rest," he said, sheathing his sword and then reaching under her legs to lift her.

"*No*," she said emphatically. There was something in her voice, some tone of command that stopped him. He had one arm around her shoulder already, the other in the crook behind her knees, but he hadn't lifted yet. "Please, Gentle Duke," she whispered. "Just help me stand. Trust me."

He had trusted her so far. He let her legs drop back and then rose up himself, hoisting her up with him. He heard the groan of pain, saw the whiteness of her face, and then she was on her feet.

"Bring my flag," she whispered, planting her hand on his chest to steady herself. Her face was full of pain and determination. He didn't want to leave her side for a moment, afraid she'd crumple to the earth, but somehow she fought the pain long enough to remain on her feet until he returned with her battle flag.

Her eyes brightened when she took it. Leaning heavily on the pole, she sucked in her breath to endure the agony of her injury.

"We are so near the top of the ramparts," Alensson said with frustration. "If we could but distract the enemy a moment, more ladders could be fixed." He looked at her. "You are *not* going to climb up another ladder. Not like this. There must be another way!"

"Distract them?" Genette said, looking at him. She cocked

her head, as if listening to something he couldn't hear.

"What is it?" he pressed.

She smiled despite her obvious pain. "I know how now. It makes sense. Thank you." She bowed her head and then whispered something under her breath. He could not hear the word, but he felt it ripple and shudder, as if a heavy stone had been hurled into a pond. Her banner began to flutter as a breeze tousled it. Then the stitching on the fabric began to glow.

Alensson blinked in surprise and amazement as the images she had crafted by thread suddenly leaped off the banner, still aglow, and hovered in the air before their eyes. The fleur-de-lis patterns, fluttering like butterflies, expanded and multiplied as they rose higher and higher. She gripped the pole, her leg twitching from the pain in her back, gritting her teeth as she held fast. The glowing shapes blossomed in the sky, rising up to the top of the wall, painting the air with color and movement. It was dazzling to watch, mesmerizing to see.

There was a shout of victory as the first men reached the ramparts. The clatter of steel striking steel followed, and the battle began to shift, the momentum changing as it had done in Lionn. Now that the first wave of warriors had successfully scaled the walls, the ladders were thick with men trying to find their way up.

The colorful strands from her banner fell apart and Genette drooped. She nearly collapsed, but he caught her shoulders.

"I'll be all right, Alen," Genette said, wincing as she put a foot forward to steady herself. A cheer and a cry came up from the army. The defenders began to flee from their positions. There were no more catapults flinging giant stones after that.

Genette used her banner like a crutch as she hobbled toward the walls, gazing up at the fighting in the ramparts. A sad smile came to her mouth. Her other hand gripped the sword pommel. The look of pain was starting to leave her, and her breathing was becoming easier.

"The Fountain blesses you," Alensson said, glancing at her as they stood together beneath the walls of Foucaulx.

"It does indeed," she said.

"You saved my life." The swell of gratitude in his heart made him feel like weeping.

She turned her head and gave him a peculiar stare, one that seemed to penetrate to the deepest part of his soul. "The Fountain has great plans for you, Gentle Duke. You will survive this war." She shook her head subtly. "I will not."

CHAPTER SIXTEEN

The Raven Scabbard

Foucaulx, the final major obstacle on the road to Ranz, had fallen. There was celebrating in the camp, and the Earl of Doone made arrangements for a garrison to defend the city while the army marched on to the sanctuary to crown the king. Alensson was battle weary, but he was also concerned about Genette and what she had whispered to him before the fall of the city. There had been a sadness in her voice, along with a certainty that disturbed him deeply. She had fore-warned him to move before that piece of rubble could squash him. Had she seen a fate in store for herself? Was something preventing her from moving out of the way?

Word came that Chatriyon and his entourage were drawing near to the city. Outriders had been sent ahead to keep the army apprised of Deford's movements. Genette was sure to be summoned when the prince arrived, so Alensson made his way to her tent. She had limped there in great pain, refusing his offer to carry her, and a surgeon had been seeing to her injuries for the last several hours.

As he approached, he remembered his previous intrusion and called out to her squire.

The lad swept open the flap. "Yes, my lord?"

"How fares she?" he asked. "Is the surgeon still here?"

"I'm here," called the man. "Is that the Duke of La Marche?"

"Aye," said the squire.

"He can come in," Genette said.

When Alensson ducked through the opening, he saw her sitting on a camp stool. Her battered armor was hanging from the spokes of its iron stand, and it was clear the young squire had been in the middle of cleaning it. The doctor stood behind her, one hand on her bare shoulder, the other on her ribs. She had covered her front with a sheet, and when she saw Alensson looking at her, he could have sworn she started to blush.

"Is her back broken?" Alensson asked the doctor, a bearded middle-aged man who was balding at the top.

"It was earlier," he answered, shaking his head. "Sit straighter, my dear. Pull your shoulders back."

She complied, looking a bit exasperated at his instructions. Alensson felt a throb of emotion akin to possessiveness—as if she belonged to him and no one else. The doctor frowned, then shook his head.

"Astonishing," he muttered.

"I told you," the Maid said, "I will be fine. Surely there are others whose injuries require more attention?"

The doctor wagged his finger at her. "When I first entered, you were in violent pain. Your shoulder was broken, your back was broken, your left arm was broken, and possibly one of your legs. How far do you say she fell?" he added, looking at Alensson.

"The distance from a cottager's roof," the duke said, remembering it vividly. "She landed on her back in full armor."

He nodded in dismay. "Her initial injuries bore witness to such a fall. But as I live, Duke Alensson, I have watched her heal before my very eyes. Her shoulder was here"—he pointed to a spot on her back—"and now it is here." He traced the path with his finger. "Truly the lass cannot be harmed."

"Thank you, Surgeon. Go tend to the other wounded."

The man flung up his hands in a helpless gesture and then collected his things. Brendin continued to clean her armor with a rag and jar of polishing wax. Keeping the sheet raised to protect her modesty, Genette slipped behind the narrow changing screen.

Alensson was upset without quite understanding why. He scowled at the doctor as he left. Then he turned to the squire. "Go fetch some food and wine," he commanded.

The young man made a furtive glance at the changing screen, then bowed meekly to the duke and forsook the tent, leaving the two of them alone.

"Why did you send my squire away?" Genette asked, coming around the changing screen in a plain undershirt with leather ties at the front.

"Because I need to talk to you and I don't think he should hear what I have to say," he answered in a low voice.

Her countenance changed to one of wariness. "What would you speak of, Gentle Duke?" she asked him, her tone very low and private.

"How is it that you are uninjured?" he demanded.

She had barely managed to hobble to her tent and now she was starting to pace, all signs of suffering and agony gone.

"Why do you wish to know?" she asked him.

"Because you take great risks in our battles. The arrow that struck your breast should have killed you. It was meant to kill you. Yet you barely bled when you pulled it out. Your bones were broken. I knew it myself without the doctor saying so. And yet here you stand. How is it possible?"

She let out a pent-up breath. "Is that all? Why does it matter how the Fountain chooses to heal me?"

He took a step toward her. "It matters because you suffer!" he hissed at her. "Your magic doesn't prevent you from injury. It doesn't protect you from pain. I don't like seeing you . . ." He stopped, unwilling to say the words until he had mastered himself again. In a low, deliberate voice, he continued, "I don't like seeing you in pain."

She was looking at him now, the flush in her cheeks was gone. She seemed to be drinking in his words. Her eyes were fixed on his face and he thought he saw a tremble in her hands. "Are you *worried* about me?" she asked him with just the hint of a laugh.

"I am," he answered truthfully. "And not because you're the Maid. Because you are *Genette*. You're from an obscure village and now you're here fighting a man's war better than any of the men." The words were tumbling out of his mouth all at once. He couldn't stop himself. "I admire your courage and your pluck. I admire your confidence. I wish I had it. But you said something during the battle. You said *I* would survive this war. And *you* would not." He shook his head. "I don't understand it. How can that be if you cannot be killed?"

Taking a deep breath, she turned away from him and paced in a small square on the floor, her hands clasped together in front of her, her index fingers steepled and pressed against her mouth. "I should not have told you that," she answered.

"Now you will worry about me needlessly."

"Then tell me what you refuse to," he said, fixing her with his eyes.

She was debating with herself. He could see the conflict tumbling around in her mind. Maybe she was communing with her inner voices, asking for permission to tell. He waited patiently, absorbed by this small slip of a girl who had already fought and won several battles. She was only seventeen years old, by the Fountain!

Then she paused and turned to face him. "Will you keep my secrets, Gentle Duke? If I tell you?"

"You know I will," he vowed.

His answer seemed to satisfy her, but rather than speak, she brought her arms down and began unbuckling her scabbard belt. He was confused by this, wondering what she meant to do. Then she approached him with the scabbard in her hands. It was made of leather and had a belt woven into the design so that it was all one thing. The raven, which he'd noticed before, was a more ancient version of the sigil of Brythonica.

"This is the source of my healing," she whispered to him, holding out the scabbard so he could inspect it.

"The blade?" he asked, his eyes on the hilt and the pommel, which did not bear the scars of war despite all the battles it had weathered.

She shook her head. "The sword is powerful, Gentle Duke. With it, I am filled with the wisdom of battles from centuries past. Holding it, I have seen visions from the days of King Andrew. I have seen the king's court and the principles of Virtus that governed it. Those principles are lost now." She gave him a reproachful look. "Our prince is but a shadow. His name is Vertus, but he has forgotten its meaning. You must remember this, when I am gone."

He closed his hand on the middle of the scabbard. "When you are gone?"

"Yes, Gentle Duke. The sword is powerful, but the scabbard is even more so. Whoever wears it cannot be slain." She raised her finger and gently caressed the raven symbol. "It comes from the drowned kingdom of Leoneyis, and its magic is of the Deep Fathoms. When it is healing me, the symbol of the raven begins to glow. Only I can see it. Yes, my body was broken by the fall. But as you can see, I am unharmed now. If others knew the source of my protection, this scabbard would be stolen from me and I would lose both magics." She put her hand on top of his. "Now heed me, Gentle Duke. Those who look at this weapon cannot help but covet it. Even you, though you are too noble to admit it. It is the sword of kings. It is the sword of King Andrew."

He felt the sudden violent urge to wrench the scabbard out of her hands. His fingers were still clenched around the middle. He was bigger than her, stronger. He could take it away by force. Anyone with the sword and scabbard in their possession could take back Occitania—nay, the world! But her hand was on top of his, so gentle and kind. The look in her eyes said, *You can take it from me. But I know you will not.*

That look was so trusting, so vulnerable. He felt sweat pop out on his forehead. He was so weak in that moment, his knees started to tremble. Oh, how he wanted the blade and scabbard for himself.

"Are you to give it to the king after he's crowned?" he asked, his throat thick. The thought of Chatriyon taking the sword made bile rise in his throat.

She shook her head. "He could not be trusted with it," she answered. "It is a weapon of great power, the scabbard more so than the blade. King Andrew died because it was stolen and replaced with a counterfeit before his last battle. He was critically wounded that day and his empire fell. He fell because someone coveted what was rightfully his." She said the words almost imploringly. Her eyes said, *Don't let that be you, Gentle Duke.*

He opened his fist and let go of the scabbard. The temptation immediately began to subside, and a smile of relief stole across Genette's mouth. She patted his hand with fondness and then strapped the scabbard back around her waist.

"Now you know my secret," she said.

"Now I know one of them," he answered. "You said you would not survive the war. Tell me why. Tell me why this must happen."

Her countenance fell as a look of sadness overtook her. "It is *my* burden to bear, Alensson," she whispered. She turned away from him. "Let me bear it alone."

He was tempted to put a comforting hand on her shoulder. But being alone with her was dangerous. He knew he should leave the tent because he *should*. He understood some important things in that moment. When he had asked her about having a boy in Donremy waiting for her, he had misunderstood her reaction. She did have feelings for someone. But they were forbidden feelings. They had been together a great deal and she had never done anything untoward with him, nor he with her. But he felt they were standing on the edge of a precipice. He backed away from her, even though he yearned to comfort her.

"I will not let anything happen to you," he said as he turned to leave. He hesitated by the tent door.

"Just promise me you'll remember what I said," Genette told him. "What I told you about Virtus. You are such a man, Gentle Duke. Gentleness is one of the attributes of Virtus that has long been forgotten. You must teach them to the king after he's been crowned at Ranz. You must be the example he looks up to."

He stiffened at the magnitude of the task. "He barely listens to me—there are so many other voices at court."

"Then your voice must win out. Do not abandon him, Alen. Without your influence, our kingdom will be brought to ruin. My mission is to set things right. Your mission is to keep it so."

A voice sounded from outside the tent, the young squire. "The prince has arrived, my lord. He wishes to see you."

Alensson looked over his shoulder at Genette, who gave him an encouraging nod.

He sighed and walked out of the tent.

CHAPTER SEVENTEEN

The Anointing

It was a surreal moment to the Duke of La Marche, riding his warhorse amidst the banners of an army led by Chatriyon Vertus himself. Crowds had gathered along the road, peasants and tradesmen who had to witness the arrival of a man they had not seen in years—a man whom the Fountain had chosen to rule by the hand of a village girl not unlike themselves.

Genette rode at Chatriyon's side, her armor glistering in the sun, her banner full of holes, the edges in tatters from the battles it had faced, but it still bore new embroideries that she had found time to work on during the journey. He watched her, blinking back the memories of when he had discovered the girl in a tavern outside Shynom. In the span of only so many weeks this girl had become both a general and a warrior. She had done the impossible. It was rare to meet one of the Fountain-blessed—much rarer to meet one such as Genette—and Alensson suspected the people had gathered to see her more than the man who was coming to be crowned.

Alensson wore his own battered armor, but it had been polished for the occasion. His wife, Jianne, was still in Lionn. Despite the risks, he wished she were with him. He longed to see her again, to banish the evil thoughts that continued to chip away at his resolve, worries that he might never regain La Marche to bestow the duchy on his child.

Some of the braver members of court were riding with the army, but most had been too frightened. No one knew when or if Deford would arrive with the back-up forces from Ceredigion. Ranz was deep in enemy territory and their stay would be brief. Some feared a surprise attack, but Genette had assured them that while they would face the Duke of Westmarch in battle, it would not be in Ranz. The road was open, and there were no garrisons left to intervene. Just as Genette had assured them, they faced no opposition as they rode toward Ranz.

Watching Chatriyon's back, Alensson felt another pang of resentment toward the prince. Had any of this man's blood been shed in their battles? Had he suffered so much as a bruise? He wore ceremonial armor, but it was just that—ceremony. It was an empty pretense. Hunger rose up in him again, and he found his gaze lowering to the scabbard belted to Genette's waist.

No, no, no, you mustn't. To distract himself, he pictured the small cottage where he had been reunited with his wife. That cottage was full of pleasant memories to dwell on. Jianne's long, wavy hair, the bright cinnamon of her eyes, the way they'd been cocooned by verdant greenery.

The spell of madness passed, and before Alensson knew it, they were riding under the arches of Ranz. He craned his neck and watched as flower petals, small and fragrant, were rained down on them like snow. They passed through the tranquil blizzard, and then they were on the main street heading to the sanctuary, which rose like a mountain before them.

The sanctuary was ancient, as defensible as the strongest of castles. The entrance had a triple archway facade—the center one was rounded and the two flanking it were more pointed. All three arches were inset into the thick stone walls. There was a huge stained-glass window above the center arch that was easily wider than the cottage in Izzt. It was circular with leaflike shapes extending from the center spoke—as if it were a bubbling fountain seen directly from above. Twin towers rose up on either side of the window, thick and impressive and full of small arches and windows. Alensson had not been to Ranz since he was a child and he still felt dwarfed by the sheer size and shape.

The company rode their horses up the main steps to the massive wooden doors, which had been opened to greet them. As the prince and the Maid ascended, Alensson lowered his hand to his hilt, scanning the crowd for any signs of trouble. The captains kept a portion of the soldiers in the city square and greenyard, taking a defensive position, and soldiers also patrolled the grounds of the sanctuary looking for trouble. The crowds from the road had followed them in and quickly filled the courtyard, but the troops kept a path clear for the king to use after the ceremony, using spears and pikes to hold the masses back. There was a lot of noise as people talked amongst themselves in hushed tones.

Once Alensson was confident there would be no disturbance, he rode his horse into the massive sanctuary. The floor was made of black and white tiles, set in octagonal patterns that formed a giant labyrinth on the floor. There was an enormous bubbling fountain at the head of the huge hall, raised from the rest of the room. The deconeus waited there with his multitude of sextons. Impressively sculpted statues stood as pillars on the eaves, holding up the massive vaulted roof. Light from the stained-glass window spread colored patterns on the floor. The subtle scent of incense hung in the air.

After dismounting, Alensson handed the reins to a squire and then followed the others on foot. As a prince of the blood himself, he had a prominent position to occupy near the prince. Genette was standing on the platform by the sextons, her face beaming with happiness. After all of their struggles, she was about to witness the fulfillment of her visions.

"Well met, my lord!" the deconeus greeted Chatriyon. He looked nervous and a little flustered. He was probably wondering what would happen to him when or if Deford arrived with the next army.

"Are you ready to do your office?" the Earl of Doone asked pointedly. He was never far from Chatriyon, and had ridden into the sanctuary before Alensson.

"I am . . . I am," the deconeus said, stumbling a bit over his words. "We have the consecration oil. Did you bring the *crown?*"

There was something in his voice as he said it. Something that bespoke significance.

"We have it," Doone said with a knowing look.

"Then it is the Fountain's will," the deconeus said. He strode forward, wearing his ceremonial vestments, and stood at the top of the steps. Then, slowly, he made his way down each one. A hush fell over the precincts. Even the horses were silent.

"Since the days of King Andrew, the nobles of each realm have been crowned king according to their right and according to the rites of the Fountain. As a child, you were given the water rite to purge your stain, cleansing your fallen nature. Now you will be anointed with oil that has been consecrated to bestow the right to rule, to preside, to lead this people of Occitania. In the ancient tongue I speak it! *Nominus. Clarinus. Debemus!*"

A ripple of *amen* came from those assembled.

The deconeus pulled out a jeweled vial and then uncorked it. He covered the open end with his littlest finger and quickly jerked the vial back to dab its contents on his flesh. Then he used that finger to anoint Chatriyon on his forehead, both shoulders, and finally on his breast.

While the deconeus refastened the lid of the vial, one of the nobles approached holding a satchel. The man reached inside and his hand emerged with the royal crown. It was an ancient, tarnished-looking thing. As Alensson saw it come out of the bag, he felt his heart flare with a pulse of sudden hatred and envy. *He doesn't deserve it.* He tried to master himself, tried to vanquish the evil thoughts, but they were nearly strangling as he watched the man give the crown to the deconeus.

Then his gaze found Genette, who was looking at him with a disapproving frown. Seeing her quiet rebuke shamed him instantly and squelched the ill feelings that had been sprouting in his soul. A trickle of sweat went down the side of his head. He could breathe again, and he quickly took in some air and forced his mind to surrender to the goodness inside of him. His heart began to slow and he felt peaceful once again.

A little smile quirked on Genette's mouth and she gave an

approving nod, even though her eyes had already returned to the king.

They both watched in silence as the deconeus hefted the tarnished crown and then gently set it down amidst the unruly locks of Chatriyon's dark hair. There was a strange feeling in the room, like the grinding of a stone door closing. It shook Alensson to his heels.

The air was suddenly filled with shouts of *Natalis!* which signified the birth of a new king. Trumpets began to blare in the open hall, gripped by courtiers who had come to witness the occasion, and soon the stone walls were ringing with so much noise and confusion, Alensson's ears were nearly split from it. He wondered if the great glass window would shatter. He winced, his ears aching, his eyes searching the hall for signs of a threat.

Then he saw Genette come down from the steps and kneel before King Chatriyon, her banner pole fixed next to her, its curtain hanging limply. The noise continued to pierce his ears and he stepped closer, trying to listen to them.

"Noble king," he heard Genette say, her voice quavering, "the Fountain's will is done." And then she started to weep. The tears rained down her cheeks as she looked up at the king with something like gratitude. It looked as if a burden had been lifted from her shoulders.

"Now I have the right?" Chatriyon asked her. "The right to move the pieces?"

What could he mean? Alensson came nearer, trying to understand. The Earl of Doone was nearby, distracted by a conversation with one of his lieutenants.

"Yes, Your Majesty," Genette said. "Yes, it is true!"

"Show it to me," he said.

Genette looked around furtively. She and the king were the

center of all eyes. "Not here, my lord," she said, glancing at Alensson. "Not in front of everyone."

"But only a Fountain-blessed can draw it out," he told her. "You said that yourself. Draw it out of the water. You said it would be here!"

The deconeus's face turned the color of chalk, and his eyes widened with surprise. Once again, Alensson felt he was skating on the edge of something he did not understand. "What mean you to do, my lord?"

Chatriyon gave him a cold look. "I didn't just come here for the crown, Deconeus," he said amidst the cacophony. The crowd outside the sanctuary had taken up the cheering.

"What did you come for then?" the deconeus asked worriedly.

Chatriyon gave him a measured, icy stare. "What's been hidden here since my father went mad. Fetch it, Genette. I command you."

The Maid bowed her head sadly and then turned and marched back up the steps, the king watching her shrewdly as she made her way to the bubbling fountain. She circled around behind it so that she would not be seen by the others. Alensson felt a gnawing sensation inside him. He broke away from the throng and went to the steps, but the sextons stopped him before he could reach the top.

"No farther, my lord," they warned him.

"My lord duke?" the king demanded in an icy tone.

"She is vulnerable," he said in a protective tone, edging closer to the sextons.

The king frowned, then nodded in agreement, gesturing for him to follow.

Alensson pushed past them. He saw her then, kneeling by the edge of the waters, her head bowed as if in prayer. She was listening to her voices. He watched her lift her head, a frown on her mouth, and then reach into the waters. The splashing of the fountain concealed her from everyone else but him. Alensson had taken part in a miracle himself when he had pulled her sword from the fountain of Firebos.

Genette did not pull a blade from the waters.

She pulled out a square brown chest with a handle on the top.

Alensson saw her grave expression as she hefted the box. The sextons stared at her, their eyes bulging with disbelief and worry. It put him in mind of the deconeus's pallor.

He had the feeling that this was a secret they had hoped to keep hidden.

CHAPTER EIGHTEEN

Stealing a Duke

At some point in the night, Ankarette Tryneowy had decided she needed to kidnap the Duke of La Marche. Or liberate him, as the case may be. The poisoner she'd caught in the act of murdering him had tipped her thinking. She also could not deny that she was eager for him to finish his tale—a task that would take longer than they had.

So she decided to escape and bring the Gentle Duke with her after all.

"You're coming with me when I leave," Ankarette told him.

He gave her an incredulous look. "I appreciate your offer to help me, lass," he said with a defeated smile. "But there is no way I am leaving this palace alive. Chatriyon's son is king, and they don't call him the spider without reason. I'm tangled in his web. I can go nowhere."

Ankarette slipped her knife out of its sheath and angled it in front of his eyes. "Spiders are my specialty," she said. "I've given this a little thought as you've told me your story, and I have a plan. Let's be quick about it. Bring me the quilt on the bed."

"The quilt?"

She nodded and gestured for it. The duke walked over to the bed, hefted the bulky covering, and dragged it over to her. Ankarette began to slice it into strips with the dagger.

"Let's talk while I work," she said, beginning another slice. She was quick with her hands and saw in her mind the shapes she would need. "I have many questions for you that are unanswered. Tell me about the chest the Maid drew from the fountain. What was inside?"

"It looked somewhat like a Wizr set. But the pieces were unique, not like the kind you'd buy from a Genevese tradesman fashioned out of alabaster or marble. It was more than just a Wizr set. There was some power within it. I don't know for certain what it did. Chatriyon guarded it jealously. In fact, he *changed* after he got it."

"What do you mean?"

"His personality altered. One could say it was the crowning. He was in the same position after being crowned—he was still poor, still dependent on others for coin and soldiers—but his mood began to alter. He started to consider the Maid a threat."

Ankarette continued to work on the quilt, grateful for the sharpness of her knife. As she listened to the story, she kept an ear facing the doorway to alert her of anyone coming up the steps.

"So the chest is still a mystery. But you did notice a change in his personality. I'm curious. Where did he keep it after it was taken?"

Alensson shook his head. "I saw it near him often. He kept

the key that opened it around his neck."

"Surely you asked Genette about the chest?" she pressed.

He nodded. "Of course. I was quite curious after seeing her draw it out of the fountain. She was very . . . evasive in her answers. She said it was the Fountain's will for the king to receive the box for a season. Those were her words. She told me that it would serve a greater good. But I could tell that she was displeased by the changes it started in Chatriyon. She noticed them too."

"Give me an example."

He began pacing, his arms folded over his chest. "He started to act impatient with Genette. Distrusting and annoyed. Almost as if he couldn't abide being in her presence. And a gloom of sorts settled on him. A melancholy. He began to chase after women in the court. He would be talking to someone, nodding and following the conversation, while his eyes fixed on some woman or other. Genette told him it was time to liberate the rest of his country. She asked him to send her and the army to conquer the capital, Pree. I was eager for that to be our next move. If Pree fell, think of it! Think of the spoils of war! Not only would Chatriyon gain enough treasure to be independent, but I could continue clearing my debts. Victory would mean ransoms as well, and I have to say, I intended to be paid for the privations I had suffered. I wanted Deford, the younger brother of the king who had ruined us at Azinkeep. The man who had been rewarded with *my* duchy. You must know how much I wanted to defeat him. But the king wouldn't hear it. Genette had won every battle since Lionn. Why he started to distrust her at that moment, I don't know. She implored him to send her. By this point, many of the towns and villages were joining our side. The balance was shifting. Duke Deford's power was waning.

He still commanded the royal army and was summoning reinforcements from his lands. He still held Pree and La Marche—Westmarch, as he called it—" This part was added with a decided snort. The duke cut himself off when he noticed Ankarette was tying the strips of cloth together.

"We're not going to climb out the window, are we?" he asked. "It's a long way to the ground, especially without the scabbard to mend our broken bones."

"We're not," she said, hurrying to make more strips and tie them together. "I only want to make them think so. Go on with your tale. Genette tried to persuade Chatriyon to attack Pree. If I recall my history, she did attack. It failed."

He nodded sadly. "Maybe it was an impossible task. Think of it, Ankarette. This city"—he gestured with his arms—"has sizable defenses. Lionn was one thing. But Pree is more secure, and it was full of enemy forces. Deford was no fool. I'm sure he wanted to ride out in battle against us, but he also knew the power of momentum in victory. After all, I'd given him that momentum years before. Deford, the cunning lion, sent a letter to Chatriyon requesting a halt to the violence. He promised to surrender the city of Pree in two weeks if they reached an agreement. Both Genette and I knew it was a trick, a stalling technique so he could fortify the city. Chatriyon was more inclined to consider it, even though it would slow our momentum. If he had listened to the Maid, if he had heeded her, it would have gone differently. Trust me, our army, although small, was courageous after such unlikely victories. They truly believed the Fountain was on our side. And they believed they could conquer Pree. So did Genette."

"What happened?" Ankarette said. "Did it go wrong because of the box?"

Alensson was quiet for a moment before speaking. "I think

so. It's something I heard Genette say to the king, something she whispered urgently to him as she tried to convince him to reject Deford's proposal. I was standing nearby, so I overheard it. She whispered to him that he would win the city because he held the chest," he said. "Not because of some truce or negotiation with our enemies. I don't know what that meant or what magic the box evoked. Chatriyon gave in to her . . . eventually. He told her that she would have a fortnight to conquer the city or he'd order her to withdraw." He grimaced. "Most sieges last for months, Ankarette. But she was convinced she could do it in less than a fortnight. She did not see what I saw, even though he warned her. I don't think he agreed out of any eagerness to conquer Pree. He intended to send her to her death. And if that failed, he could be sure it happened in his own way."

Ankarette finished the makeshift rope made out of bedding. "Would that I could hear the rest of it now, but we must make ready to leave. Here is my plan. People are quick to believe what they see—and even quicker to jump to the wrong conclusion." She went to the brazier and grabbed an iron poker, then fastened the makeshift rope to it. He followed her into the garderobe.

"We're going down the toilet?" he asked, his cheek twitching with revulsion. "We're going to jump into that cesspit?"

"No, we're going to make them *think* that you did." She set the iron poker across the garderobe seat and then flung the heap of cloth down into the darkness. "They'll arrive and find your bed in tatters. The windows will all be bolted. A quick search will reveal the false trail, and every guard in the palace will be ordered to start searching the perimeter."

"But we'll still be in the room?" he asked quizzically.

Ankarette nodded. "When the servants are ordered to

clean up the mess we're about to make, I will render them unconscious and we'll take their clothes. Everyone knows who you are, Duke Alensson, but one thing I've learned is that people don't give you a second glance if you *look* like someone of lower birth. A shave, a haircut, and a different walk will make everyone look right past you as we escape."

"And where are we going?" he asked her cautiously.

"I need to get back to my king and warn him what we're up against," Ankarette said. "And you are coming with me. King Lewis has been acting with a great deal of overconfidence. Like he *can't* lose this fight. I'm beginning to suspect I know why." She gave him a cunning smile. "Now, before we hide in the rafters, tell me about this chest. I want you to describe it to me in perfect detail. What did it look like?"

Alensson gave her a broad smile. "I like you, lass. And I am only too happy to leave this prison."

CHAPTER NINETEEN

Defending Pree

Alensson watched as the soldiers yanked the trebuchet lever. The massive timbers groaned, pivoted sharply, and then hurled a bucket of debris toward the towering walls of Pree, only for the boulders to be pulverized against it.

"By the mast," one of the soldiers said, shaking his head in disappointment. "It didn't so much as soften her."

"And why should it?" said another soldier. "The walls of Pree are eighty feet thick. It's siege ladders again, lads."

"Not for you," Alensson said. "Load it again. Throw another and then another. It may crack the shell eventually." It was only the first day of the siege. He hadn't expected the walls to crumble on the first strike.

"Aye, my lord," the soldier said, his armor coated with chalky dust and grime. "You heard the man. Fetch more rubble from yonder."

Alensson remained to watch them obey his orders, then

strode farther onto the battlefield, where the archers were sending volleys up against the walls.

He planted one knee, shielding his eyes from the sun, and gazed at the walls. "How goes the work? Do you have enough arrows?"

The archer had a gouge on his cheek and was missing some teeth. "It goes well enough, lord duke. I got a knight in the neck about an hour past and watched him tumble off the wall. That was a sight to see. How many do you reckon are defending Pree? A million?"

Alensson chuckled. "Not so many. I wonder how many inside would actually like us to win, eh?"

The archer grinned. "How far away is Deford's army? Have you heard word, my lord?"

Alensson nodded. "He's at Tatton Hall," he answered. "I'd love to take a thousand men and go give him trouble right now, but we need every man here. He's coming with reinforcements from Kingfountain. Latest word is they are three days away."

The archer pursed his lips. "Cutting it awfully close this time," he said. "If they join the city defenders before we break through . . ." He clucked his tongue. "But we've got the Maid with us. She's worth ten thousand brutes of Kingfountain. I seen her banner up there against the walls. She's got pluck, that lass. Fears nothing. I'm grateful the Fountain is on our side, my lord."

"So am I," Alensson said, clapping the man's shoulder. The last he'd heard, Genette was in the command tent talking to the king. It was unusual having the king amidst the army for once, taking an active role in the decisions, however far his tent was from actual danger. But when Alensson looked up, he saw her white banner near the front walls, just as the archer had said. She was rallying the soldiers to fill the moat with bales of wood to create makeshift bridges that would allow them to reach the fortifications with the ladders. The archers and crossbowmen from the city were brutally picking the soldiers off, one by one. The dead were left on the field, many with multiple arrows protruding from them. Some were writhing, their screams ghosting over the battlefield.

"You look like you've a mind to join her," the archer said with his gap-toothed smile.

"I do indeed," Alensson said, rising and swinging his shield around from the back strap.

"Mind your head," the archer grunted, then fitted another arrow, pulled, and sent it winging. Alensson watched as the arrow hit its mark and a soldier tumbled from the wall. "Got another one! You're a bit of luck, my lord! I'll see if I can clear the whole wall for you."

The men tittered and laughed and Alensson grinned at them before securing the shield to his forearm. Then he started walking forward, his heart beating wildly in his chest as he entered the vale of death. He passed men twitching and moaning, their bodies impaled by feathered shafts. He kept his gaze on that white flag.

A horseman rode up to him from the camp. "Duke Alensson!"

"What is it?" he asked, turning back.

"The king wishes to see you. He's ordering a retreat. Come back to the camp."

He frowned. "Darkness will give us some cover. Does he mean to wait until nightfall?"

"No," the herald said, shaking his head. "He means to pull back from Pree. Deford's army is getting too close for comfort."

"But if we take Pree, Deford's army will be on the run!" Alensson snapped, his anger flaring. How could Chatriyon expect them to overwhelm the defenses of a city like Pree in a single day? Yes, Deford's army was coming. But they were so close to victory!

"Tell that to the king. He'll not listen to me."

"Nor is he likely to listen to *her*," he growled. "I'll be right there. Let me be the one to tell the Maid."

"Thank you, sir," the herald said. His relief was obvious as he turned his stallion and spurred it away.

As he walked toward the walls and closer to the imminent violence, he thought on the last few days since the coronation at Ranz. They were at a crossroads of sorts—the future hung on the hinges of Chatriyon's decisions. It was said that Duke Deford had brought the young lad, the King of Ceredigion, with him to also be crowned at Ranz. This was the pivotal moment, the time for action.

An arrow struck the turf right ahead of Alensson, snapping his attention back to the matter at hand. The sycophants of Shynom were tired of war and bloodshed. A negotiated truce was more to their liking. Peace through bargaining. And they pleaded with Chatriyon to form an alliance with Brugia, their neighboring kingdom across the sea. With Brugia on their side, they could push Deford back on his heels with diplomacy rather than battle. Chatriyon's only ally was Atabyrion, and it was a small, backwater kingdom that had lost many men during the wars.

This was all totally against Alensson's nature and character. Occitania had been sundered by blood. And it would be rebuilt the same way.

Raising his shield before him as he walked, he made his way to the thickest part of the danger, for that was where the

Maid had stationed herself. He heard her voice ringing out amidst the commotion of battle. She wasn't urging the men onward. She was shouting to the defenders on the wall.

"Surrender to us quickly, by the Fountain!" she yelled. "If you do not surrender before nightfall, we will come in there by force! Surrender! Or the Fountain will bring death upon you without mercy! These walls will not save you!"

There was a jeering sound from one of the Ceredigic soldiers above. "Shall they not, bloody tart?"

He saw two crossbowmen rear up from the wall suddenly, aim at Genette, and fire the bolts at her. He was close enough to see their movement, but too far and too encumbered by his armor to reach her in time.

Genette cried out in pain as one of the bolts sliced through her thigh. The blow made her stagger and nearly drop her standard. Her squire, the lad Brendin, seized it with both hands to steady it and the second bolt struck the boy's foot, pinning it to the ground. The boy yelled with pain, wrenching on his leg, but he was trapped painfully. Alensson started running toward them, trying to reach them to offer them the protection of his shield.

There was an angry red gash on the Maid's leg—her armor had been slit clean through by the broadhead bolt. But it was not bleeding, and Alensson knew it was because of the scabbard she wore.

Still struggling to free himself, the squire lifted his visor higher so he could see his foot. It was a painful wound—the lad wouldn't walk for months after this. But just as Alensson reached them, a third crossbow bolt struck the lad's chest. He toppled to the ground, dead before he fell.

"No!" the Maid screeched. "No!" She rushed to the boy's side, her face filled with horror and anguish. Her standard lay in the grass, still gripped in the boy's hands.

Horns began to blat from the command tents. The signal —retreat.

Genette looked up at Alensson, who had positioned himself between her and the wall, his shield lifted high to protect her. He took the impact of a shuddering bolt on his arm, feeling the power of it bruise him. The Maid knelt there, cradling the lad in her arms, staring into his unblinking eyes with distress and grief.

"He's dead," Alensson said softly. "There's nothing you can do." He had compassion for her loss, but he needed to get her out of there. They were too vulnerable where they were and the king had ordered the retreat. Even if it was the wrong decision, it was his to make—unless they managed to convince him otherwise.

"Brendin, poor Brendin!" the Maid moaned. She looked up at the sky, tears streaking down her lashes. She turned her ravaged face toward Alensson. "Why are we retreating? We are so *close* to victory!"

Alensson looked at her in disbelief. "The king orders it, Genette. Come with me. We must persuade him to continue the attack."

Soldiers were already peeling away from the walls, carrying their siege ladders as the defenders' cheers of triumph rained down on them.

Genette set the boy down and wrenched the standard from his dead fingers. "Attack!" she yelled at the fleeing soldiers. "Come on! This is our chance! This is the Fountain's will! The city will fall to us!"

"Never!" cried the defenders from the wall. "Kill the strumpet! Bring her down!"

Alensson saw the situation start to spiral out of control.

Some of the troops were hesitating. The horns had sounded the retreat. It was an order from the king. But the Maid, who had guided them to victory so many times before, was telling them to keep fighting. Who should they obey? Alensson saw the confusion it was causing. Men would be killed if they hesitated too long.

The long, loud blat of the horn sounded the retreat signal again. Farther down the wall, the Occitanian soldiers were falling back, oblivious to the tension at the heart of the scene. Soldiers were dropping, hit by arrows sent raining down on them. The Maid stared helplessly at the melee, tears mixing with the dust and dirt on her face.

"Fight on!" she pleaded. "The Fountain is stronger than these walls! It will aid us! Believe in me!"

Alensson believed. But he knew the nature and disposition of men. Their brothers in arms had been slain before their eyes, and now their comrades were fleeing to safety. They saw the gash in the Maid's leg, her own squire lying dead at her feet. And their faith in her began to crumble. Men will follow if someone leads, but they are more inclined to listen to other men. Besides, the king was leading them out of harm's way while the Maid wished to lead them into more danger. One by one, they turned their gazes away from her and began running back to the camp. Some glanced at her, but most lacked the courage to look her in the eye. Genette pleaded with them to resist, to have courage. But no one listened to her.

Alensson watched her shoulders sag, watched the defeat register in her eyes. He knew in that moment how he must have looked after the battle of Vernay.

"Come, Genette," Alensson said, gripping her arm. "The king commands it. We will not back down without a fight. We must persuade him to continue the attack tomorrow. You and I. Come with me."

"He won't listen to us," she said through her hot tears. "And we would fail if we tried," she added bitterly, her teeth clenched to stifle her sobs. She stared up at the walls, her brow wrinkling, her lip quivering. "With this sword, I could destroy those walls," she whispered to him. "The Fountain would have brought them tumbling down. If only he'd believed. If only."

She turned and started to kneel by the body of her squire. "I must bring him."

"You're wounded," Alensson said. "I'll carry the lad."

"Thank you, Gentle Duke," she said, putting her hand on his shoulder to steady herself. She swayed slightly. "I'll need my strength for what lies ahead."

"And what's that?" he asked, wrenching the bolt out of the dead boy's foot. He lifted the boy in his arms and found him surprisingly heavy. He was tired, so very tired, as he started toward the camp. The sound of cheering from the walls nearly drowned out her next words.

"To bring the lad back alive," the Maid whispered.

CHAPTER TWENTY

Breath

The camp was in commotion as Alensson carried the limp body of the dead squire into it. Genette used her banner pole as a crutch and walked with a pronounced limp from the gash on her leg. The tents were being brought down in a hasty manner, and all around them there were signs of retreat. The king was abandoning the siege of Pree after one day. Rubbish and filth had been left behind and supply wagons lumbered down the road, driven by cranky teamsters with pole whips.

"To my tent," the Maid gasped. Her tent was one of the few still standing.

She hobbled ahead of Alensson and opened the flap, allowing him to duck in and bring the body. He was breathing fast and hard, tired from carrying it so far, sickened by the awful duty he had assumed.

"On the pallet," she directed. The tent was darkening quickly from the advancing dusk. She quickly lit a taper and then some candles to ward away the gloom. The air smelled like dirt and sweat. There were screams all around them as the wounded were brought in from the battlefield. Most were dragged to wagons to be carted off for healing elsewhere. Alensson knew many wouldn't survive the night.

"I'm going to Chatriyon," Alensson said, watching as Genette knelt stiffly by the body.

"Don't go yet," she said, looking up at him worriedly.

He hesitated at the threshold, unnerved by what she had said she was going to do. Reviving the dead was a blessing from the Fountain. Few in history had been able to accomplish it, but he did not doubt that someone of Genette's faith and abilities could do it.

"Should I be here?" he asked her, feeling dirty and tired and frustrated and a host of other feelings. He grappled with the desire to choke the king if he could not dissuade him from making such a monumental mistake. Chatriyon was not one to change his mind quickly, though.

"Yes. The Fountain wishes it. And I'll need your help, after it is done."

"Help? What can I do?" He wanted to flee from whatever arcane magic she was about to invoke. But he was also curious, so he came over and knelt beside her and the pallet.

Genette's hair was a wild, untamed mess when she removed her chain hood. There were smudges of filth on her cheeks and nose. Then she pulled off her gauntlets to free her hands, and he saw the bruises on her knuckles.

She was finally getting her breath back after her injury. The glow of the candles illuminated her face, and he saw their points of light shining in her eyes as she looked up at him. A strange expression crossed her face, one of tenderness and gratitude. Then she unbuckled her sword belt and the mystical scabbard woven into it.

"What are you doing?" he demanded.

She laid the scabbard on the boy's chest and brought his hands up to rest against it. "It will do no good to revive him if he's so wounded. This will hasten his healing."

Her lips grimaced in pain and he watched as the wound on her leg began to trickle blood.

"But what about your wound?"

She shook her head. "The bolt just grazed me. I will be fine."

"You need a healer yourself."

"I don't have time, Alensson!" she said in scolding tone. She averted her eyes and sighed. "I am sorry. I shouldn't have yelled at you. When I revive him, I will lose all my strength. I'll be helpless as an infant." She looked up at him. "I trust you, Gentle Duke. With all my heart. Bind my wound and let me rest. I will recover soon, have no fear." She looked down at the body again. "Have no fear. What's done is done."

He put his hand on top of hers. "What do you mean by that?"

"What's done is *done*," she whispered. "I knew this would happen. I knew it, yet I believed he would become the man he could be. I hoped."

"Who? Chatriyon?"

"Yes," she answered wearily. "The Fountain warned me." Then she looked him in the eye with heart-wrenching tenderness. "I knew this would happen, Gentle Duke. All of it. I chose it willingly."

"You speak in riddles, Genette," he said with frustration.

"I know. I know," she nodded, her shoulders slumping. "If I say more, I'll lose my courage. I cannot falter. Even if Chatriyon does, I cannot. Just know this, Alensson. I *chose* to answer the Fountain's call. Now it bids me to heal this boy. You must watch it. You must hear the word of power. Someday it will save the life of the heir of La Marche. A little babe —stillborn."

Her words burned the inside of Alensson's chest as if she'd grabbed a poker from the coals and jabbed him with it. A stillborn child. His wife was pregnant with their first child. Would the child be stillborn then? Would Genette's word of power be able to save him? A mix of grief and hope and fear battled inside him, and he didn't know what to say, let alone what to think.

"I will only say the word of power once," Genette said, cupping her hands together and placing them on the corpse's waxlike hands. "You must remember it. You must never forget it, Gentle Duke. Promise me."

"I swear it," he said. "On the—"

"It is enough," she said, cutting him off. She leaned over the boy's face, the peaceful face beneath the thatch of thick flaxen hair. Alensson felt his skin prickle and gooseflesh spread down his arms, across his neck. He shivered and started to tremble. Her face was serene and, despite the smudges, filled with unearthly beauty.

"*Nesh-ama*," she breathed and then planted a gentle kiss on the boy's cold lips.

There was a distant rushing sound like a waterfall.

And then the boy began to breathe.

Alensson watched as the boy's chest rose and fell and color blushed his cheeks. The squire's fingers stiffened against the scabbard of the sword. Then the black wound on the boy's chest began to shrink before his eyes. The duke felt as if he were in a holy place and could not utter a word for fear of disturbing the reverence.

Brendin's eyelashes fluttered open. He stared up at them in confusion, but with a look of tranquility. Genette stroked his fair hair tenderly, then Alensson watched helplessly as her eyes rolled back in her head and she slumped to the ground unconscious.

♦　　♦　　♦

The Duke of La Marche had helped knights get in and out of armor many times. But getting Genette out of hers was fraught with peculiar sensations. She was a woman, not his sister, not his wife—of no relation to him at all. But she was his friend, and their friendship had been forged in the furnace of war. A sister in arms, truly. He removed the battered breastplate, bracers, and greaves.

Her skin had turned chalk white and she was listless and unresponsive. The doctor he had summoned lifted her eyelids, checked her pulse, and tried to rouse her with hartshorn—which failed. The bandages the doctor wrapped around her leg were soon soaked with blood. He used needle and thread to stitch the wound shut, but the bleeding did not stop. Alensson paced in the tent, gazing down at her and fearing that she had traded her life to save the boy's. Her breath was too shallow to hear and her chest rose and fell at distant intervals.

The squire was sleeping on a pallet, clutching the sword to his bosom. Alensson had inspected the lad's foot where the bolt had pierced it—all that remained was a pink scar.

"I can't stop the bleeding," the doctor said worriedly, shaking his head. He had a bowl full of bloody water and stained rags. "I think I have some woad in my tent. Here, press your hand against the wound rag until I return."

Alensson knelt by her side, doing as the doctor had asked,

and the man rushed from the tent. He glanced at the boy, wondering if he should take the scabbard away and bring it to her. He knew it would heal her wound. But the boy's injuries had stolen his life. While the external injuries had been healed, he did not know how long it would take for the scabbard to heal the inward ones.

He heard a faint whisper from Genette's mouth.

Looking down, he saw her eyelids fluttering. She was so weak she couldn't move at all. He pressed the bandage even harder against her leg, willing it to stop bleeding.

"Are you awake, Genette?" he asked, bending close to her mouth.

"Alen . . . sson," she whispered.

"I'm here," he said, his heart churning with worry. "I'm going to bring the scabbard."

"No," she whispered. "Or he won't . . . recover. I'll not die yet. Not yet, Gentle Duke. Just weak. So weak."

He felt a surge of relief, but while he believed her, it did not stop him from worrying. He was still looking down at her pale face and seeping wound. "The doctor is getting some woad."

"Pretty yellow flower," she mumbled. Her head lolled to one side. She blinked her eyes open fully, gazing up at him. "I'm cold," she said.

Keeping his hand pressed against the wound, he pulled the blanket up to her chin. She closed her eyes again. "Promise me."

"What? Did you say something?"

"Promise me."

"Promise me."

He strained to hear her over the commotion of the camp. He leaned so far forward that his ear was nearly to her lips. "What? Promise you what?"

"That you'll not kill the king," she said. "He must live. Even if I must die."

A piercing pain shot through his heart. "I don't understand."

"I know. I know. There is so much . . . you don't understand. Promise me that you won't kill him. Or his child."

"I wouldn't kill a *child*," Alensson said indignantly.

"Lewis won't always be a child," she said with sigh. "Promise me, Gentle Duke. Please. Even if you don't understand. Promise me. The game must go on."

"What game? What are you talking of, Genette? Tell me!"

"I can't. You must find out . . . for yourself. Promise me." She gave him a pleading look. "Or my death will be worth nothing."

"Have you seen your death, Genette? Do you know when it will be?"

She stared at him and then slowly nodded. It was the first time she'd moved her body since breathing life back into Brendin. "Promise me. Please."

He let out his breath. She had given everything to see Chatriyon crowned. She had suffered and she had bled and she was bleeding still, yet she was determined to see him king. It didn't matter that Chatriyon was ungrateful, that he was perhaps unsuited to leadership.

It was not an easy promise for Alensson to make, and he did not make it lightly. Still pressing the soaked cloth to the oozing wound on her leg, he rested his other hand on top of hers. "I promise you, Genette of Donremy."

A rustle of the tent fabric announced the doctor's return.

"What took you?" Alensson grumbled, turning and glancing at the doctor. The man looked haggard and spent as he crossed the tent to where the Maid lay. There was a stalk of vibrant violet-tipped flowers in his hand. Violet, not yellow.

When Alensson gazed down at Genette, she was looking at him, her mouth turned into a frown. "That's not woad," he said.

The doctor's eyes were full of panic. "He ... is ... outside," he panted. His voice was hoarse.

As Alensson rose, the flap rustled and a man came through it, dagger in hand. A poisoner, no doubt. The doctor quailed, letting out a moan of fear, and scrabbled away from the Maid. Alensson noticed a sticky substance on the tip of the dagger. The poisoner lunged at him, bringing the hilt down toward his neck to stun him, but the duke hiked up his shoulder and caught the blow that had been intended to knock him out. He kneed the poisoner in the stomach and grabbed at his face with his blood-slick hand, the one that had been staunching the wound moments before. Their two bodies collided as they wrestled each other for control. The poisoner's knee slammed into Alensson's groin, but he was protected by his armor, and when the dagger came slicing down at his forearm, it glanced off the metal bracer.

The duke swung his elbow around and caught the poisoner in the teeth, tearing his lip. Then he tackled the man to the floor and buffeted him on the face.

The dagger came stabbing at his side, right beneath the armor. The chain hauberk stopped it from piercing, but he felt the pain of the jab in his ribs. Alensson grabbed the man's wrist and forced it down to the floor through sheer strength. The poisoner spat in his eyes, bloody spittle, and Alensson butted his forehead down on the man's nose, breaking it. That finally stunned the poisoner, who groaned and went limp beneath the blinding pain.

The duke pried the dagger from his fingers and then

brought the blade up to his throat. "Who sent you?"

The poisoner coughed and gargled something unintelligible.

"Answer me!" Alensson roared, pressing the flat of the blade to the man's throat.

"Lord Bannion," the poisoner said with a cough. "She was supposed to die at the wall!"

Lord Bannion was the king's chamberlain.

Alensson was temporarily stunned: He knew who the order had truly came from. Was Chatriyon going mad already? Then he increased the pressure enough to nick the man's neck with the blade. "Oops. I slipped," he growled.

The poisoner's face began to twitch in horror. Then the convulsions started to rack his body.

CHAPTER TWENTY-ONE

Abandoned

The Duke of Westmarch's army arrived at Pree two days later, descending on the city like black storm clouds that promised to bring the lash of lightning. The rest of Chatriyon's army had already melted away, but Alensson waited outside the sanctuary of St. Denys, a small burg on the outskirts of Pree, astride his horse, holding the reins of Genette's steed, waiting for her to finish inside. She had demanded that he never speak of the miracle of her squire's recovery.

"Shouldn't we be on our way, my lord?" grumbled one of his captains, eyeing the road nervously for signs of outriders from Deford's army. He stroked his graying red beard anxiously and glanced back at the sanctuary.

"Patience, Jeremy," Alensson said, although it was a virtue

he was struggling to find within himself. "She'll be out soon."

"I don't have time for patience," the soldier griped. The city of Pree was ominously silent, like a child waiting fearfully for the rebuke of an angry parent. The city had withheld the short-lived siege, but the many outlying towns, like St. Denys, would suffer the wrath for helping Chatriyon wage war. Alensson ground his teeth together, wishing with all his heart that the situation had been different. He had hoped they would already be in Pree by the time Deford arrived. How glorious it would have felt to repel him from the city. Unfortunately, it was not the Fountain's will for his revenge to be satisfied.

"There she is," Jeremy said with relief. "We cannot leave here soon enough."

Alensson watched in surprise as Genette left the sanctuary wearing one of the royal tunics he had provided for her. She had gone in wearing armor, but it was missing.

Jeremy gave Alensson a puzzled look.

The duke watched her limp, seeing how her leg still pained her despite the scabbard she once again wore at her side. The Maid marched up to him, and there was an almost sour look of determination on her face as she took the reins.

"You left your armor?" he asked her softly.

Genette put her good leg up in the stirrup and winced as she mounted. "My work here was unfinished," she told him. "So I left my armor in the fountain."

That earned another baffled look from Jeremy, but Alensson nudged his mount closer to hers. "You put it in the water? To hide it?"

She gazed at him, eyes narrowing slightly, and then nodded. "The Fountain bade me to do this. It will be needed . . . later."

"Will we take back the city of Pree then?"

She looked at him seriously. "Chatriyon will regain his palace, Gentle Duke."

"We should be going," Jeremy murmured impatiently. "Deford's army is hardly more than a stone's throw from us. Someone will warn him we're still here."

The Maid looked at the captain and snorted. "We are not in any real danger."

She turned and looked back at the sanctuary, staring at the bubbling fountain set inside the doors. The sexton bowed his head to her from the doorway. Genette's strength was returning slowly this time, and he couldn't help but wonder if it was because she was heartsick.

"Why did you send Brendin away?" Alensson asked her. "After the scabbard healed him? You will need a squire, Genette, even if you don't have your armor."

She gave him an enigmatic look. "Where I am going, I will not need one. Let's rejoin the army."

"And be quick about it," Jeremy huffed, jerking the reins and starting out at a clop.

Alensson gazed at the walls of Pree rising over the cropped tree tops at the edge of the village. He saw the flags in the distance, taunting him.

"You'll get your chance, Gentle Duke," she told him, reaching out and touching his arm lightly. "If Deford is here, it means your lands are unprotected."

She knew just what to say to make him smile.

♦   ♦   ♦

The king had retreated to the royal castle of Montjuno, a fortress between Lionn and Pree. They had reclaimed it during their journey. Supply wagons from Shynom arrived regularly, as did a host of courtiers come to surround the king like so many buzzing flies.

When Alensson and Genette arrived from Pree, they found the mood much changed. Instead of treating the Maid of Donremy with the awe and respect they had once demonstrated, many of the soldiers greeted her with black looks, curled lips, and whispered conversations. Alensson had told the king he'd killed a poisoner who had been sent to murder the girl. But he had not told the king he knew who'd hired the man. Chatriyon had feigned shock and outrage and promised to send his captain to investigate, but nothing further had been done.

As they walked through the crowded hall, Alensson saw several courtiers bustle up to Chatriyon to warn him of their approach. The king wore his crown and a sumptuous jeweled doublet made of purple velvet and stitched with costly gems.

Genette was limping as she walked, and although Alensson would have slowed down to accommodate her, she kept a pace that forced *him* to keep up.

When she reached the king, Genette dropped down on one knee. Her wince was probably undetectable to anyone other than Alensson, but the king waved her back up.

"No need for that, my dear," he said graciously. "Your leg is still troubling you. Cousin, help her up!" The king gestured for Alensson to assist her back to her feet, but she managed it on her own. "So you've managed to arrive at last. You took your time in coming."

Alensson felt a hint of censure in the tone. "She was grievously wounded in the attack on Pree, my lord."

Chatriyon's eyes narrowed. "I know that, Cousin. But surely *you* could have come, Alensson? I've been in need of your advice." He cut a glance at Genette, his eyes narrowing coldly.

The duke felt his anger heating up, but kept control of his face. "I am here now, my lord."

"Thankfully." The king pitched his voice lower, but there was so much commotion in the hall—drinks being served, women flirting with men and men with women—that it would have been difficult for anyone to overhear them. "I have received word that the King of Brugia is warming to the thought of an alliance with us. Deford is married to Philip's sister, you know, so their alliance is more than one of practicality. But things are changing. The tide is beginning to turn. Now that I've been crowned, Philip is looking at me as the rightful heir of Occitania and not the little brat from Kingfountain. I've been advised to cease hostilities and let diplomacy do its work." His eyebrow lifted. "What do you think, *Cousin*?"

Alensson glanced at Genette, whose expression reflected the same anger and resentment he felt. After all the success and victories they'd had, why stop? The only reason they hadn't taken Pree was because Chatriyon had called it off too soon. He hadn't even given them a chance.

"My lord," Alensson said, trying to master his tone. "Isn't it better to negotiate from a position of strength? You don't need Brugia's help to regain your kingdom. You have soldiers willing to fight in your name, willing to fight and lose their blood on your behalf."

Chatriyon winced. "Yes, yes, but it's all rather *bloody*, don't you think? Consider how many *lives* will be saved, Alensson! We are shedding the blood of our brothers. They are my subjects as well. This is a civil war. Don't you realize that? If I can persuade Philip of Brugia to join me, it will permanently alter the balance of power between us and Ceredigion. Deford will be forced to make a truce with us. And then we can regain much of what we lost. Including *your* lands!"

Alensson was trembling with anger. "You think Deford will *give* up La Marche? He won't, my king. It must be wrested from him. And I cannot think of a better time to attempt it than right now. If you want to play peace instead of war, so be it, but let me take those who will follow and harry Deford's lands—*my* lands! Diplomacy can take years to achieve results. And it would all but hobble the momentum we've built thus far. The kingdom is tottering like a vase on a small table and you want to steady it before it falls!"

Chatriyon's look was so patronizing. "Of course I do, Cousin. If the vase falls, it breaks! What's the use of ruling a kingdom that's been broken to pieces?" He chuckled to himself, shaking his head. Then he turned his gaze on Genette. "And what is your *opinion*, dear girl?" In the past, he had attested that she spoke for the Fountain. But the coronation had changed him. It was remarkable how sudden the change had come. The king looked uncomfortable in her presence, as if her act of breathing annoyed him.

She looked him full in the eye. "You have the power to *take* your kingdom back," she said in a low voice. "If you will use it. It is your decision, my lord. But you must remember that you cannot choose the consequences."

He cocked his head in confusion and misgiving. "What do you mean?"

"You know what I mean. You know what the Fountain wills, my king."

"Yes, I think I do," he said with an almost lazy tone. Then he turned back to Alensson. "I will heed your advice, Cousin. Take what men you can and go around Pree. It will only help hasten the negotiations if you're there stinging Deford's flanks. But when I call you back, you must come. Agreed?"

Alensson felt something was wrong. The king had given in too easily. Here it was again, the sensation that something else was afoot, something the duke wasn't seeing. "Thank you, my lord. I will take Genette with me, and she will—"

"No, I don't think so," Chatriyon said solemnly.

"My lord?" Alensson asked.

"You heard me. No, I will have duties she can perform. An army is always in need of good captains. There are cities to hold, garrisons to maintain. I will keep her near me."

Alensson felt his heart warn him. "She inspires people, my lord. More soldiers would join the effort if she came to support my assault on La Marche. She's skilled on the battle-field."

"I'm sure she is," Chatriyon said with a yawn. "I'm sure you want her near you for *other* reasons as well."

It felt like the king had punched him in the stomach. "What did you say?"

"I don't judge you, Cousin. But she's too important. No, I order you to ride out tomorrow with as many soldiers as will come. I think a hundred ought to do. The Maid will stay at Montjuno, where I will look after her myself. The two of you should spend more time apart. People are starting to *talk*, Cousin."

If Chatriyon weren't the king, Alensson would have smashed his fist into the man's mouth. It took all his self-will to keep himself from striking his sovereign. In that moment, he felt the ambition in his heart swell so much that he wondered if it would consume him. As he stared at the king in outrage, he began to understand what was going on. He understood why Chatriyon had called off the siege of Pree.

If Genette had indeed defeated Pree in only one day, it would have established her reputation forever. Chatriyon was crafty enough to know that if he kept her as his champion, he would be shackled to maintaining her standards in his court. For a man of many hungers, it was not an appealing prospect. And while each of Genette's successes had drawn more men to the fight, they were fighting for *her* and not for the king. Oh, Alensson could see it in the cunning look in Chatriyon's eyes. He was asserting his control and humbling the girl, without whom he would not be wearing his crown.

It was deplorable. It was cowardly. And it was obvious why the king was trying to shame Alensson and send him away—he was her protector. If one poisoner could be sent, why not another?

"If that is your will, my king," Genette said, bowing her head to him.

CHAPTER TWENTY-TWO

The Squire's Gift

The wind was surprisingly fierce as it battered the curtains of Alensson's tent, the thunder of it momentarily drowning out the noise of the night crickets. The tent was much smaller than his previous one, for it needed to be packed and moved every night as they made their lightning raids through the inheritance of his youth. A small oil lamp burned nearby as he read the latest missives arriving from Shynom. The air smelled pungently of horse manure.

He sat on a camp chair, hunched over, still wearing his torn hauberk beneath the filthy tunic he'd been wearing for days. He rubbed the stubble on his chin, scowling at the news, his mind twisting for a solution to his quandary.

"You're grimacing," Jeremy said, twisting strands of his graying beard, shaking his head, and peering over his shoulder. "Ill news, my lord?"

Alensson sighed. It had been two months since the king had separated him from Genette. She'd been sent to take a town that showed no sign of surrendering. It was too fortified to assault without siege weapons, not that Chatriyon had bothered to supply her with any, but she had gone willingly enough. In other words, he'd sent her to kick against a stump while his negotiations with Brugia progressed. Maybe Chatriyon had sent Alensson to La Marche to get him out of the way as well, but at least his duty was more enjoyable—after all, he had been sanctioned to be a thorn in Deford's side. He had stayed on the move, stopping to strike at a garrison for two days before slinking away and hitting another, making Deford chase him all the while. The king had expressly forbidden him the battlefield victory he craved, but the duke honestly didn't think he would win without the Maid helping him. He'd written letters begging the king to send her to La Marche to help him. She'd wanted to come. But Chatriyon had remained implacable. Now the situation had finally come to a head, and he would have to make a decision—one that would define him for the rest of his life.

He remembered that Jeremy had asked him a question, and he let out a pent-up breath. "I received a letter from Genette," he said gruffly. "Before I knew her, she couldn't write her own name. Now look." He waved the letter. "She's not just dictating letters to a scribe. This is her own handwriting."

"What does she say?" Jeremy asked. "Is she still hammering fruitlessly at Compenne?"

"No," Alensson said, shaking his head. "She abandoned it."

"Really? Where is she now?"

"She's heading to Shanton."

Jeremy's brow wrinkled. "The border city? Why there?"

Alensson rolled up the letter and stuffed it into his saddle-bag. "I learned from her that Chatriyon is giving that city to the King of Brugia." He frowned with resentment. "Obviously His Majesty didn't see fit to consult with me on the matter. Giving Brugia a foothold in Occitania is dangerous. If you let the wolf's snout inside the henhouse, he'll soon be eating the hens."

Jeremy chuffed loudly and in surprise. "I truly didn't believe the king would be such a fool. But why is the Maid heading there?"

Alensson smiled ruefully. "Because the city of Shanton isn't keen on being surrendered to the Brugian army. They're holding out, and they asked the Maid to come help them."

"They asked her to defy the king?"

He gave his captain a knowing look. "She says she's obeying the will of the Fountain. She bids me to join her in preventing Brugia from taking over. Apparently they've sent a strong force to threaten the mayor of the city. She sent this message six days ago, so she's probably already there."

Jeremy's brow wrinkled with concern. "And what are you going to do, my lord? The king wants you here to keep the pressure on Deford. I don't care how accomplished the man is, fighting three fronts at once would cause anyone grief. Surely Deford doesn't want Brugia intervening."

"Of course not," Alensson said, rising and beginning to pace. "Remember that Brugia and Ceredigion are currently allies, bound by marriage. King Philip must tread carefully, because if he provokes Deford too much, he'll get invaded himself."

"And Ceredigion controls the Brugian city of Callait, does it not?"

"Indeed. They have a foothold. And there's another reason why it would be foolish to give Philip one with us. What if he's deceiving Chatriyon? What if the foothold is a pretext to help Ceredigion? It could be disastrous for them to have a fortress inside our realm. I can see why Genette is so upset. She called the king a few . . . unflattering names in her letter." He grinned as he recalled them.

"How fares your wife?" Jeremy asked after another moment's pause. "The babe is due before the winter, aye? Or was it spring?"

"The spring," Alensson said.

That opened up another festering sore inside him. It must have shown on his face, for Jeremy said, "Is she not well?"

"It's been a difficult pregnancy thus far," Alensson said, continuing to pace. He clenched his fist, wishing he could punch something. He hated being so far away from his wife, especially since he knew how much she suffered. He knew his decisions affected not only himself but also Jianne and their unborn child. It was a torturous position to be in. "She can hardly keep any food down. She says this is normal, but she's suffering and lacking the comforts her station deserves."

"Is she still in Lionn? Surely her uncle's attending to her needs?"

Alensson shook his head. "No, Lord Hext is at Shynom trying to negotiate his brother's release from prison in Ceredigion. She went back to her cottage in Izzt." He ground his teeth with frustration. "Would I were there instead. But what could I do? I'm no nurse, no midwife. I'll go back for the winter months, and she says she's content to wait until then." He let out his breath, feeling torn and conflicted. Genette wanted him at Shanton. The king wanted him to stay in La Marche. His wife needed him. What was he to do?

Jeremy rose from his bench. "I'll give you time to think about your answer then. Your men will follow you no matter where you lead them. Maybe it's time we attacked the palace of Kingfountain, eh?" He chuckled softly. "That would surprise them."

"Indeed," laughed Alensson. "As you said, my mind is in turmoil. Grant me some time to ponder the dilemma before I give orders for the morrow."

After his captain's departure, the only sound was the chorus of the crickets. Alensson took a drink from his wine flask and winced at the bitter taste. He rummaged through his saddlebag again until he found the pile of letters he'd bound with a strap of leather. They were all from Jianne. He carefully untied them and started to read them over again, admiring the penmanship and savoring the words of love and encouragement from his wife. There was such a difference between her letters and Genette's. He paused, his thoughts drifting to the Maid once more. She had seemed so certain that the Fountain would deliver Pree into their hands. Yet she had failed. Rather, the king had pulled back his forces too soon— he hadn't given the Fountain's magic time to aid them. Alensson had thought on that decision over and over since they'd abandoned Pree, and he still believed the king hadn't wished for her to be successful. How would he take her actions now? If she'd truly gone against his wishes, it would give Chatriyon justification to declare her a traitor. Would he dare do that? If he did, did that mean Alensson would be considered a traitor for helping her?

He looked down at the letters again, banishing the Maid from his mind as he read his wife's words. He fancied being at the cottage, tiptoeing inside, and startling her with a surprise, folding his arms around her middle and nuzzling kisses against her neck. Pangs of loneliness and frustration spiked inside his heart. Jianne was so far away it felt as if she were on a different world. He wasn't a prisoner of Ceredigion any longer, but he did feel like a prisoner of the crown. His fate was bound to Chatriyon's—a king whom he no longer respected, a king who no longer valued him, despite all the years his family had served.

The thought made him brood angrily. He pored over a few more of the letters and then tied them up again and delicately returned them to the saddlebag. Each was a treasure that brought a little balm of comfort. He would get his duchy back. He would make sure Jianne was given all the comforts she deserved. He would get his duchy back. He would make sure . . .

"My lord?" said a voice outside the tent.

"What is it?" Alensson asked, wrestling with his feelings of futility.

One of the soldiers parted the tent and poked his head inside. "My lord, there's a lad here to see you."

Alensson frowned. "Who is it?" It was highly unusual for a local village lad to wander into his camp uninvited.

"He says he knows you. The lad's name is Brendin."

Genette's squire. Alensson hurried to his feet. "Send him in."

The soldier held open the tent and the tawny-haired boy came inside. He was holding a long bundle, tied off with ropes and straps. It was much longer than a bedroll. Alensson's mouth went dry.

The boy looked nervous. There was a furrow in his brow, just beneath the hairline. He looked anguished. The memory of this boy lying dead on a pallet flashed through Alensson's mind, so vivid it made him relive the clash and fury of the siege of Pree.

Alensson's gaze fell to the bundle in the boy's arms. It was clutched to his chest like a treasure. The young duke's mouth went dry. He thought he knew what it was even though it was concealed by blankets.

"What do you bring me?" he asked softly, his skin prickling with apprehension.

"*She* told me to bring this to you," Brendin said. "She bade me to wait until the second full moon and then find you. She told me you'd be camped outside the village of Doeg. She made me . . . she made me swear an oath to the Fountain that I would obey her."

The boy set the bundle down and quickly knelt by it, untying the knots that bound it. Alensson's heart hammered in his chest. It wasn't possible. But then the boy began to unroll the blanket and *there it was*. Nested inside was the sword he had discovered at Firebos in the raven-sigil scabbard.

"She said . . . she said this is for you," the boy murmured, looking up at him with tears in his eyes.

Alensson stared at it, feeling the hunger twist inside his belly, twined now with the sickening sensation of fear, as if the blade really were a serpent.

"My lord!"

The voice came from outside the tent. It was the captain.

"What is it?" Alensson asked hoarsely, unable to take his eyes away from the treasure before him.

Jeremy thrust his way into the tent, nearly stumbling over the kneeling boy. He looked around in confusion and then met Alensson's gaze.

"Word just arrived," he said breathlessly. There was a panic-stricken tremor in his cheek. "She's been captured, my lord. A rider just came from Shanton with the news. The

Maid has been captured by the King of Brugia!"

CHAPTER TWENTY-THREE

Escape

The king's palace at Pree was abuzz with the news that the Duke of La Marche had escaped his confinement, and everyone was on the lookout for him. Although Ankarette's pulse was racing, she kept a calm demeanor and walked unhurriedly down the passageway. Two male servants walked behind her, carrying two chests between them. The chests were stacked atop each other, the top one smaller than the bottom one. The men were sweating from the burden.

"Careful, you fools," Ankarette snapped as they came around a corner and nearly collided with a squad of soldiers. "Those plates are worth more than your wages." One of the men grunted an apology and they continued.

The porter door at the end of the corridor was manned by several soldiers wearing the colorful plumage of the King of

Occitania. A crowd had assembled there—people with trollies, and servants carrying crates and chests outside the palace walls. The soldiers were inspecting each of the larger chests. They offered no explanation, but their purpose was clear. A large chest could be used to conceal a man.

Ankarette joined the end of the line. There was an imperious expression on her face as she glanced back at the servants. "Tell me you have the carriage ready outside," she said with a haughty tone. "My lady will be furious if we are late!"

"The driver is waiting even now, mum," said one of the servants, wiping his sweaty forehead across his sleeve.

"It better be," Ankarette said, stepping forward as the line shortened. "Come along. Don't dawdle."

"Yes, mum," said the other, and both heaved at the chests again.

As they reached the guards at the end of the line, Ankarette gave the servants another scolding look. Then she flashed a dimpled smile at the captain of the soldiers. "Any word of the duke's capture, my friends?" she asked boldly.

"Rumors is all, my lady," he said, quickly sizing up the two chests. Both were too small to hide a body. He waved her past. "They say he escaped in the night through a privy hole. Messy business. The hounds are on the hunt, but with the smell, it'll be difficult to follow him. Where is your mistress headed?"

"Chateau Grif," she answered. "Thank you, Captain." She gave him another winning smile and he offered a gallant bow in return.

"Come on," she said, glancing back at the servants again. Then she gave a toss of her head to the captain, acting as if their incompetence was a sore trial in her life. The captain chuckled and waved them through.

As they reached the carriage awaiting them in the crowded courtyard, the two men hefted the bundle up onto the baggage well and secured it with ropes. The driver hopped off the perch and opened the door for her.

"My lady," he greeted, showing a false tooth and a crooked smile.

"Thank you," she offered, keeping her nose high in the air in case someone was watching her, and then ducked into the carriage. The window curtains were already closed, so she quickly went to work on the false panel beneath the seat facing the back wall. She could hear the grunting of the men outside, their low jokes, and then one of them slapped the chests.

That was the signal.

The driver climbed back up onto the perch, clicked his tongue, and gave the beasts a little snap with the whip. Both of the men clung to the back of the carriage as it began to lumber across the courtyard. Ankarette sat on the carriage seat and folded her hands in her lap, feeling exhausted from the long night's interview. The carriage made it to the end of the courtyard before being halted again by the gatehouse guards. Just as she'd expected.

She parted the curtain as a soldier approached. "What is it, sir?" she asked impatiently.

"Are you alone in the carriage, my lady?"

"Of course I am," she snapped. "See for yourself."

The soldier nodded and twisted the handle. He poked his head inside, looked both ways, and nodded when he found her alone. "Apologies. It's the king's orders that every wagon be searched upon entering and leaving."

She settled back on the bench and folded her hands across

her knees, staring away as if the conversation utterly bored her. The soldier nodded to the driver and then secured the door again. With another click and whistle, the carriage trundled through the gate and across the moat bridge, entering the hive of Pree.

As soon as they were past, Ankarette knelt by the bench and lifted the seat. She'd already removed the plank and she could see the edge of the larger bottom chest. She pried loose the nails and then pulled the edge of the chest open, revealing the soles of two heavy boots.

"Are you quite comfortable, Alensson?" she called into the void.

"It may be a bit crowded, but it's better than a stinking privy hole," he said in a muffled tone. Ankarette smiled as she grabbed his ankles and began pulling him into the carriage to join her. He wriggled and squirmed to help, and soon he was sitting on the bench across from her, his gray hair askew, a mischievous smile on his mouth.

"A cunning lass," he said. "Cutting the boxes in the middle like that and stacking them was an inspired idea. If they'd opened the top one, they would have seen my head and shoulders."

"If they'd opened the top one, they would have found themselves with daggers in their ribs," Ankarette answered with a shrug. "One poisoner and two Espion would be more than a match for those simple guards at the porter door. I had planned for the possibility that I might need to kidnap you earlier in the evening. Your eagerness to escape only made the task easier. Now sit down. I have some questions before you continue your story."

"I assumed you would," Alensson said. The carriage jogged and tottered a bit as it went across the uneven cobblestones.

He parted the curtain with his fingers, glancing worriedly and hopefully at the scene, a small smile of relief twisting one side of his mouth until he let it fall back into place.

"She gave you the sword and the scabbard," Ankarette said pointedly.

"And you want to know where they are *now*," he replied with an evasive smile.

"Yes, that is true. As I told you when we met, that was my mission—to find out where King Lewis was hiding them."

"And now you know from my story that they weren't taken from her when she was captured," he added.

"Exactly. She was given over to Deford's men eventually after being in the custody of the King of Brugia. While tracing the origins and history of the blade, I spent some time in Brugia to see if I could discover rumors of it there. It's safer visiting Brugia than Occitania at the present. I have it from reliable sources, who were poisoned and quite cooperative, that the sword they took from the Maid when she was captured did not have the markings. I knew nothing of the scabbard's power until your tale, so naturally I'm eager to find it as well. It would be a great asset to my king."

"It would indeed. As I said, the blade once belonged to King Andrew. The scabbard also did, though it originated in Leoneyis. The histories of the legends of the Lady of the Fountain show that when the need arises, the blade and scabbard will return to the land."

"But they have both been missing since the Maid's war," Ankarette said. "She brought them back and then they were lost. She gave them both to you." She could hear her own eagerness in her voice. "You mentioned before how much you coveted them. Then they were freely given to you. Why would she do that?"

He looked away from her, staring at the curtain, his face clouding with fatigue and sadness. "I don't have the sword anymore," he whispered.

"I didn't think so," Ankarette said. "You've been imprisoned several times for rebelling against King Chatriyon. The only reason Lewis didn't execute you long ago is because you're somewhat of a hero among the people. You are noble in a court that is lewd. You are still her Gentle Duke."

He wouldn't meet her gaze. "That was many years ago. I was very young. I was no stranger to suffering, but I did not realize how much I'd be schooled in it later." He sighed, shaking his head. "You wanted the full story, and I will give it to you, Ankarette." He looked her in the eye. "These are painful memories. I've not shared them with anyone in a very long time. But I trust that you will keep my secrets. And share my pain."

She reached over and laid her hand on top of his. "I'll tell you what I know and you fill in the gaps. There is comfort in sharing another's pain. I've seen my own share of sadness as well."

A crooked smile stole across his mouth. "I don't doubt it."

Ankarette released his hand and then cupped hers together in her lap. "King Chatriyon refused to ransom the Maid. Not that he could have afforded it, even if he were so inclined. She was taken by the King of Brugia but held in custody at the castle of one of his liegemen, the Count of Luxe, who had gone with him to Occitania."

"You are well-read, Ankarette," he said approvingly. "Very few remember the name of the Count of Luxe. Do you know it?"

"His name was Peter," Ankarette said. "I know this trite piece of history because my master's wife, the Queen of

Ceredigion, is his granddaughter."

An ironic smile crossed the duke's mouth. "Isn't it strange how events twist and turn and come around again? We all play parts upon some grand stage. The Fountain wills the roles." He shook his head. "Yes, Peter of Luxe had a daughter named Jaquette. She was born the year Occitania fell in the Battle of Azinkeep. You remember that Deford was married to the King of Brugia's sister?"

"Yes," Ankarette said. "You mentioned that in your tale."

"She died. Some thought a poisoner did it because they were childless." He shrugged. "I don't know if that is true. But his second wife was her."

"Jacquette," Ankarette said with a nod. "She was seventeen when they married, but it was also a childless marriage. It didn't last that long before Deford died. And yes, he was poisoned. She married again to Lord Rivers and they had a large brood of children. My mistress, she who now reigns at Kingfountain, was their eldest."

Alensson sighed. "So now you know that Genette did not have the sword when she was captured outside Shanton. Once I saw the blade, I understood why Genette's leg had taken so long to heal. She had entrusted it to her squire and then sent him away to await news of her capture. When it happened, he was to bring the blade to me."

"And why to you?" Ankarette pressed.

"I thought it was because she wanted me to rescue her," he replied. His eyes twinkled. "And so I tried. You already understand, Ankarette, that my wife was having a difficult pregnancy. I hadn't forgotten Genette's warning that the heir of La Marche might need the same magic she'd used to save Brendin. I needed to free the Maid from that awful dungeon —for her and for my family. I disobeyed my king's orders. I was willing to risk *anything* to set Genette free."

CHAPTER TWENTY-FOUR

Risk

Alensson's stallion was wearied by the pressing ride, but the duke was impatient to arrive. The lush valley spread before him, the air full of gnat clouds and the pleasant odor of honeysuckle. His heart started pounding faster when the roof of the cottage came into view from his vantage point on the road. The stallion wanted to linger and crop grass, but he gave it an encouraging nip with his spurs, and it continued to labor down the gravel road, bringing up puffs of dry dust. A meadowlark trilled from the nearby trees, and Alensson was lost in its beautiful song for a moment.

The beast managed the final agonizing steps to the cottage door. Before the young duke was out of the saddle, the door flung open and his wife emerged from within, holding her swollen belly. Alix Felt looked worriedly from the doorway, but her face melted into relief upon recognizing him.

"Alensson!" Jianne gasped. She leaned against the door frame, looking as surprised as a child who'd seen a jongleur's trick. The smudges under her eyes wrenched his heart.

He had left his armor and royal tunic with his captain, Jeremy, so he could conceal his identity while he traveled. He wore a hunter's garb now, clothes that would be comfortable for living off the land, which he intended to do until he succeeded.

"Hello, my love," he said, reaching her in moments and sweeping her into his arms. Her growing womb was as taut as a melon, and it felt strange and exciting when it pressed up against him. He kissed her ear, then her neck, then her mouth, and she responded with a fiery vigor that proved they'd been away from each other for too long.

"What are you . . . doing here?" she tried to get out amidst the flurry of kisses. Alix discreetly slipped away to give them some privacy.

"I had to see you," he answered huskily. "Let's go inside."

"What about the horse?"

"I don't give a badger about the horse! It's half lame right now. It won't wander off." He waved at it with his arm. "Go find a water trough, beast! Off with you!" He grinned at Jianne, his heart swelling inside his chest as he walked back into the cottage with her, one arm around her shoulders to support her.

"I'm not made of glass, you know," she said, her arm squeezing around his waist.

"I wish Izzt were not so far," he said, turning to shut the door behind them. The small kitchen smelled of bread, baked squash, and there was a pile of greens she'd been in the middle of cutting. Again he felt the lack of coin and thus the lack of servants who could have tended to her needs. "It cost me dearly to come this way first, but I had to see you."

"I wouldn't be comfortable at Shynom anymore," she said shyly.

"What do you mean?" he pressed, leading her to a bench at the table and helping her to sit.

She looked down at her hands and then up into his eyes, giving him a knowing look. "The court has changed, Alensson. It has always been a hive of scheming and plotting, but recent developments have altered the tone. The women are more ... brazen. I suppose that's the word. More haughty. You should see what's fashionable now. The gowns, I mean." She shook her head. "I would blush wearing something like that. We lack money, Husband. There are those who are willing to lend, but they wanted certain ... favors."

Alensson's face went tight with anger. "Who?"

She shook her head. "I don't want you to worry, Husband. I made it very clear that I wasn't needful of money." She sighed. "The court has changed so quickly. But that is not why you're here. You didn't come because you were worried about me." It wasn't stated as a question.

Alensson rose from the bench and began to pace restlessly. "It is not the only reason."

"Tell me," she pleaded. "When I heard that Genette was captured, I feared you might do something rash."

He chuckled under his breath. "I am doing something rash," he said. Then he looked at her. "So I needed to forewarn you."

Her eyes closed and she began to tremble with fear. "What are you saying, Alensson?"

He approached the table and planted his palms on the surface. "During the siege of Pree, Genette's squire, he was only a lad, took a crossbow bolt to the heart. It killed him instantly. She brought him back to life, Jianne. The Maid did. But before she did it, she turned to me and said, you must hear the word of power. Someday it will save the life of the heir of La Marche. A little babe—stillborn."

Jianne shuddered at the words and covered her mouth in horror.

Alensson felt a gush of tenderness and fear. "When Genette was captured by the King of Brugia, I went to Shynom to plead with the king to ransom her. I begged him. I tried every device under the sun to influence and persuade him, even promised to give the crown a portion of my lands once I reclaim them. Nothing was enough to tempt him. He wants her gone." He felt his lips twisting into a sneer. "She, the savior of Occitania. Jianne, we nearly took Pree in one day. One day!" His voice had raised to a shout, but he wrestled it down. "One day," he whispered. "The king would not hear me. He ordered me to return to La Marche but to stop attacking Deford so boldly. He's trying to negotiate a peace between the three realms—Ceredigion, Occitania, and Brugia. To restore some balance. Pah! We could have won it all back and more! But with each of her successes, she grew more powerful. He would have been beholden to her. *Limited* by her. And so he betrayed her, and now . . . now she'll languish in a Brugian dungeon for years as I did. Or worse, they will sell her to Deford, who will execute her." He paused. "There is some magic at work here. I can sense it. Some Fountain magic, though twisted."

Jianne's tears streamed down her cheeks. She reached out and put her hand on his atop the table. "Don't go," she begged.

He jerked his hand away. "How can you ask that of me! I

know what it is like to languish in prison. You are still several months away from giving birth. Let me try, at least!"

"But if you are captured, Alensson!" she said desperately. "I . . . waited . . . I waited so *long* for you! How can you ask me to endure it again? Think of our child growing up without a father."

He was trembling beneath a surge of violent and conflicting feelings. "But the child will be stillborn," Alensson whispered hoarsely. "She knows! Genette always knows! The Fountain whispered it to her. The child *will* be stillborn. She told me the word of power, but I am not Fountain-blessed!" He pushed away from the table and paced, shaking his head. The look on his wife's face . . . If he'd sent a letter, he wouldn't have seen it, but it was an unworthy thought. She deserved to hear the news directly from him, and it would have been unbearable to take such a risk without first seeing her.

She looked down at the table, where her tears had gathered in a splotchy pool. "What will you do?" she said with a whimper of emotion.

"I'm going to Brugia," he said. "I know the language. I can pass as a merchant, a mercenary, whatever. I've heard she's being held at the Count of Luxe's castle in Beauvoir. I will go there in disguise to see if I can get work at the castle."

"But if someone finds out who you are . . ." she moaned.

He shook his head. "How would they guess? I've ordered my captain, Jeremy, to continue launching raids against Deford. Everyone thinks I am there. The king forbade me to try to rescue her." He clenched his teeth. "But I will not obey him. His heart has become blacker than flint over these past months. He has forgotten who put the crown on his head." He shook his head no. "But I haven't. And I will do anything to save you and our babe, Jianne. I am determined to do this. If I can free her, then I will bring her here secretly. We will *both* be here when the babe comes."

Jianne looked miserable. He was breaking her heart with this news, but he could not allow fate to take its course, not when he knew he had the wits and courage to enter his enemy's lands and take back what was theirs. The Maid of Donremy belonged to Occitania.

"Hold me," Jianne murmured, rising from the bench. He wrapped his arms around her, and she pressed her face against his chest and sobbed. They stood silently for a long moment, feeling the weight of the situation crushing against them. He tried to reassure her, to give her courage. But she was terrified by the great risk he was taking.

"What if they've taken her to Kingfountain?" she asked him, looking up into his eyes.

He frowned. "Then that is where I will go to find her," he whispered, knowing it wasn't the answer she wanted to hear.

Her eyelids closed and she nodded in resignation. She would not thwart his goal, although he could see she did not support it. Even the risk of losing their child wasn't enough for her to willingly risk losing him.

"I love you, Jianne," he whispered.

Rather than answer him, she pulled away and walked to the window. She put one hand on her lower back, the other on her belly.

His entire soul was scorched with the desperation of the situation. She hadn't noticed the sword and scabbard belted to his hip. There was power in its magic and he could feel it. There was protection for his quest.

But it still meant parting from her once again.

CHAPTER TWENTY-FIVE

Beauvoir Castle

Finding out where they were keeping Genette—Luxe Tower —had proved ludicrously simple once he arrived in Brugia, disguised as a wandering mercenary in search of a lord. News of her capture and confinement had traveled far and wide. He managed to hold his tongue when people slandered her in his presence. The most common one was the Maid of Donremy was a water sprite come to wreak havoc on mortals with her magic. One man insisted he knew someone who had been at Shynom when she had presented herself to Chatriyon. The tale he'd heard was that a servant had spilled a cup on water on her and she hadn't gotten wet. He did not dare contradict these tales, even the lurid ones, including a rumor that the Maid was not truly a maid at all but one of the king's lovers. Some even insinuated that she was *his* lover.

He had learned the language as part of his childhood education, but one of the guards he had met in his long captivity had given him the chance to practice its nuances better. Getting to Brugia was easy enough after paying a fare from a Genevese merchant.

Alensson was used to being a beggar, and he quickly found work guarding a merchant caravan bound for Luxe Tower. While he traveled, he kept alert for news of Genette. Negotiations for her ransom were underway with the palace of Kingfountain. Despite the Brugians' efforts to drive up the price they'd get from Deford, Chatriyon still wouldn't bid for her. As the weeks passed, Alensson picked up more of the local dialects, but being a mercenary gave him a lot of flexibility, and people didn't expect him to be a learned man.

When the caravan reached the city of Luxe with its load of pickled sardines and cucumbers, the caravan captain offered him permanent work if the count wasn't interested in hiring him. Alensson thanked him for the offer, but he needed to find a position that would give him better access to the tower. To Genette.

He applied to see the castellan of Beauvoir, but the guards sent him away. The man was too busy, they said, so Alensson found a room at one of the three inns and prepared to hunker down.

The news he had dreaded arrived the next day.

Deford and Philip had finally reached an agreement. The Maid had been sold to Ceredigion for ten thousand marks. A ship with the gold would be arriving shortly with orders to bring the girl to the palace.

That meant he needed to find a way to get her free before the ship arrived.

◆   ◆   ◆

Beauvoir castle was smaller than a duke's palace and very rustic. The park had beautiful hedges, sculpted lawns, and several small servants' cottages situated at odd angles from one another. The main structure of the castle had a steeply pitched roof and several towers, including a narrow bell tower in the center. The walls were gray and blockish, and the circular towers at opposing corners had cone-shaped turrets with brims that resembled peasant hats topped with weather-cocks. The grounds were open to the citizens of the village, so it was easy for Alensson to wander the parks without notice during daylight hours. But the moment he tried to approach the grounds, he was immediately accosted by the guards and warned to stay away from the castle itself. He bowed meekly and wandered back.

There was a lush wooded holt, thick with trees and un-tamed scrub, on the western side of the grounds. Some of the fanciest hedge work bordered it, but there was no fence or stone wall. After watching for a moment to make sure no one was looking, Alensson stepped over the hedge and disap-peared into the wood. From that vantage point, he was able to get closer to the castle. He discovered the rear of the castle contained a dry moat filled with clumps of earth and nasty weeds. A steep shelf of rock covered in vines led from the foundation of the castle down into the moat, which would make it very easy to climb up onto the castle grounds. He nodded with satisfaction and hid amidst the trees, watching. After a time, he noticed the guards were patrolling the ground below the tower, coming and going according to a set routine.

He circled farther into the woods and found the remains of a stone bridge with three arches that stood up in the empty moat. The bridge was riddled with vines and it connected to the rear of the castle with an iron porter door. It was a sturdy-looking thing, possibly still in use, so he leaned against one of the shaggy oak trees and watched to see if the door opened or shut frequently. It did not open once while he watched that afternoon.

From his vantage across the dry moat, he could see the back tower of the castle with its strange hat-like roof. There was a window on the upper floor facing him, and he had a compelling feeling that it was where Genette was being held. It was the farthest point from the main doors and the gardens. The tower was quite high, and there was no way to scale it.

Alensson rubbed his mouth. Why had the moat been drained? The grounds were obviously well watered, so it couldn't have been done out of necessity. He ventured as close to the edge as he dared, not wanting to be seen, and squinted down at the soft earth mixed with rocks at the bottom of the moat. It was dry, but newly so—he could see how high the water level used to be. It appeared as though the water source feeding the moat had been dammed and diverted by the many aqueducts in Brugia. Perhaps the moat had been left to dry out deliberately to prevent Genette from leaping out of the tower window and swimming away. He tapped his lip, confident of his assessment. The earth would be softest at the bottom.

He spent the remainder of the day skulking around the woods, studying the castle, and looking for weaknesses. It was small enough that even if he managed to overcome a guard and take his uniform, he'd probably get noticed as a stranger. He wished he could insinuate himself into the ranks of the castle guards as he'd originally planned, but time was not a luxury he had. He fumed with frustration, trying to determine how he could get Genette out before the ship from Ceredigion arrived with the treasure.

As the daylight faded to dusk, he began to settle down for the night, knowing he would soon run out of light. He'd found her—he was certain of it in his heart—and he would not leave until he figured out how to free her. The guards became more infrequent and the air was cool but not frigid. He'd spent some time gathering brush and leaves for another layer of warmth. Once he was settled, he pulled out a meat pie he'd purchased earlier and saved for his supper. Sitting with his back against the tree, he wolfed down the salty pie and then licked his fingers, savoring the juices.

He stared up at the tower. How could he get her free? His mind worked over the possibilities. Could he use the sword's magic? Would it help him fight off the guards? It was a dangerous idea, but one that appealed to him. Then the sword and scabbard would be taken away, and they'd be of service to no one—or worse, they'd be in the enemy's possession.

The night sounds settled over him—buzzing mosquitos, crickets and bulrushes, crackling leaves and twigs. Then he stood and began pacing, both to keep his body warm and to stir his thoughts. The moon hadn't come up yet, and it was dark enough he wouldn't be seen by a guard. He needed to be patient. The area was guarded, and he might be wrong about which turret she was in. He saw no sign of light coming from it. Maybe it was empty? Or maybe it was made to *appear* empty. He stalked this way and that, wondering what he should do.

He stared at the upper window. Could he toss a pebble that high? Some small stone to make a noise? If he could determine whether she was indeed up there, it would help him plan their escape. He gathered a handful of rocks from the edge of the moat and crept to a spot that was just across from the tower.

Pulling his arm back, he hurled the first pebble at the tower window. When he missed it completely, he shook his head and cursed himself. Then he readied the next one, stepped back, and threw it as hard as he could. He knew there were shepherd boys with slings who would have been able to break the window from this distance. His second attempt struck the tower, but it was way too low. The stone clattered down the wall and then bounced several times, making a terrible racket. He swore under his breath.

After six more attempts, he returned to his little nest to prepare to sleep. He lay awake for a long time, staring at the castle, willing his mind to conjure up a plan to free her. He fell asleep during the middle of his silent prayer.

♦   ♦   ♦

A noise in the woods snapped Alensson awake. He sat up, the twigs and leaves crackling as he shifted. Several guards with torches were making their way through the thick expanse of woods with a pair of hounds.

Alensson's heart began to hammer with fear and he cursed himself for being thickheaded. Yes, no one had bothered searching the woods during the day, but it made sense that the guards would add it to their pattern at night.

"I'm a fool," he muttered to himself. They were still a good distance away, but he could not stay where he was, and he suspected the dogs probably already had a scent. Breaking free of his cover, he scattered the leaves he'd gathered as quietly as he could. If he climbed a tree, they'd have him pinned down within the hour. His instincts told him to go deeper.

Like a cat, he stalked to the edge of the moat and studied it quickly. He scrabbled down the ravine and landed amidst the soft earth, weeds, and hidden rocks. His heart thundered in his ears, and he knew the moat walls would make it more difficult for him to hear the approaching guards. The moon was out now, and if the dogs tracked him here, the guards would likely see him from above, but then he remembered the dilapidated bridge. He rushed over to the supports quickly and slunk into the shadows they provided, keeping an eye on the ridge of the moat for any signs of the night watch. The perimeter of the grounds was probably also being protected, so it would be near impossible to escape Beauvoir without a fight. Had he made a mistake in coming here?

The guards approached his former camp, and he watched their torchlight illuminate the area, casting moving shadows that stretched and yawned. He was concealed within an arch of the bridge, but he still felt vulnerable. There were some voices he couldn't make out, and then a hound was suddenly snuffling at the top of the moat. It could probably smell his sweat.

One guard approached the edge of the moat and gazed down before tugging at the leash and pulling the beast away toward where the other one was going. Alensson felt a little thrill of hope when he realized the guards were coming toward the bridge. He imagined they would use it to enter through the porter door. Did they have the key? Probably not, he reasoned, or someone attacking them would gain access. He had no qualms about killing men or beast if need be, but it wasn't his first choice, especially if there was a chance it wouldn't get him what he needed.

If there was a password at the door, he might be in a position to hear it. He softly stepped through an arch, moving closer to the foundation of the castle. His boots made a hissing sound amidst the weeds.

There was a sharp knock on the iron door overhead. Alensson positioned himself as close as he could, his stomach wriggling with worry.

A little portal gap opened. "Who is it?"

"It's Bromin. The dogs have a scent. I think someone was hiding in the wood and went into the moat. Tell Captain about it. I think he'll want a full search."

"You sure, Bromin? I don't want to wake him for naught."

"It could be nothing, Gollenbock. But with ten thousand coming to fetch her, I wouldn't put it past someone to send in a poisoner, you know? I'm trusting the hounds on this one. Just to be sure."

"Stay there. I'll fetch Captain."

Alensson knew some of their names, which would be helpful, but now he needed to escape before all the guards were awakened to search for him. Knowing the guards and dogs were nearby, he crept quietly away from the arch, hugging the rim of the moat ravine and increasing his pace with every step he took. The moat didn't surround the entire castle, just the back half, so he needed to climb some vines and roots to get out. If he made it back into the woods, he would go as far as he could and fight his way clear. It would be a long night still, but if he could hold out until dawn, when other people would appear to add distraction, he would have a much better chance of escaping. He didn't know how long it would take for the captain to be summoned.

Alensson crossed the dry moat and then looked for handholds to start climbing back up. As he searched, he heard a sound above him and froze, his heart suddenly in his throat.

He looked up slowly, expecting to see a crossbow aimed at his head. There was no one there. His knees were trembling. Turning, he looked around and then heard another noise. It came from high above him. From the tower.

In the moonlight, he saw someone poking out of the window of the tower, a black smudge against the light gray stone wall.

Then he heard a whisper falling down like rain. "Alensson!"

It was Genette. He stared up at her, his heart beating in relief. She knew he was coming! The Fountain had told her! His heart began to thrum with confidence and hope. He could do this. Somehow he'd figure out a way for them both to escape.

He watched in horror as she leaped from the window.

CHAPTER TWENTY-SIX

Broken

She fell.

There was no time to rush and catch her. There was no warning whatsoever except that one whispered word. She soared from the window in a giant leap and then he saw her plummet to the bottom of the moat in a heap. The sound of cracking bones hung in the air—sickening and terrifying.

For a moment, he disbelieved what he'd seen, and then he rushed to her side, unbuckling the scabbard from his waist as he moved. She was sprawled out amidst the dirt and rocks, seemingly lifeless, the air crushed out of her from her shattered ribs.

"Genette!" he gasped in shock and despair. She tried to lift her head, then collapsed. She was still alive, if barely.

He dared not roll her over, so he laid the scabbard across

her back and offered a silent and impassioned plea to the Fountain to save her life. His healing skills were completely inadequate to save her. He knew that. But he believed the Fountain's magic could do what he could not.

Listening fearfully for the sound of approaching guards—they, too, must have heard her fall—he knelt amidst the debris, his hands clasped together tightly, his heart hammering wildly. She couldn't die. If she died, so would his child. Tears pricked his eyes and he mutely shook his head, still not able to believe he'd witnessed what he had. He treasured her friendship, how she had made him into a better man. The thought of losing her devastated him.

There was no sign from the scabbard to show whether it was working, but she was breathing. Then, as he stared at her still form in the moonlight, he saw her shoulders start to rise and fall with greater vigor. He heard little cracks and snaps coming from her body, and it made him shudder at the enormity of the healing taking place in an instant.

Then Genette let out a sigh. "You came?" she croaked.

He was still concerned about the guards finding them. How was he going to rescue her and get her away? Her body was fixing itself, but it would take time. And that was something of which they had precious little.

"Of course I did," he whispered, bending low. "They've sold you to our enemies."

"I know," she answered. "They arrive on the morrow. I don't . . . want . . . to go to Kingfountain."

"I'm going to take you away. There's a little cottage tucked into the valley of Izzt. You will rest there. You will get stronger. I need you to come with me."

"I can't, Gentle Duke."

It was like a physical blow. "You need to come, Genette.

You said yourself, you said the child needs your magic."

"I know what I said, Gentle Duke. It was a prophecy . . . of sorts. My whole body hurts," she added with a groan.

"You just fell from a tower. No, you jumped! Why did you jump, Genette?"

She moved her head, wincing with the effort. There was blood trickling from her mouth. "It was the only way . . . to save *you*."

He stared at her in surprise. "What do you mean?"

"Nnnghh," she grumbled. "This hurts so much, but I feel the magic healing me. My legs and hip aren't broken anymore. You shouldn't have come, Alensson. I don't want to go to Kingfountain, but I *must* go there. I must speak to the boy king of Ceredigion. I don't want to, understand. But my voices . . . the Fountain bids me. I must make a warning before I . . . before my *duty* is through."

Alensson shook his head, gazing at her almost with anger. "No."

"I must, Gentle Duke. I must go there first."

"They won't ransom you, Genette. If you go there, they will kill you. They will throw you into the river and let you rush over the falls."

She pursed her lips. "It's not easy to kill someone who is Fountain-blessed. As you can plainly see."

"Do you think they will let you keep the scabbard?" he chuffed. "No."

"Of course they won't. But the scabbard needs . . . it needs to go to Kingfountain, Alensson. You must bring it there, for I cannot. That is why—" She stiffened suddenly with pain and moaned weakly. He felt absolutely helpless and terrified in the face of her suffering. "I'm sorry . . . I'm sorry," she panted. "It just hurts so much. Do you think a waterfall . . . .hurts this much?"

"I have no idea," he said in despair. Kingfountain? He had to go there next?

She squeezed her eyes shut. "Hold my hand."

He leaned over her, wishing he could take her pain on himself. Her arm was stretched out before her, elbow bent. He put his hand on top of hers and squeezed it very gently, watching to see if she flinched.

"It's the only part that doesn't hurt," she gasped. Her thumb grazed his. "I had to jump, Alensson, because you would have been captured tonight," she explained in an almost matter-of-fact way. "You were very foolish to come here and hide at night. The Fountain whispered to me that you'd be caught. That you brought the sword and that it would be taken away from you. You are not following the will of the Fountain."

"But how am I to even *know* the will of the Fountain?" he said, feeling desperate and confused and shaken by the knowledge tumbling from her lips. "How was I to know?"

"You knew before you left the cottage," she whispered. "You've been seeking your own will for so long, Gentle Duke. All now is confusion and despair. So I had to go alone to fulfill the Fountain's will in all things. Even though I do not want to. When I learned you came, when I learned you'd be captured, I paced and paced, trying to understand what I could do to save you. This was all. The Fountain said if I fell, it would draw attention to my escape. They would forget about seeking the intruder they know is here."

She blinked, gazing at him adoringly. "If I was to save you, I had to jump. I'm afraid . . . I'm afraid of heights, Alensson. Truly I am. I've always been afraid, but the Fountain gives me the strength to conquer my fears. Scaling the battlement walls that day in Foucaulx was ... it was my test. Sometimes we must face our greatest fears. If we obey, the Fountain will bless us." A crooked smile came on her mouth. "I knew if I fell, I wouldn't die because you would come to me. You would save me. So I must ask you now to save yourself. Hide in the bushes over there, behind us, against the wall of the moat." Her voice was getting stronger and stronger. "The magic is healing me quickly. When the guards come, you must hide and let them take me."

"But I want to take you away!" His heart was full of anxiousness and confusion.

She shook her head slowly. "That cannot be! If you carried me, how far would we get before the hounds found us? Hmmm? No, you must heed me. You must believe in me still, Alensson. Go before me. Go to Kingfountain. Both scabbard and sword must go there. You must bring them there."

"What about Jianne? What about my child?"

She closed her eyes. "I know this is difficult, Alensson, but you must trust me. I serve the Fountain's will. There is nothing more I could want ..." She stopped, swallowing, then shook her head slowly. "It is such a temptation. Please, you must stop asking that. It tempts me. But I will be strong. I will do my duty."

"What are you talking about?" he said, growing even more confused.

"I've seen what happens, Gentle Duke. The game must go on. Trust me. Please, you must ... just ... trust me. I save you. Then you save me. At Kingfountain."

Alensson heard the sound of hounds and the crunch of boots, and panic seized him. The guards had descended into the moat and were coming from the direction of the bridge he had hid under.

"If you hide in *that* bush," Genette whispered, her gaze piercing him. "They will not find you. It's a thorn bush. It will hurt. But there are berries in it that will confuse the hounds. And they will find me because your scent leads them here. Take the scabbard. It will protect you from the thorns. Then *heed* me, Alensson. Wait for me there. Stay at the sanctuary of Our Lady. They cannot arrest you there. You will be one of many pilgrims who will come and pray at the fountain of Our Lady. There you will find a little boy. Nine years old. He'll have cropped black hair. He's Fountain-blessed. Give the boy the scabbard, *not* the sword. If I have the scabbard, I will survive the falls. The boy will help me get the scabbard when I need it. Trust me, Gentle Duke. Do your part. Go to King-fountain and wait for me."

Her voice was racing with concern as she spoke, her eyes glittering in the moonlight. "Take it and go! Go!"

"But your wounds!" He didn't want to take it from her. What if he used the sword to fight the guards and the hounds? Would there be time to escape?

Her fingers dug into his hand, snapping his attention away from the violent thoughts. "Please, Alensson! You must hide in the thorn bush. Please! Or all is ruined!"

From the corner of his eye, he saw the light of torches coming their way. The guards were sweeping the entire length of the moat. In moments, the light would expose them both. He wrestled with indecision, wanting to obey her—he *believed* in her—but not wanting her to be taken away, not when he was so close to rescuing her. She had literally fallen from the sky to him.

"Please, Gentle Duke," she whispered, squeezing his hand.

He bowed his head, kissed her hand, and then snatched the scabbard from her back. He slid the sword into it and dashed over to the thick foliage-wreathed thorn bush growing from the base of the moat like a nest. The hounds barked at his movement, and the guards released their leashes to let them bolt. He heard their snarls and growls and the padding noise of their paws as they charged ahead of the guards. Alensson held his breath and plunged into the thorn bush, feeling the sticks and thorns jab and poke him as he wrestled himself farther into it. He winced with pain as he was pricked and pierced all over his arms, side, and legs. The bush was too short to conceal him, so he was forced to crouch. Stings and cuts covered his body—an exquisite agony—but he was certain it was nothing compared to what Genette had suffered from her fall.

The hounds reached her still body and began barking fiercely as they sniffed her from head to toe. She lay there still, her back rising and falling as she breathed.

Alensson watched as the guardsmen arrived next, their lanterns showering light on the area. While he hadn't noticed before, she was still dressed in men's clothes, a bloodstained tunic and pants that she'd worn previously into battle.

"Bless me, it's *her*! It's the Occitanian strumpet!" Alensson could only grit his teeth as the guards discovered the body.

One of them gazed up and pointed. "She jumped from the tower!"

"How could she . . . ? She's dead? The count will be furious if he doesn't get his money."

Another chuckled with disbelief. "She's afraid of King-fountain. I knew she was a coward."

"She's breathing."

"No!"

"I swear it, look! She's breathing!"

"She survived? She must have broken every bone. Go get

the castle physician. Let's make a pallet and roll her onto it. No one will believe this!"

Genette let out a soft moan and tried to move, her action frightening the guards.

One of the hounds came up to the thorn bush, sniffling and snuffling. Alensson could smell its horrid breath as it gazed at him through the leaves, branches, and berries. A low growl sounded.

He remained still, but his heart was racing.

"Chut! Come over here, dog. The girl's right here! Get over here."

Alensson was grateful all the guards were trampling the area with their boots, hiding the evidence that he had been there. The dog poked its snout at the bush, snuffling and growling. Alensson held perfectly still, his body sliced and stabbed in dozens of places. He could see a thorn impaling the skin of his forearm. He felt it ache and throb, but no blood oozed from the wound. The magic of the scabbard kept him from bleeding.

But he wished Genette had been able to keep it instead.

He watched as she was laid on a makeshift stretcher and carried away from him down the length of the dry moat. His throat was thick with gratitude and despair. Despite her fear of heights, she had jumped from a tower window to save him from getting captured again.

Huddling in the thorn bush, he silently wept.

CHAPTER TWENTY-SEVEN

Kingfountain

As a boy, Alensson had always imagined visiting the fabled city of Kingfountain. Kingfountain was as ancient at Pree, the two capitals existing in defiance of one another for centuries beyond counting. He was no scholar, no student of lore, so he did not know what had driven these kingdoms to be perpetual enemies. He only knew there was an implacable enmity between them—one he felt in his heart as he approached the docks in a trading vessel and saw the stunning waterfall exploding off the rugged ridges and hills. There was a constant wrestle between feeling impressed and feeling spiteful.

The palace rose up on the eastern side of the river, impregnable and secure. No army could attack that bastion without great labor and difficulty. Hulking in the middle of the river was the enormous sanctuary of Our Lady, his destination. The ivy-covered walls surrounding it and gated parks were inviting and peaceful. There was something genuinely comforting about the shared forms of worship between Ceredigion and Occitania.

He climbed the steps from the Genevese docks to the lower city on the west side of the river and joined the throng. He'd spoken only Brugian while on board the vessel, for Occitanians were not welcome here. Though it was almost certainly in his mind, he felt a menace, a brooding sensation that every citizen, every merchant could sense he did not belong. The noise of the waterfall was omnipresent, growing louder as he came closer to the bridge. The streets were full of carts and merchants, selling muffins, pies, sausages, skewered fruit, joints of pig, and other aromatic delights that made his stomach growl. He dispensed a few coins into a merchant's grimy hand in exchange for a skewered piece of pork, which he ate as he sauntered down the street, watching the urchins zigzag around in games of tag and theft. The streets bore pennants from the house of Argentine, fluttering in the lazy breeze that wafted in from the river. Alensson tried to look like a man with business, not the overwhelmed novice he was in this place. The raven's-head scabbard was strapped to his waist, and the pommel of the sword swung lightly as he walked. Had the citizens known that he carried the blade of their ancient king Andrew, they would have torn him limb from limb and striven after it in a frenzy.

The sights and smells of Kingfountain enveloped him. The fashion of his tunic, heavy leather belt, and sturdy boots helped him blend in with those around him. The wounds from the thorns had closed and healed quickly, removing the pox-like scars. How many of the Maid's injuries remained?

He thought of her and then he thought of his pregnant wife . . . Would the babe truly be cursed if he did not succeed in bringing Genette home with him? Her instructions had been very specific. Find a lad who was Fountain-blessed at the sanctuary of Our Lady. A nine-year-old lad with dark hair. And yet . . . he'd already seen dozens of dark-haired lads just walking the streets. How was he to know upon sight if the lad was Fountain-blessed?

After finishing his meal, he entered the bridge spanning the tumultuous river and ventured closer to the island that held the sanctuary. The percussive clop of hooves suddenly filled the air—someone was approaching from behind Alensson. The crowd began to make way and he did the same, pressing back out of respect when he realized he was seeing a nobleman arriving at the city. It wasn't a duke, probably an earl or the like. Alensson saw many lowering their heads in respect, but he couldn't do it. Rather than look down, he raised his steely gaze.

Alensson saw the badge before he saw the man. The tunics of the knights accompanying the nobleman were emblazoned with the symbol of a lion, paws raised, and muzzle open to a roar. An arrow pierced the maw in a grotesque way that made Alensson's cheek twitch. This was one of the Northern families, he believed. He couldn't remember the name.

As the knights passed, his gaze fell on the earl. To his surprise, there was a young boy riding behind the noble—it could only be his son—and the boy's small arms clasped his father's waist. Something about the boy stood out to him. Maybe it was his serious eyes or the half-frown on his face. But in that moment, it felt as if the grinding wheel of time had suddenly slowed. He saw the boy's sand-colored hair, his stern expression. He noticed the way he clasped his father's middle, his cheek pressed against the cloak. The boy's eyes met his, for some reason, out of the crowd. The two looked at each other and Alensson felt a strange dizzy feeling, as if he were suddenly in two places at once. There was something about that boy, something that pressed against his thoughts in a strange way, giving him the uneasy feeling that he had witnessed this scene before.

And then it was over, the wheel surged forward again, and the noise of the earl's men faded. Alensson stared after them, noticing the boy, still gripping his father, had turned in the saddle and was staring back at him. Alensson nodded to the boy, coaxed by some preternatural feeling, and then he was lost in the crowd that filled in the gap made by the horsemen.

He did not know what had summoned those strange feelings, and it unnerved him that such a young boy had taken notice of him amidst the crowd. Why had he not bowed his head to the earl's son meekly like the others and let the entourage pass without giving him any attention? He cursed inside his mind—he'd let his imagination run rampant—and walked vigorously until he reached the sanctuary gates.

The Duke of La Marche was well-versed in the strange traditions of Ceredigion. He had heard that many unlawful men resided on the sanctuary grounds, where the king's law could not pursue them. The privilege had been in existence since the beginning of time, it seemed, and no one had ever offered him a satisfactory explanation as to why grown men still heeded it. It was said that the protections of sanctuary would last until the river stopped flowing, which would never happen considering it was fed by mighty glaciers in the North that provided the unending supply of water to the river. There were many stories about knights who had rebelled against kings and sought—and found—protection at the many sanctuaries in the realm. For this reason, Alensson felt a middling portion of peace upon entering the gates.

As he had done at Beauvoir, he instantly began walking the grounds, seeking to understand the location. There were many fountains throughout the outer courtyard, and individuals and families were clustered around them. Many were tossing coins into the waters. As he drew closer, he noticed the heap of rusty coins on the bottom of each. It was another shared tradition, he knew, not to remove the coins. If someone was caught stealing them, a crowd of violent citizens could instantly rise up, seize the offender, and throw him or her into the river.

He also wandered the grounds behind the sanctuary and was surprised to find a small dock there. He thought that very strange considering the violent pull of the waters, but perhaps goods were sometimes sent from upstream. From this angle, he saw the profile of the palace up on the hill. The sight took his breath away and spread a sick feeling through his heart. He had never seen the like—there were many levels of walls and bulwarks built into the hillside to provide rings of protection to the castle atop. He sighed and shook his head, seeing the futility of attacking such a place. But with the thought, he imagined seeing Genette's face and her confident look. If the Fountain had bidden her to do it, he had no doubt she would have attempted it—and he had no doubt she would have succeeded.

After walking the grounds, he went to the sanctuary itself and took a seat on a stone bench. The black and white tiles of the marble floor were arranged like the squares on a Wizr board. Despite the constant tide of traffic in and out, the floor was swept and clean. Judging by their clothes, the families who visited came from a vast array of backgrounds, but all were welcome on the grounds.

Alensson lingered, watching and observant, for a long while, but the day was passing quickly and he knew he'd need a place to spend the night and possibly the next few days. Were there places to sleep on the island? There had to be, didn't there? If not, where did the sanctuary men stay after the gates were shut?

He approached the sexton with a submissive air, wringing his hands nervously. "Excuse me," he said, hoping the accent wouldn't betray him. "I didn't want to bother the deconeus. I need to spend the night. Is there . . . is there a room?"

The sexton looked at him with concern and Alensson felt his worry begin to mount. Perhaps he should have taken refuge in one of the inns on the bridge.

"You will need to see the deconeus, I'm afraid," the sexton said. "He is the one who grants permission. Come with me."

Choosing to risk his luck and trust the Maid because she had sent him there, he followed the sexton and was led to an anteroom and told to wait there on a stone bench. He folded his arms, feeling a dark cloud of foreboding close in around him. He had been among soldiers from Ceredigion often enough that he thought he could mask his identity.

Soon the door opened and the sexton gestured for him to enter.

The deconeus was a middle-aged man with well-silvered, close-shorn hair. He had an arched nose and an imperious stance, bull-chested and not fragile. He looked down at Alensson with wary eyes. "Soldier or mercenary?" he asked curtly.

Alensson didn't know the names of the nobles well enough to dissemble, but if he earned the deconeus's disdain, he might escape a closer interrogation. "Mercenary, my lord,"

Alensson said, hastily bowing his head. "Was a bit too friend-ly with the captain's wife, if you understand me. I didn't do anything, to be sure, but he flew into a rage and threatened to kill me. I thought . . . I thought I'd find protection here for a few days. Hopefully he'll forget about me after a while."

The deconeus chuckled to himself. "Well, you're a hand-some man, I can see how this *misunderstanding* may have hap-pened." He rubbed his mouth, giving Alensson a keen look. It wasn't distrustful, though—it was the look of a man doing business in his head. "You'll only be here a few days?"

Alensson raised his hands helplessly. "I think so. I won't be any trouble."

"Of course you won't be any trouble," the deconeus quipped. "On this island, inside these gates, you are under my authority. Not even the Duke of Westmarch could arrest you here if he had a mind to do so. Why did you flinch?"

Alensson realized he had reacted to the deconeus's mention of his rival's name.

"You weren't courting the *duke's* wife, were you?" the de-coneus asked, appalled.

"No! No!" Alensson said, laughing weakly. "I was stationed at Pree recently when the duke arrived. We're all still bleeding from the lashes he gave us."

The deconeus nodded and sniffed in through his nose. "He's not a patient man, I assure you, and he's no friend of mine. You'll be safe here. I will let you know if your captain comes looking for you. May be best to stay in your cell for a few days."

"A cell?" Alensson asked, imagining a dungeon.

"We have a lot of *visitors*," the deconeus said with an oily smile. "They tend to stay a while. Each room is divided into smaller cells. You'll be sharing yours with several other men.

It costs five florins a day, but you must get your own food. You can pay a lad to go outside the gates and fetch you a meat pie or whatever you like. Three pents—I'll take a week's worth right now. If you're a mercenary, you should have some wages?"

The cost to stay was likely dependent on the newcomer's ability to pay. The deconeus had sized him up, and now he was asking for a price higher than an inn but for worse accommodations. Alensson had a sense that the price would be raised the longer he needed to stay.

"Most fair, my lord," Alensson said, bowing meekly. The deconeus held out his hand, and Alensson turned and counted out the florins from his coin pouch. He'd deliberately concealed additional funds elsewhere. He tried to look distressed at the loss of the money as he handed it to the deconeus.

"There we are. All is settled." He turned away from Alensson. "Tunmore, take this man to his cell."

"Yes, Deconeus," piped up a small voice, startling Alensson. He hadn't noticed anyone else in the room, but he realized the giant of a man had been blocking his view.

A young boy with short-cropped dark hair circled around the deconeus. As soon as Alensson laid eyes on him, he felt the whisper of the Fountain.

CHAPTER TWENTY-EIGHT

The Deconeus of Ely

The carriage wheels struck an overlarge stone, giving the cart a ferocious shake that nearly sent Ankarette and Alensson crashing into each other. The poisoner stared at the duke in surprise and wonderment.

"The lad's name was Tunmore? John Tunmore?" she asked, her insides seething with the new information.

The duke gave her a wizened smile. "I take it that you know the august Deconeus of Ely?"

Ankarette's mind was whirling. "He is my . . . my mentor," she said, shaking her head. "He is scrupulously strict about keeping his secret. Only the king and queen know he is Fountain-blessed. And myself," she added wryly. "He is the one who taught me to use the Fountain magic. You say he was just a boy at the time?" She laughed to herself. "I cannot even imagine him so young."

"And surely I am as old as the mountains!" Alensson said with a gruff laugh, folding his arms. The carriage had settled back to its normal pattern again. "Yes, the lad was Fountain-blessed. The corruption of court taints everyone it touches, so I do not know how he is today, but he was a serious boy. A sober child. He supported King Eredur's rival originally, did he not?"

"Yes, he did," Ankarette said. "During the story you have been telling me, Deford was named protector of the child-king of Ceredigion. He was the lad's uncle—"

"Uncles and nephews," the duke murmured. When Ankarette gave him a quizzical look, he motioned for her to continue.

"The boy was already the King of Ceredigion. Deford was planning to bring him to Occitania to see him crowned king of this country as well. But Chatriyon, as you said, was crowned at Ranz instead. Deford had his nephew crowned at Pree, defying tradition. But this was several months *after* Genette's death, and it caused a lot of political upheaval in my kingdom. The Maid's impact on Ceredigion did not end with her capture. Tunmore was young back then. I hadn't even thought to consider that he was alive, let alone a participant!"

Alensson nodded his head and wagged his eyebrows. "Of course you didn't. No one did. He was the one who smuggled the scabbard into the palace." He sighed. "It's still there, for all I know."

Ankarette leaned forward, her eyes riveted on his face. "Still?"

He stretched out his long legs. "I don't want to get ahead of myself, but the story is coming to an end. Genette's story, that is." A mask of pain and sadness wrinkled his brow and his eyes. "This boy was being trained as a novice at Our Lady. His life had been dedicated to the faith at a young age, but rather than resent it, he embraced it—both because of the opportunities and because he could actually *hear* the Fountain's whispers. Imagine what it was like for him, being so young and attached to the grandest sanctuary in his realm. All the while the Fountain whispered to him that the Maid of Donremy, whom everyone *hated,* was actually a true messenger of the Fountain. He did not tell anyone what he knew." He shook his head and laughed softly. "Think of that! I've always regretted that I never thanked him for his help. He's come to Pree on occasion in a diplomatic role, but I was never permitted to see him. He's very good at keeping secrets."

"He is," Ankarette said in awe, amazed that her mentor had never told her any of this.

Tunmore had recognized her gifts when she was dabbling with the magic as a young lady-in-waiting to the Duke of Warrewik's eldest daughter. He had sensed her using it to discern the intentions of one of the duke's royal visitors, for the Fountain-blessed could always sense the magic another Fountain-blessed was using if they paid attention. Some who possessed the power were never schooled in its use and didn't learn how it was depleted and replenished. Tunmore had given her lessons in the use of her power, and it was he who had recommended that she be sent to Pisan for training as a poisoner.

She noticed that Alensson was studying her face, keenly interested, and she felt a little flush creep into her cheeks. "I'm sorry. Go on with your story."

"We're both exhausted, Ankarette. It's been a long night, a

long journey. Perhaps we could rest for a while?"

"You must tell me what you know," she said, shaking her head. "We'll leave this wagon at Ranz and then take horses toward Westmarch." She saw him flinch. "I mean, La Marche. Now that I know so much about your history, I have ill feelings toward Lord Kiskaddon, who is the Duke of Westmarch now. You *never* won your duchy back. That must have grieved you."

He let out a deep breath. "I won't lie to you, lass. I can't hear the name of Kiskaddon without grinding my teeth. No offense against the man, though. I have wasted enough years stewing in my regrets. Well, what's done is past. The Fountain's will is inexorable. Fighting against it only leads to suffering." He sighed. "When it whispered to Genette to leap from a window to save my life, it only did so to ensure she would suffer an even greater fall."

Ankarette shuddered at the thought. "The falls at King-fountain?" she said.

Alensson nodded. "So imagine this," he said, spreading his hands. "I've arrived at the sanctuary as Genette bade me do. She told me to look for a boy and I discovered him quickly. He escorted me to my cell, asking nothing, saying nothing. But I felt myself seething inside, like a kettle in the kitchen under too many coals. I started to speak to him in low tones, asking if he believed in the Fountain. He nodded, saying nothing. Then I asked him . . . I asked him if he believed in the Maid of Donremy. He jumped so fast and high, you'd have thought I had stuck him with a needle. He stared at me, frightened."

"Did he know who you were?" Ankarette probed.

Alensson shook his head. "No, I never told him. I took him aside and put my hands on his shoulders. I knelt down and looked him in the eye, face-to-face. You can tell a lot about someone if you look closely. I asked him again if he believed in the Maid. Tears came to his eyes, lass. He was shaking with fear and I knew why. The girl was a hero in his mind. Everyone around him said all sorts of horrible things about her. But he knew the truth and felt as if he was the only one who did."

She stared at him keenly. "Did he tell you?"

The duke smiled. "He did. He was shaking like a leaf, but he started gushing words after that. He told me the Fountain had whispered to him that a man was coming with a sword. He had seen the sword and the raven scabbard in a vision. He was afraid of me, because I was a stranger to him, but he knew from the Fountain he could trust me. I told him that the Fountain had sent me to help the Maid. That she had told me about him, had even described him to me. You should have seen his face, Ankarette. The Maid knew about *him*. He would have done anything to help her. And he did. I asked if he could get me into the palace, but he said no. I asked if *he* could get into the palace, and he said he often ran messages from the deconeus to the king's men. He knew the palace very well. He even knew some of the secret places within its walls." Alensson closed his eyes and massaged his forehead. "I told him that he needed to bring the scabbard into the palace and give it to the Maid when she arrived. No one ever thinks a young boy is a threat. He could pass unnoticed through the halls. He was scared to death of being caught, but he was also courageous and determined. And so the boy Tunmore promised to fetch me another scabbard to trade for the one I held. He showed me to my cell and said he would come for me later." He paused, parting the curtain of the wagon to look outside.

Ankarette heard it shortly after. The sound of riders coming up from behind the wagon.

"I think we may shortly have some visitors," he said warily, glancing back. "They're wearing the Spider King's badge."

The poisoner frowned with displeasure. Getting Alensson back into the secret compartment of the double chests would be difficult and noisy. She glanced out the window on her side of the carriage and spied eight riders, their stallions lathered and obviously trying to keep a punishing pace. She had to decide quickly.

"What shall we do, lass?" he asked her with his wry smile.

"Fight them," she answered confidently. "There are only eight, and then we won't need to get horses at Ranz."

His smile turned into a grin. "I was hoping you'd say that."

CHAPTER TWENTY-NINE

Trial of Innocence

The news of the Maid's arrival at Kingfountain days later spread through the sanctuary like wildfire. A crowd was already starting to gather by the time Alensson rushed to the gates. Within the hour, the courtyard within the gate and the street without it had swollen into a crushing river of human bodies, all jostling with one another for a better position. Some of the city urchins had even climbed atop the gates and dangled their legs from above. Every window from every shop was open, and the streets were jammed with those eager to catch a glimpse of Deford's prisoner. Alensson was uncomfortable in the crushing throng, but he simply kept one hand on his sword hilt and the other gripping the bar of the gate. The commotion of talking and gossip nearly overwhelmed the noise of the falls rushing past on both sides of the sanctuary island. The prodding of strangers and jostling of the crowd disturbed him, while the sickly reek of unwashed bodies choked his senses.

After an interminable wait, a cry arose from down the bridgehead, and suddenly the street was a writhing mass of onlookers, each craning to get a view. A phalanx of soldiers bearing royal tunics and banners rode on horseback and cleared an opening so that the cart bearing the Maid could lumber past. Alensson's pulse raced and he squeezed up to the pocked iron bar, smelling its rusty scent as he pressed his face slightly through the gap.

The citizenry of Kingfountain took up howling against the Maid, jeering obscenities at her and flinging spoiled fruit at her cart. There were at least fifty soldiers in front and fifty behind, but they would be useless against the swelling mob if a riot started. The indignities hurled at the Maid burned in the duke's ears, making him bare his teeth at the willful humiliation. The street vendors had even stopped hawking their wares to join in the abuse of the young woman. He watched the advancing phalanx plow through the crowd as if trudging through a snow-packed landscape.

As the first ranks of soldiers passed, Alensson saw the wary looks they were giving the tumultuous panoply. A fearful dread began pounding in his heart. What if they rushed the cart and seized her and threw her into the mouth of the falls? In the days since Alensson had been at Kingfountain, he had witnessed only one such outrage, a man caught thieving at one of the fountains. He'd been unceremoniously accosted and rushed to the ledge, and his corpse had later been found on the river shore below. The duke was terrified by the mass of life, the frenzied rabble who had been taught to hate Genette. What if she was murdered before his very eyes and she wasn't even granted a trial?

The pandemonium on the bridge outside the sanctuary was so great he could not hear the clacking of the wagon wheels as the cart followed the ranks of royal guardsmen. Smashed fruit and sludge dripped from the bars of the cart as it passed, making Alensson squeeze the bars of the gate in impotent fury. He saw Genette within, seated on the wooden floor, her hands bracing her body as the cart bumped and jostled. She was thinner than when he'd last seen her, her dark hair speckled with tomato seeds and other stains. But as the cart lumbered past Our Lady, she lifted her head and stared up at the sanctuary beyond the gate, taking in its vast architecture and sky-piercing spire. If she heard the taunts and deprecations of the crowd, there was no sign of it in her expression. A rotten cabbage exploded against the bars, and Alensson wanted to throttle the villain who had hurled it, but Genette still did not flinch. A slight smile brightened her face as she stared up at the shrine dedicated to the Fountain. She made a quick sign of obeisance with her hand, a prayer, and then her eyes fell to the gate of the sanctuary.

Their eyes met.

He was relieved she'd seen him, for he'd worried the cart would bear her away before he could alert her to his presence.

Her shoulders slumped in a grateful sigh, and this time her smile was so bright it pierced his heart and brought tears to his eyes. She crawled to the edge of the cart, fastening her hands on the bars, and she looked at him with tenderness. With his gaze fixed on hers, he nodded once and inclined his head respectfully, as if she were the duchess and he a mere village boy. She took his meaning. He had done as she had bidden him.

◆　　◆　　◆

For the next three days, the boy Tunmore brought Alensson daily tidings of the trial occurring at the palace. The trial was attended by most of the nobles of the realm, along with many of the prelates, including the deconeus of Our Lady and his protégé, John Tunmore. They were restless, anxiety-ridden days.

Alensson desperately wished he could find a way to gain entrance to the trial itself, but the notes the boy took in his ledger book were articulate and thorough. Despite his young age, Tunmore recounted details so vividly that Alensson almost felt as if he were there. They conjured images and moods and emotions. The boy had captured Genette's tone and willfulness so well, it was as if she were speaking to him from the page. The people were astounded that such a young woman was managing to defy and out-argue the brightest minds in the royal court.

On the third night, Alensson paced the sanctuary grounds as darkness fell and the torches were lit. Then he spied the young man approaching, his ledger clutched tightly to his chest.

The sense of doom in the boy's countenance made his heart jump in his chest. "What happened today? You look grave."

The boy sighed, his face pinched and worried. "The king's court does not want justice. They are only interested in arriving at guilt. Tomorrow she will be condemned."

It was the result he'd expected. Hadn't Genette told him that she was going over the falls? It was why she had asked for the scabbard. And yet he nearly swooned with worry.

"What charges against her have been worthy of death.

Sedition? Treason?"

The boy shook his head. "No, they cannot try her for treason because there has not been a coronation in Occitania yet. She was quick to remind them of that. Their grounds for sedition were equally difficult to enforce. No, I'm afraid they are planning to condemn her for wearing men's clothes."

"What?" Alensson asked, baffled. "When did this come about?"

"Today," Tunmore said. "She debunked their other accusations with logic, so today they have charged her with acting against her maidenhood. She has fought in battles and worn armor. She dresses in men's clothes. She has defended herself by saying that she does it to protect herself. She said that none of the Occitanian soldiers ever tried to molest her, but once she was captured by Brugia, she has had to be vigilant day and night for fear. They have tried to persuade her to give up the soldier garb now that she's *safe*." The boy had a scoffing look. "But she insists she is no safer in the palace of Kingfountain than she was at Beauvoir."

Alensson clenched his fists. "If only I could know what she wants me to do," he seethed.

"I think . . . I think that *I* could see her," Tunmore said softly.

Alensson dropped to one knee and gripped the boy's shoulders. "Tell me how!"

He glanced both ways to make sure they were alone. "As I've said, the guards recognize me at the palace," he said in a stumbling voice. "No one looks at me twice. I know where they are keeping her. If I said I bore a . . . a note. From the deconeus." He was stuttering now, his face white with fear. "It would be a lie, but if I did, I think I would be allowed to see her." His lips trembled. "But if the deconeus found out . . ."

Alensson tightened his grip on the boy's shoulder. "Lad, you must have courage to do the Fountain's will. You are not an ordinary boy. I sense in you the same power that she possesses. You must do as you suggest."

The boy shivered. "I'm afraid."

"So am I, lad. So am I. But you must talk to her. She knows . . . she knows the future, lad. She'll know what we must do to help her. If you brought the scabbard to her in the cell, they would only take it away from you." He released his grip and rubbed his lip. "She must get it."

"I know where they stow the boats they use for executions," the boy said. "I've hidden the scabbard in the palace, but I could bring it to the boat if I knew which one it was. Perhaps she'll know?"

Alensson gazed eagerly at the child. "Yes!" He gripped his shoulders again. "Lad, there are times when a boy must act like a man. This is one of those times. The Fountain will guide you. Trust in it. Go seek the Maid. Her name is Genette. Tell her . . . tell her that her *gentle* friend awaits her orders."

The boy blinked at him. "Did you *serve* with her in Occitania? Are you one of her soldiers?"

Alensson felt he could trust the boy. "I am," he answered. "I am here on her orders. Talk to her in the dungeon. Hide the scabbard on the boat. Where is it now?"

The lad squirmed again. "I've hidden it." It was the same answer he'd given before.

"Where?" he pressed.

The serious eyes met his. "In the Deep Fathoms."

The duke had no comprehension of what it meant to hide something there. But then a memory surfaced: Genette drawing a chest from a fountain that had looked empty moments before. It was a power the Fountain-blessed had.

"Go see her," he said, clapping the boy on the shoulder. "You are destined for great things, John Tunmore."

The boy looked pleased by the compliment. "They are holding her in the dungeon, not the tower. They say she jumped out of the tower at Beauvoir and survived without a broken bone."

Alensson felt a flash of pain at the memory. "I've heard the same," he said. "And yes, she did survive. She *must* survive now too."

"Go," Alensson said, jerking his head. The boy nodded and departed, clutching the ledger to his chest once more. Alensson watched until the shadows smothered the lad. He disliked using a child to achieve his ends. He'd grown rather fond of the lad over the last few days.

And then he remembered his pregnant wife. Her time was coming due, and it was seeming less and less likely he'd be able to return in time with Genette. The worry in his chest was so fierce he almost couldn't breathe.

CHAPTER THIRTY

Into the Falls

Alensson could not sleep. He lay awake, arms hugging his chest, listening to the garbled snores of his cell mates as he lay on the itchy wool blanket covering his dingy stray pallet. He listened to the omnipresent murmur of the falls, which could not even be escaped within the stone walls of the sanctuary. The sound was a constant reminder that Genette was likely to meet her fate today. She would be bound by arm and ankle, handed into a wooden canoe, and then ceremoniously dumped into the raging river—the form of execution trial most common in both Ceredigion and Occitania. He wished he could have sat with her in her stone cell that night, holding her hand and giving her a morsel of comfort before she faced the falls.

The corridors had fallen quiet hours ago, and he occasionally tossed and turned, seeking to ease the pain in his hip. The rank smell of the blanket was normal to him now. After his five-year imprisonment, he'd learned to be comfortable in solitude, a feeling that drove most men mad. His thoughts turned again to his wife, Jianne. Had she sent for a midwife already? How close was she to her confinement? He had not contacted her in weeks for fear of discovery. She was undoubtedly as worried about him as he was about her.

What would happen to the people he cared for so deeply?

His ears picked out the cautious tread of a boy's shoes coming down the hall. The slow, steady cadence spoke of his fear of being discovered roaming the sanctuary at night.

As Alensson crept away from his pallet, he heard one of his cell mates grunt and then emit a loud snore. The disruption made him freeze his motion, waiting to hear the rhythm of the man's breathing start up again. It did. There was no door covering the cell, only a stiff, tattered curtain. Alensson parted it and then slipped into the hall.

The boy was inching his way toward him, his hands patting the wall as he counted the way down. A trio of torches burned in a rack at the far end of the hall, stretching the boy's shadow to the point where it almost touched Alensson's boots.

The lad saw him and then came forward.

"Did you see her?" the duke whispered.

Tunmore nodded gravely. "I'm sorry it took so long."

"Did you have any trouble?"

"Quite a bit, sir. But nothing I couldn't manage. I don't think anyone will send word to the deconeus. If they do, I don't have an explanation."

Alensson smiled. "You're very young. Just say you were curious, and that will explain it all away." He dropped down to one knee to put their faces at an even level. "You spoke to the Maid then? What did she say?"

Tunmore flinched and glanced back the way he'd come. Had there been a noise?

"I did speak to her and the Fountain spoke inside my heart. She knew . . . she knew my name. It was almost as if we'd always been friends. She's very pale, very tired." He glanced back again, looking unnerved.

Then Alensson heard it to. The soft clip of boots coming down the corridor. A swell of panic rose up inside his chest. Had someone followed the boy back to the sanctuary? Their time together was suddenly very limited. Alensson gripped the lad's shoulders. "What does she want me to do?" he whispered urgently.

Tunmore kept glancing back at the corridor, his eyes widening with fear. His nostrils flared and he started breathing fast. "She said she didn't want you to watch her go into the falls tomorrow. The waters won't kill her because she is Fountain-blessed and water is of the Fountain. But she said it would *disturb* you to see it."

A flush of anger shot through Alensson's heart. "And she's worried about *me?*" he growled.

The boy nodded. "She said the Fountain has its own purpose for you. You must go to the North. To North Cumbria. There is a castle there called Dundrennan. Beyond the castle, high in the mountains, you will follow the river to its source. She will meet you there in three days."

Alensson's mind whirled. The prospect of going even farther into his enemy's country alarmed him. "Dun—Dundrennan? Was that the name?" he asked.

The boy Tunmore nodded. "It's the duke's castle. If you follow the river, it will take you there. She said to dress warmly. There will be ice."

His heart hammered with dread as the bootfalls drew

nearer. Because of the torches, there were no shadows on the floor to show how close the interloper was.

Alensson pressed his back against the wall and ducked behind the curtain of his cell. The sound of the boots grew louder and faster as the man broke into a run.

"Oy!" the man called. "You, boy! Hold fast in the name of the king."

Alensson's blood froze. He pressed his wrist against his mouth to stifle the noise of his rapid breathing. His heartbeat pounded in his ears. The lad's pursuer passed Alensson's curtain, but his bootfalls were quickly followed by another set.

"Did you find the brat?" asked the second man.

"He went down that way and disappeared. I thought I saw him talking to someone, but couldn't see for sure in this blasted darkness."

"Why didn't you carry a torch?" asked the second man.

The two men met up just outside Alensson's cell. Terrified they'd pull the curtain back and see him, he carefully tiptoed to his pallet and slunk down onto it, putting his back to the opening and pulling the covers up to his shoulders. He was shivering with dread.

"I wasn't that far behind the lad. He came here from the palace!"

"He did?" asked the other man in confusion. "In the middle of the night?"

"Yes. One of the palace Espion caught him carrying a long box through the halls of Kingfountain. Thought he was a thief."

"These sanctuary men are all cutthroats," the other said disdainfully. "They steal during the day and then hide here at night. Over half should be thrown into the river."

"You can't do that, man! Think what the citizens would do! Superstitious fools. The Espion tried to follow him, but the boy was crafty. He knows the palace well."

"Humph! Definitely a thief then."

"Strange that he didn't steal anything. He stashed the box he was carrying somewhere. When I was sent, I caught him leaving the grounds. Sure enough, he came here to Our Lady. There's a gang of boys running amok these days. Urchins, all of them. Well, whoever the boy was, he's slipped away. I didn't get a good look at him."

"Well, best we leave before the sexton arrives with a lamp. Come on."

"All right. But I hate the thought of someone stealing His Majesty's treasures. If I find that brat, I'll wring his little neck. You're stationed here. See what you can find out. Ask around."

"I will. Best to go."

The sound of their bootsteps faded. Alensson took deep gulps of air and gripped the pommel of the sword Genette had given him as he waited for the boy Tunmore to return.

He didn't.

◆　　◆　　◆

When it was dawn, Alensson decided to leave the sanctuary. He had wrestled within himself for the remainder of the night, tempted to disobey the Maid's instructions. Part of him felt he should witness the canoe entering the river, that it was his duty to her despite what she'd said. But he knew himself, and perhaps Genette also knew him well. Would he be tempted to jump into the river to try to save her? He wasn't Fountain-blessed. A rash action like that would end with his death, more likely than not. The more he thought about it, the more he realized he couldn't trust himself. So he heeded her wisdom and pushed his way roughly through the crowds loitering on the bridge. Everyone was gathering to witness the spectacle, and he was moving against the flood.

With a snarl on his mouth and fire in his eyes, he marched through the throngs, earning a battery of curses and contempt. More and more people tried to crowd onto the bridge to watch. When Alensson finally escaped the confinement of the press, he increased his pace and rushed beyond the city gates. He took a road leading north that followed alongside the river, though at a distance. Walking in long furious strides, his arms folded across his chest, he brooded on what was even now happening back at Kingfountain. Each step brought a variation of the same question. Had it happened yet? Was it about to?

Those endless questions were what finally drove him to abandon his determination to honor Genette's wishes.

Once he made the decision, he ran to the river's edge. He was about a mile upriver, close enough to see the mossy flank of the sanctuary island. The icy waters rushed by at breakneck speed. Swimming across the river would not be possible. Looking back at Kingfountain, he spied a series of docks wedged behind the castle, down at the water's edge.

The crowd was still gathered around the river, and when he squinted hard enough, he made out various men, soldiers mostly, though he also saw the cassock of the deconeus. This was the moment. There was a canoe fixed to poles, and he could see them lowering someone into it, someone who went willingly and without struggle.

Alensson's heart flamed with agony as he watched the deconeus stand over the prostrate girl. The man made a little benediction with his hand. As soon as he stepped away, the soldiers hefted the poles the canoe sat on and marched the little boat to the end of the pier. And then, unceremoniously, they tilted it and the canoe landed with a splash.

He squeezed his fists, shaking with fierce emotions. Did she know he was there? Did she know he was watching her after all?

The canoe was quickly gaining speed. Suddenly the brash duke stepped away from the tree, cupped his hands over his mouth, and screamed her name over the roar of the river.

"Genette!"

Could she have heard him? He prayed to the Fountain that she had. He watched with sickening horror as the canoe accelerated, caught in the current that would bring her to an inexorable fate. Was the scabbard with her? Was her fate sealed?

He watched the tiny canoe fade into the distance, following the river to the left bank of the island. It quickly veered out of sight, but he knew when the boat went over the edge. He knew because of the cheers that rose from thousands of throats overlooking the falls.

When he heard the noise, he started to weep.

CHAPTER THIRTY-ONE

Secrets of Ice

The fur blankets, thick boots, gloves, and thick wool cloak that he had purchased in the city of Dundrennan could not evict the chill that had settled into Alensson's bones. Even his whiskers had a dusting of snow. He climbed the majestic peaks through rock and ice and fierce winds, following the thundering waterfall up to its origin, a snow-capped mountain wreathed in winter's chill year-round. It was the source of the water that made the land fertile. It was impressive, cold, and mysterious, and although his toes felt like stones, he pressed on, huffing his way up trails better suited to goats than men.

His exertions up the cliff face rewarded him with a view of the verdant valley below, including the gray citadel that was the fortress of North Cumbria, tucked between thickets of fir trees so dark they were nearly black. He could only hear the wind and the ruffling of his cloak. The community was too far below for its noises to filter to the upper heights of the mountains.

The Maid had said she would meet him at the ice cave in three days. He'd done his best to close the distance, barely stopping to rest and eat. His strength had flagged, but his determination was prouder than the solemn boulders around him.

The trail arrived at a small plateau where he found a great boulder fixed with iron chains. The thought of being chained there made him shudder. Something heavy pressed on his mind as he stared at it, and he felt an unmistakable premonition. Had he been to this lonesome perch before? It felt like it, yet he had never been so far north in his life. He walked up to the stone and rubbed it with his gloved hand. Snow cleared away, bone-dry like sand. The iron chains were heavy and fastened through stout rings.

Unsure of what he was seeing, he pressed onward, following the crevice of the river as it wound through the upper gorges of the high mountains. He continued on his way, chafing his hands and hunkering inside his layers of fur and cloth. The ice caves were a mystery, and he wondered how he would find them.

But he did.

When he reached the end of the river, which had shrunk to a small trickling stream that was sluggish with chunks of ice, he saw the maw of the cave. A strange power emanated from it, and enough daylight remained to illuminate the interior. He marveled at the colors as he ventured cautiously into the cave. The inner walls were rich with shades of silver, blue, green, and turquoise. Ice; all ice. The rippled, supple edges and contours were all the effect of wind and weather.

This was a hallowed place. He could sense it deep within his bones. There were ancient secrets contained here, mysteries related to the origins of the world. As he ventured into the cave, the stream solidified into a giant slippery sheet of ice strong enough to support his weight. He had to walk carefully, though, for the footing was treacherous.

Wandering into the convoluted corridor, he gazed ahead, looking for any signs of life or magic. When he reached the far end of the cave, he found himself facing a wall of ice. The pommel of the sword began to glow, startling him. He sensed the blade's magic responding to the proximity of the wall. Carefully and cautiously, he withdrew it from its sheath. The blade had a textured, warped pattern, much like the curious flowing shapes of the ice walls. The sword had been birthed in a cave like this, he intuited. It drew its powerful magic from the very depths of the Deep Fathoms.

What was he supposed to do? Alensson approached the wall, holding the blade before him so that its light shone on the surface. A misty breath came out of his mouth as he exhaled, and he shuddered with cold. Was he supposed to yield the blade to the wall? How? He waited, listening, trying to make sense of his strange and mercurial feelings. Something wasn't right. He was missing something.

Only Genette would be able to invoke the magic, he realized. He needed her.

♦　♦　♦

Alensson spent that black, freezing night alone in the cave, with only the frail light from the sword to assist him. He waited throughout the next day, tromping around in the cave, climbing the rocks and peaks outside to build up his warmth again. He was freezing to death, he realized. The food supplies he had bought in Dundrennan were dwindling. Drinking water from the stream only made him colder, and it barely slaked his thirst. Where was she?

As he waited, his mind kept returning to the boulder and the chains he had passed on his way to the cave. It could not be coincidence. Would the Ceredigic bring her there when they discovered she'd survived the falls? Though she'd asked him to meet her here, she hadn't told him how *she* would come. Should he go search for her? Or should he wait? Why wouldn't the Fountain speak to him?

Alensson gritted his teeth and marched in circles in the ice, fearing he was losing his wits. The thought of his wife's cozy cottage nestled against the castle wall. How he longed to sit in front of the hearth with Jianne. The babe was coming within the month. He had to get back to his family. But what good could he do them if he did not return with Genette?

As the sunlight began to slip away on the fourth day, he could abide the suspense no longer. He would march back toward the boulder and wait for Genette there. His calves were aching, his feet felt frozen and hard and painful. With a fierce scowl, he started back down the mountain, hoping to make it to the boulder. He regretted his decision the instant he left the cave. The wind was even colder outside. Although he hadn't realized it, the protection of the walls had helped him stay warmer. The wind was a knife and it slashed at him viciously. He'd never felt so miserable and cold.

But as he marched along the rock and ice, he saw a flicker of light ahead. Piercing light—man-made light. He blinked, wondering if his senses were now conjuring things that weren't real. The night wind blew against his cloak, whipping it furiously. He squinted and clutched himself tighter, but the light didn't change. *Torches.*

As he got closer, the images resolved into a coherent scene. There was a fire, a brazier with three sturdy iron legs and three posts for torches. It was full of wood and delicious heat, and his soul hungered to join the soldiers huddled around it. But his mind was sharp enough to see that the soldiers wore the colors of the King of Ceredigion. There were six of them there, gathered around the fire, some squatting, some sitting, hands chafing to keep warm.

And then he saw Genette.

His heart raged with dismay when he recognized the half-frozen creature chained to the boulder. He had never heard of this form of execution before, and it horrified him. She was wearing only a shift, a thin night-dress that offered no protection whatsoever against the elements. Her hair was down around her face, her head bobbing up and down as if she was wrestling to stay awake. There were dark stains, likely blood, on her shackled wrists, and it had frozen to her skin.

"Are you sure you don't want to join us at the fire, lass?" one of the soldiers taunted. "I can think of a few ways to make you warm!"

"It's a long night for sure. People die in these mountains all the time," another said. "We all know you're not really a maid. You're a strumpet. Come on, we'll even pay you!"

How long had they been torturing her? How long had she endured their foul words and shameful goading? It was unconscionable to him that a woman would be treated so. The cold he had been suffering was nothing compared to this torture. As he drew nearer, he saw her shift ruffling in the wind.

"If you're truly Fountain-blessed, save yourself!" one of them goaded. "Or doesn't your power work on ice? You may have survived the falls, lass, but you won't survive this."

"I'll bet you five florins she won't last until dawn."

"I'll bet you ten she dies before midnight."

"Ten? I'll take that bet. She's tough, this one. She'll make it till dawn. Then she'll die."

Liquid rage replaced the cold in Alensson's bones. He continued to march up to the camp, not caring if they heard him. He drew the sword from the scabbard and gripped it tightly in his hand. There was no warning voice telling him to stop. The Fountain wouldn't even speak to him directly now. So be it. He had made his decision.

"What's that sound?" someone asked. "Do you hear it?"

"I hear the jingling of coins, man. Now give the money to Turner. He'll hold it for us and pay each man his due. Eh, Turner?"

"I hear it too."

"Shut it man, it's just the wind!"

"There are bears in these mountains. Grab a torch, I say. See what it is."

Alensson saw a few heads turn his way as he approached, his boots crunching in the ice.

"It's a man."

"Who are you, man? Lost?" His voice quavered a bit, betraying his alarm. "This is the king's business. You can't stay here," another said.

Alensson continued to advance on them without speaking, fury roaring inside him like the brazier the men were cowering around.

He struck down the first man, sending a spray of hot blood across the snow. Alensson felt the power of the sword singing up his arm. Then it was five against one, an unfair match under any circumstances, but the soldiers had not been expecting an enemy. They'd been paid to stay with a victim until she was dead. Well, Alensson was determined *they* would be the ones to meet an unpleasant end. He moved like water, running through the second man while the others scrabbled to their feet, reaching for their swords and shouting in terror.

The remaining four men were not ready for him, but they were not unskilled. He crossed blades twice with another man before dispatching him, then was forced to defend himself as the final three charged him at once. Despite the cold, despite the agonizing circumstances, his mind felt clear and supple. This blade had seen countless battles. Images of ancient kings, jousts, tournaments, and wars flashed through his mind. He saw the hall of a great palace, but instead of a throne, he saw a table unlike any other. It was a circle of wood, a slice from a giant tree trunk more massive than any he had ever seen. On instinct he deflected a thrust, then spun around and smashed his elbow into the soldier's nose. Stomping on another man's boot, he whipped his blade around to thrust it into the flesh of the man with the broken nose.

Pain struck his arm as one of the remaining two managed to stab him, but the pain was nothing compared to his fury. He howled at the man like a wolf and went after him, bashing away his defenses before ending his life abruptly. That left only one, one man who was running and slipping in the snow and ice to escape. Alensson turned the blade upside-down, closed his fingers around the hilt, and then lifted it and hurled the sword at the fleeing man like a spear.

He had never done that in a battle before. The blade's magic had planted the thought in him, and it had worked—he watched as the blade pierced the man from behind and sent him into a snowdrift.

Alensson rushed over to where Genette was.

Kneeling in the snow beside her, he hurriedly removed his

cloak and wrapped it around her shoulders.

"Genette! Genette!" he called urgently, shaking her shoulders.

"*Gentle* duke," she murmured, swayed, and collapsed against him. He hugged her close, but her half-frozen body was rigid against him.

"I'm going to get you off this mountain," he said. "I'll carry you the whole way if I must."

"The key. The one with . . . the badge. Has the key."

Alensson hurried to the corpses and found the one with the badge. After a quick search, he discovered the key ring and hurried over. His hands were shaking, his fingers clumsy as he tried to force the key into the lock. It was difficult to twist the cold metal, but he finally managed to free the bar that locked the cuffs together. His eyes fell to the frozen blood on her wrists.

"It's not painful," she said, shaking her head. She looked like a child who was half-awake, groggy at the first rise. Alensson put his arm around her and then lifted her up and carried her to the brazier. The tongues of flames were lashing violently in the wind. He set her down in front of it and then unfastened one of the soldier's cloaks to wrap it around himself.

The sound of her teeth chattering reminded him they were still in danger. "I was waiting for you at the cave," he said. "I should have waited here. I . . . I had a feeling."

"No," she responded. "I asked you to wait for me there. You did the right thing."

"If I'd come sooner—"

"Shhhh," she soothed. "If you'd come sooner, you would have been killed, Alensson. I didn't want that."

He stared at her in wonderment. "What do you mean?"

She sighed. "I must fulfill the mission the Fountain gave me. I chose this, Gentle Duke. I knew I would die here . . . tonight . . . on this lonely mountain."

"You are *not* going to die!" he snarled furiously.

"And I knew you would be here with me. Holding vigil until the last. I knew that when I first saw you. When we first met." A shy smile came over her mouth. "I have done what the Fountain bade me to do. You have always been there for me, Alensson. Giving me strength. Having you near me has made the burden easier."

"Why are you talking like this?" Alensson said in frustration. "I've rescued you. I'm going to take you down from this mountain. I will get you back to Occitania. You *must* come with me, Genette, or my child will die!"

A look of sadness passed over her. "I know, Alensson. I know he will." She let out a trembling sigh. "He will be stillborn. Do you remember what I told you?"

"You said you knew the word. You said there was a word of power that could revive him."

She nodded. "Not your son, Gentle Duke. The *heir*. Your time as Duke of La Marche is over." She paused, and when she spoke again, her voice was very gentle. "You will have no children. You never will. There is another the Fountain will put in your place. It has always been so. A future duke. A babe stillborn. He is the one I saw in my vision. The babe will come when you are about to die. You must know this, Gentle Duke. Your pain, *our* suffering"—she reached out and squeezed his hand—"has saved the lives of countless of our countrymen. They will never know what we did for them. They will never say thank you. They will, eventually, forget your name. But I will not forget you. You were the one who gave me courage to carry my burden. Remember this, Gentle

Duke. Remember this when you are trapped in the king's palace in Pree." She reached up and touched his face. "One night, a poisoner will come to you. She will not come to kill you. You will tell her our story so that she can save the heir's life. Our story will give her courage to do what must be done." She squeezed his hand and then leaned over to kiss him on the cheek.

He was startled by all she had said and found it impossible to react to the news with words. Grief, sadness, resentment, despair all buffeted inside him. He wanted to shake his fist at the sky; he wanted to lament the cruelty of his life. Then he felt her lips brush against the edge of his eyebrow. "*Tardemaw*," she whispered. It was a word of power.

A feeling of heaviness slammed into him—an exhaustion so profound he could not fight it. He collapsed into a puddle of melting snow.

CHAPTER THIRTY-TWO

The Maid's Grave

As Alensson slept, he dreamed. He knew it was a dream, for only in dreams were the colors so vibrant. He was walking in a garden, listening to the babbling of fountain waters. The sky was such a clear blue, he imagined he could reach up and stir it like a pond. Butterflies flittered with exquisite wings, light and free, and the birds had heartbreakingly bright plumage—red, orange, purple, yellow. The ground was spongy, a woven mass of grass so thick and soft it was like walking on a cloud. It was strange how slowly the awareness stole over him before he noticed the young woman walking at his side.

It was Genette, he realized, and she was smiling at him peacefully.

"Where are we?" he asked, amazed at the butterfly that

landed on her outstretched hand.

"It's an in-between place, Gentle Duke," she said. "In between dreams and awake. In between life and death. It's one of the gardens of the Fountain."

"Am I dreaming?" he asked, amazed at the fresh, sweet smell of the grass. It felt as if his entire being was keenly attuned to the sensations around him.

"Of course you are," she answered. "It is the stuff of dreams."

Memories stirred sluggishly in his mind. Memories of a cold mountaintop, frigid snow, leaden feet. But it was all fuzzy and far away. There was something wrong in his heart, some hidden grief that he could not quite remember. It lay buried beneath an overwhelming sense of peace.

"Am I dying?" he asked her.

Then he noticed she wasn't wearing the soldier's tunic he'd so often seen on her. No, she was dressed in the simple frock of a peasant girl from Donremy. Her hair was long and dark, but there were little hints of gold in it. Had it always been so, or were his powers of observation different here? The bruises and smudges on her skin were gone. She looked comfortable and calm as she strode barefoot in the grass beside him. She was the picture of innocence, and a protective, gentle feeling swelled in his heart.

"No, Gentle Duke. I asked a gift of the Fountain before I died. I wanted to bring you here."

He was confused. "*Before* you died?"

She nodded, her hair bouncing slightly. "When I was young and first began hearing the water sounds of the Fountain, I would close my eyes and imagine what it was like. In my visions, I was always brought here, to this garden. This is where I learned to hear the whispers. This in-between place was just as much my home as Donremy. I tried to share it with others, but none believed me. None trusted me enough to let me take them here. I was the only one who could see it. Sometimes, when I was younger, I wondered if I was sick for seeing these visions that no one else could." She gave him a delighted smile. "Before I died, I asked the Fountain to let me show you."

He felt a rush of gratitude and intense emotions swell inside him. "When I awaken . . . you'll be gone."

She nodded cheerfully. "It is difficult being so different. To be the only one who hears or sees. Thank you for believing in me. It meant so much to me to have someone else believe in me."

He smiled at her, but felt on the verge of tears. "I won't see you again."

She shook her head. "Not until your time in the mortal coil is over. That filthy world with all its greed, anguish, and sorrow. So much of it brought upon itself because people don't understand what truly gives meaning to life. I have done what the Fountain sent me to do. I am ready to be in a different place."

A stab of bitterness welled in his stomach. "You crowned a false king. He betrayed you, Genette!"

She patted his arm with her hand. "I know, Gentle Duke. I hoped his better nature might persevere, but I knew what he would do. My mission was not to help Chatriyon, but to save our countrymen. To preserve their lives from a devastating flood. That threat has been averted now. You have to know the rules of the game. Chatriyon has been taught. It is his choice how he plays the game. If he'd chosen to be a good king, he would have earned much wealth and prosperity. Sadly, he will be a *dark* one. But it is his choice."

Alensson sighed heavily. "I'm not yet ready to go back to that world," he said gravely, feeling the grief bubble up inside him. "My child will be stillborn. My wife may perish as well. I've lost the scabbard and cannot heal them. It will be painful to go through all of that. It feels so . . . different here."

A tender smile softened her face. "I know, Alen." She slowly shook her head, her eyes serious. "But your turn is not yet finished. You will bear those griefs as I have born mine. Knowing the future does not make it any easier to endure. But you still have a role to play. The Fountain needs you. It always has."

"To do what? Help another lad claim my duchy?" he asked, but could not quite summon the bitterness and resentment he had once felt.

"Was it ever truly yours?" she asked him delicately. "Was it not a gift from the Fountain to your ancestors? We hid the scabbard in Kingfountain because it's intended for someone else. The sword will be reclaimed one day to aid a new king, a righteous king. It is so simple to limit our view of the world to our immediate surroundings," she added, gesturing to the resplendent garden. She sidled a little closer and held onto his arm as they walked. "There are worlds beyond imagining, Gentle Duke. Worlds without number. There are times and seasons for them all. I go to join the ranks of others who have gone before me. But I will wait for you, Alen. I will wait until your journey is done. And when it is finished, I will meet you and Jianne and your unborn child here in the garden. I will care for them while you linger. You will feel differently then. Believe me. Trust me. Farewell, Gentle Duke. For now."

She released his arm and it felt as if tree roots had squirmed through the grass and entangled his feet, forcing him to a halt. She kept walking ahead, looking back at him with an inviting, promising smile. His heart was breaking as he watched her leave.

"Genette!" he called after her. There was a stab of sunlight in his eyes, forcing him to look away. He blinked rapidly, trying to see her through the blaze.

And that was when he awoke.

♦   ♦   ♦

He was cold, though that was hardly an adequate word to describe it. His body was rigid and stiff and his face was numb from being pressed against the ice. The prick of light in his eyes came from the actual sun, cresting a snowy peak with brilliant wonder. It hurt to look at it, but he could still hear the murmur of the fountain water from the garden in his dream. There were clouds in the sky and the sunlight bathed them in dazzling hues that made him want to weep for their beauty. His vision drifted lower, finding the boulder. He saw the Maid chained there, frozen. Dead.

As his senses began to return to the pain and cold of his mortal confinement, he registered the sound of crunching bootsteps and garbled voices. With half-veiled lids, he saw the soldiers inspecting the camp.

"They're all dead, including the girl," one of them said, sniffing against his leather glove.

"I can't believe it. Deford will be furious. He won't believe this." The second soldier's tone was incredulous, full of awed disbelief.

"I just don't understand. All the nightwatch were slain by sword, yet there is not one bloody sword among them. The girl is chained to the rock like when we left her. Did they all go mad and kill themselves?"

"I don't know. I don't know what to make of it. Where is

Brant?"

"He's over there. Oy, Brant! What did you find?"

Alensson's body was painfully stiff, but he didn't dare move. There was no way he could fight at the moment, and he knew he was in trouble. These were all the king's men and he wasn't one of them. If they noticed he wasn't wearing the tunic—

Then he noticed that he *was* wearing one of the soldiers' tunics. His own cloak was draped across him, covered with freshly fallen snow. How had this happened? Then he remembered and the grief crashed over him like storm-driven waves onto a rocky shore. He had fallen asleep when Genette had kissed his eyes and uttered the word of power. What had she done in the interim?

"This one fell trying to escape," a man shouted from a distance. "He's got a wound in his back from a spear by the looks of it. No spear around, though. No weapons at all. Whoever killed them left."

"Are you sure the girl is really dead?" one of them asked worriedly. "Someone could have switched her body for another!"

"You think me daft, man? You guarded her just as I did. Tell me that's not the strumpet from Occitania. She's frozen to death. But I'd know that face, that hair. You want to know what I thinks? I thinks one of these fools tried something foolish with her. You know what I mean. And she cursed them to kill one another. If we hadn't bound her to the stone, she'd have escaped all right. And then we'd all be in the river. At least she's dead."

"At least she's dead," his partner agreed thankfully. "What do we do?"

"We fetch a wagon and bring them down to Dundrennan.

What else do you think? There were six soldiers who come up here last night. And there are six soldiers left. They're all dead. We have the bodies to prove it, including hers."

Alensson wondered if Genette had hidden one of the bodies beneath the snow or shoved it off the edge of the mountain.

"This mountain is cursed," a soldier moaned. "I'm never coming up here again."

"Nor me either," said the other. "Let's stack the bodies over there."

Another soldier marched up to them. "At least they'll be getting a ride down the mountain, eh? Lucky sods."

"Don't joke," someone said, rubbing his gloved hands over the arms of his cloak. "This place gives me a strange feeling. It's over, though. The Fountain didn't save her after all. It was all a riddle. A farce."

"Aye. You two grab that one."

"Yes, sir."

Alensson feigned the mask of death as he listened to their approaching footsteps. His mind was sharp, but his limbs were still unusable. One soldier grabbed his ankles. The other hoisted him beneath his arms. His heart throbbed with pain and wretchedness.

"Come on, lift. Don't make me carry the bulk!"

"I am lifting! I thought we'd only be carrying one corpse back down the mountain in the wagon, not this lot too."

Through his lashes, Alensson saw that he had been positioned right near the brazier. All the torches were out, but there were still some smoldering coals left in it. Genette had kept him by the fire while she had willingly frozen to death. She'd positioned him so that his back and neck were to the brazier, his face toward her so that she could look at him in her final moments. His heart ached for her, for his wife, for the child he'd not see until his own death. How different things could have been had Chatriyon chosen better things. How different indeed.

As they lugged him away, he cast a final look at her stiff body, watching as another soldier unlocked the chains. Her mouth had frozen into a smile of victory.

CHAPTER THIRTY-THREE

Black Knight

Ankarette and Alensson were hidden in a hollowed-out trunk near a gurgling stream. They had rested there for several hours and continued their hushed conversation until the crack of wood nearby had alerted her. There was something dreadfully wrong. Ankarette's senses were taut with danger. It was not possible that their pursuers could have found them this quickly. The riders who had accosted their wagon had been the outriders of a larger force bent on hunting them down. They had scarcely stolen the mens' horses and tunics when the sound of approaching soldiers reached them. Ankarette had sent the two Espion into the woods on the left and urged them to return with reinforcements. Then she and the duke had taken the strongest of the beasts and ridden on ahead, only to find a picket of stakes blocking the road. At first

Ankarette had thought the pickets were a trap, but then she'd realized these were the border defenders of Occitania, here to alert King Lewis of troop movements from his rival on the throne in Kingfountain.

She and the old duke had plunged into the woods on the right side of the road in the hopes of losing their pursuers. Then they'd ditched the horses to provide a false trail and found refuge in the hollow trunk. But their pursuers hadn't taken the bait.

All her ruses were failing.

The forest was thick, full of moss-covered trees, and furrowed with deep ravines and gulches. There were plenty of places to hide, but the poisoner knew she could not stay still.

"I don't understand how they keep on our trail," Ankarette said in a low voice, deciding it was better to flee before they were surrounded. The two departed the trunk and hiked side by side eastward, trying to reach a break in the woods. She knew Eredur's army was nearby. If she could only reach it, they would be protected, and she knew her king would value the prize she had brought.

The duke was breathing heavy in short order. He was much older than her, but still had the strength for a long march. "It's happened to me before," he said darkly. "Every time I've risen against the king, he knew where to find me. His spies are everywhere."

She shook her head. "This is more than spycraft, Alensson. I can sense Fountain magic at work. It's subtle and I cannot determine the source . . . but it's coming from behind us. He sent someone who is Fountain-blessed to hunt you. What I don't understand is why they let us get this far. Why didn't they stop us from leaving the city?"

"I don't understand it either, Ankarette." He dodged a low-hanging branch and then lifted it so she wouldn't have to duck. He had not lost his courteous manners.

There was a call coming from the woods on the left. It could have been a bird, but she recognized it as a human sound. The soldiers were trying to flank them, to encircle them.

"This way," she said, tugging at his sleeve, leading him toward a ravine with a trickling stream at the bottom that joined the one they had left. "There was a river that leads to the king's camp," she said. "I remember seeing it before I left. I think we are drawing near. This brook may feed into it."

"Which river was it?" Alensson asked. "I can tell you."

"It was the Sienna River. The one that leads to Pree. The army is encamped on the other side of Montreux Bridge."

A wise grin passed over Alensson's face.

"You know that bridge?"

"Of course I know that bridge," he said with a chuckle. "That's where Chatriyon murdered his rival, the King of Brugia. Is that were Lewis and Eredur plan to meet?"

"It is. I've not heard this story."

"It was famous back in its day. But it's long been forgotten. Are we going down into the ravine?"

"I think we should," Ankarette said.

He shook his head. "This will lead to the Sienna. It would be wise for us to follow it for a while, but let's not go down there just yet. Once we're there, it'll be easier for them to trap us. Let's save it for a final hope. Agreed?"

"Agreed. As long as we're heading in the right direction."

"We are . . . I know this wood. Let me tell you this story quickly. It may save your king's life. I'll keep my voice low."

"Thank you," she answered, keeping alert for noise of their pursuers. She could hear them in the woods. They weren't troubling to keep their silence. The occasional spurt of voices or cracking of limbs announced their presence. She was determined to bring Alensson to safety. Perhaps their hunter had a special gift from the Fountain that enabled him to pursue someone?

"Montreux Bridge is just ahead," Alensson said, pointing. "The Sienna is too difficult for an army to cross. The bridge is notoriously stone and quite defensible. What's not well known is that a secret trapdoor was built into the flooring on the other side of the bridge. The side your king is encamped on."

"A trapdoor? To what purpose?"

"Murder, of course. Before a negotiation, the king's men will erect two timber cages on the bridge, and the two sides will meet in the cages. The doors are locked. The arrange-ment ensures only a few men on each side are involved in the negotiation and the cages prevent them from attacking each other. But there is the trapdoor. At the king's signal, the soldiers hidden under the bridge come through the trapdoor and kill those inside the cage on the enemy's side. That's what happened to the King of Brugia when he came to negotiate peace with Chatriyon. This was before Chatriyon was crowned king at Ranz. This deception was the reason Brugia sided with Ceredigion during the troubles that followed. Chatriyon's father often relied on murder and duplicity too. He bribed several lords to betray the King of Ceredigion before Azinkeep. Unfortunately, they were discovered and sent over the falls. The best way to win a battle is to prevent one."

"So you are saying that Lewis is only pretending he will negotiate peace terms with Eredur in order to assassinate him?"

"Yes, my dear. That is precisely what I am saying. Eredur thinks he came to fight a battle. I assure you that Lewis has no intention of fighting a battle. He knows his history, Ankarette. He knows about Azinkeep, Vernay, and Pree. He knows the costs of losing. And Eredur has a fearsome reputation on the battlefield. One side is playing Wizr. The other side is playing with wooden staves. There are two different games going on. Best you know this. Best you realize what's truly happening."

"Thank you for the warning," Ankarette said. "I hadn't known that bit about the betrayal of Brugia."

"Not many remember the past." His breath was coming in ragged pants now and she hoped they reached the safety of her king's army soon. He would be such an asset to Ceredigion, and she really thought Eredur would like him. He would be a great addition to the king's council. If he survived that long. The Maid's prophecy about his death rattled her. She glanced backward, hopeful she wouldn't see anyone yet.

"Do you have any . . . further questions for me?" Alensson huffed. Another whistle came from the right. The enemy was getting closer.

"Let me see if I can lay it out," Ankarette said, searching the woods. She caught a shiver of movement—a man ducking behind a tree behind them. He was trailing them from a distance. She considered the possibility of doubling back to kill him, but she didn't dare leave the duke unguarded. "The last time you saw the Maid's sword was when you threw it at that man's back, wasn't it? The soldier who was fleeing from you. There was no sword on the scene, which means Genette took it somewhere. Do you think she hid it in the ice cave?"

"Possibly," came the answer. "I have never been able to prove it, for I never returned to the North."

Ankarette nodded. "So you don't believe that Lewis has it. He allows people to believe he does, but it's likely a bluff."

"Indeed. He's quite good at those."

"You were carried off the mountain with the corpses in a wagon. No one bothered to check if you were alive. And no one guards a wagon of corpses. You slipped away the first chance you got."

"You are a crafty lass, Ankarette. So far, you are right."

"And since Genette disguised you as one of the king's soldiers, you had no trouble making it back to the borders. You returned to the cottage as quickly as you could. Had your wife delivered the baby yet?"

He let out a deep, ragged breath. "I was not there when she first went into early labor. Alix stayed by her side. I arrived just before it was over. The babe was stillborn, as you know." His voice softened as he spoke the words. "Jianne was so weak, so heartsick, that she died a month later. Alix pleaded with tears for her to hold on, to come back to us. I was her nurse, her constant companion. She said she had to leave us, to be with the child. She told me she understood why I had left. And then . . . she was gone." His voice was a mere whisper at the end.

The poignant recollection throbbed in Ankarette's heart. She was a midwife herself and knew some of the remedies that could have sustained Alensson's wife. But even the surest remedies wouldn't work if someone was determined to fade.

"You never remarried," Ankarette said, struggling to find her voice.

He looked back at her. "I did."

She gave him a startled look.

"You must understand, Ankarette. It is the privilege of a king to decide whom his nobles will marry. Even though I was penniless. Even though I was scarred by the ordeals of my life, Chatriyon arranged for me to marry the daughter of one of his sycophants. Someone to keep an eye on me. It was not a pleasant memory, and I was not a good husband. To be honest with you, I was quite bitter during those years. But we had no children. And when she died, I was considered too old to sire an heir. I could not stand being in Chatriyon's court." He stumbled on a tree root and caught himself on a trunk. Sweat trickled down his cheeks. His strength was flagging, but they were so close. Ankarette thought she could hear the rushing water of the Sienna River.

"Do you need to rest?" she asked him, coming close and putting her hand on his back.

He shook his head and limped onward. "No. I am sturdy. We're almost there."

"I've heard that Chatriyon's court became rather . . . debauched," Ankarette said knowingly.

"Yes, you could say that. Remember how the Maid's presence inspired a higher degree of morality? After her death, it was as if Chatriyon descended into a bleak frame of thinking. His turn was sudden, though, you have that right. It was not a gradual descent. The peace negotiations with Ceredigion lasted for years. Deford's wife was poisoned and he remarried a pretty young lass. Your queen's mother, as we discussed. They didn't have any children, so the duchy was passed to the Kiskaddon family as a reward. They became loyal to Eredur when he won the throne, so he allowed them to keep it. They call it Westmarch, but in my mind it will always be La Marche. And it will always be mine. Do you think Eredur will . . . ? Well, it's best not to hope."

Ankarette heard more snapping of wood and saw flashes of color from uniforms. The noose was beginning to tighten.

"We're not going to make it, are we?" Alensson asked in a low voice.

Ankarette's skin prickled with unease. "We may have to fight our way to freedom. But I will see you safely to Eredur."

"It's me they're after," Alensson said. "Somehow, they always find me. I've enjoyed getting to know you, Ankarette. You are a wise soul. I've looked forward to meeting you for many years now. Genette saw you in her visions. That should make you feel special, I hope."

"It does indeed," Ankarette said. "But don't despair. I'm not out of tricks yet."

"La Marche!"

The voice rang through the trees behind them.

When they turned, they saw a knight advancing wearing black armor. He had a chest under one arm and a sword in his other hand. As soon as Ankarette saw him, she felt a shuddering sensation—as if a stone boulder were grinding against the ground. It made her dizzy, and her vision went blurry.

"I'm sorry," Alensson whispered to her. "You did your best. But you must survive this fight."

And then he shoved her into the ravine.

CHAPTER THIRTY-FOUR

Secrets of the Grave

Ankarette struck the bottom of the ravine, cushioned by mud and the sluggish, murky waters. She hadn't anticipated Alensson's action and had been mentally preparing to engage the black knight. As she began scrabbling back up the side of the scrub-choked hill, she heard a quick exchange of voices. Her soaked, muddy gown clung to her in ways that hampered her movements.

"You've stolen away for the last time, La Marche," said an angered, vengeful voice. "The king will not pardon your treachery this time. He bids me to kill thee, and I relish the command."

"You might try," said the old duke. "I will not go back to Pree."

"Aye, but you will. In a barrow. It's almost a pity to strike down one so old."

"At least I'm not a slave," Alensson taunted.

As Ankarette pulled herself up on her elbows at the edge of the ridge, tearing her sleeve on a jagged piece of root, the two men struck each other with swords. Both were skilled, but it was clear that the younger man was more fit, stronger, and had the stamina to endure the conflict. She noticed the black knight had set the chest down before making his approach. It struck her that this might be the very chest that the Maid had withdrawn from the waters of Ranz on the day of Chatriyon's coronation. She was keenly interested in seizing it.

The two combatants locked swords, their hilts trapped, and the taller, darker knight pressed his advantage, bending Alensson back. The old duke's face twisted with pain and anger as he tried to resist but could not. Ankarette brought her leg up and around, then used the twisted roots to pull herself the rest of the way.

Alensson let go of the sword and grappled with the knight, trying to wrest him away. The knight pummeled him viciously in the stomach, then brought his elbow around and smacked the duke's face. Alensson whirled like a top and then collapsed on the ground.

Ankarette saw the rest of the hunt closing in, at least a dozen soldiers. She drew a thin knife from the sheath in her boot. But just as she brought her arm back to throw the dagger, the black knight plunged his sword into the old duke's heart.

For a moment, she looked on in disbelief as the blade skewered the old man. There was an almost exultant grin on his face. Then he lay back against the ground, perfectly still, the smile still on his face.

A hot flood of rage filled Ankarette's heart. "You murdered an excellent man," she said in a low, dangerous voice.

The black knight was heavily armored. All she needed was a patch of skin for one of her poisons to destroy him, but he wore gloves, thick boots, and a hauberk under his black tunic. Shoulder guards protected him along with bracers. His most open feature was his face. The man looked to be in his thirties, and he had a swarthy look and a pointed beard.

"I would argue with you about his *excellent* qualities, Poisoner," the knight said snidely. "He was a traitor to his king."

"His king is the traitor," Ankarette said. "But you already know the measure of the Spider King. Spiders are my specialty."

"Oh, I have no doubt, lass. No doubt at all. You defeated Marrat, who was sent to kill him. We still haven't found the body."

"Look in the moat under the privy hole," Ankarette suggested.

The knight smirked. He kept his blade at the ready, preparing to try to deflect her dagger if she sent it at him. He paced in a semicircle, then switched directions. It was harder to kill a moving target.

"Come on lads," the knight shouted to the soldiers. "We have a poisoner to kill."

Ankarette was outnumbered. She eyed the chest. Should she snatch it and try to run? Alensson's chest was struggling up at down as he lay dying. He gave her a subtle nod, the only way he could communicate in such a moment.

Then the black knight rushed her, swishing his sword around him in wide circles. Without armor, she was completely vulnerable. As he rushed, she dived to the side, doing a front roll that closed the distance between her and the chest. She grabbed the handle.

"Get her!" the knight roared.

Ankarette hefted the burden, much heavier than she'd expected it to be, and then started toward the nearest trees. Two soldiers rushed at her. She flung her dagger at the first, catching him in the shoulder. The blade was poisoned, so she knew he'd die in seconds. The older soldier tried to stab her with his sword, but she spun around and swung the chest, clubbing him on the chin with it. The man flew backward from the force of the blow, his eyes rolling in his head.

Having broken free of the ring, Ankarette started to run, every branch snagging at her wet clothes, ripping and tearing and clawing at her skin. Another man came at her from the side, trying to cut her off. She heaved the chest at him, and he instinctively dropped his sword to catch it. Ankarette snatched up his fallen blade, stabbed him with it, and then grabbed the handle of the chest as he fell. There were too many, and the chest was slowing her enormously.

She heard the twang of a crossbow, but before the curse could leave her mouth, the shaft embedded in the chest of one of the men chasing her. It had come from the woods behind her. Whirling, she saw soldiers wearing the tunic of the Sun and Rose, the royal insignia of Ceredigion. Hope bloomed in her chest.

Thirty knights from the king's guard came charging onto the scene, swarming around her and engaging the soldiers of Occitania in a skirmish. Ankarette watched as the black knight scowled and fled, rushing away from the onslaught.

Her breath was hot and loud in her own ears, and her strength was flagging quickly. She hadn't slept in two days and had been in constant peril since entering Occitania. Was it too late to save the duke? She knew the word of power that could bring him back from death . . .

"Ankarette!"

She whirled again and saw the Deconeus of Ely approaching through the woods, wearing a dark cloak to cover his vestments. She recognized his tall stride, his bulk, the hawkish nose and close-cropped hair. A feeling of relief went through her. He was someone she trusted, someone who had been her mentor and friend, and now she also knew him as the young boy who had smuggled the scabbard to Genette on the eve of her execution.

"Where is the duke?" Tunmore asked fervently. "Is he dead?"

"He's over there," Ankarette said, pointing. "Come with me."

Together they rushed through the crowded glen as the soldiers of her king chased after the Occitanian defenders. They reached the spot where the duke lay, blood staining his shirt. His eyes were glazed over and vacant, but still—he smiled. Ankarette felt his neck and there was no thrum of a heartbeat. Her shoulders sagged in despair and sorrow.

Tunmore knelt down next to the body, his own face grim and sorrowful. He laid a hand on the duke's shoulder, his brow crinkling.

"You knew him, didn't you?" Ankarette's voice was just a whisper. "He told me that he always regretted not thanking you."

Tunmore stiffened with surprise, looking uncharacteristically moved by the sentiment. "I met him when I was a lad." Then he looked up at Ankarette, his eyes full of emotion. "I didn't know who he was at first. But then I learned what she called him. He was her Gentle Duke." He frowned, his lips pursing with deep emotion.

Ankarette stared at him. "I never knew until he told me the

Maid's story."

"He told you? I don't doubt it." He paused, staring into her eyes, then said, "What I've always wanted to know is how she really died. Up there on that mountain. It rocked my faith when I was a child. But I am a man now. I think I am ready to hear the story. If you'll tell it to me, Ankarette."

She nodded slowly and then let out a deep sigh, gazing down at the waxy skin of the man whose story had so moved her. She touched his stiff arm and stroked it. But she would let Alensson tell his own tale. He had taught her the word of power—*nesh-ama*. She began summoning her Fountain magic, preparing to invoke the word.

The rippling shudder of the magic began to quicken inside her. She bowed her head, drawing it into herself, filling her soul like a cup from a spring. Tunmore could sense her using the magic. A jolt seemed to run through him.

"What are you doing?" he asked.

"I can bring him back," she answered, not opening her eyes.

"Wait," he said, putting a hand on her shoulder.

She opened her eyes and gazed up at Tunmore.

They were alone in the glen. The soldiers had ridden off to chase the black knight and his men. The deconeus gave her a solemn stare. "She told me not to."

"What?" Ankarette asked, confused.

He glanced around once again, making sure they were truly alone. "The night I went to her cell, she told me things about my life, my future. She said that I had a role to play. She was the one who told me to wait for you both here with soldiers to help drive our enemies away. She also told me that you would try to revive the duke. That you had the power to do so." He shook his head. "He's gone to the Deep Fathoms.

273

And she is waiting to take him there to join his wife and child. You cannot use the words of power against the Fountain's will, Ankarette. If you do, the magic will destroy you."

She caught her breath, staring down once again at Alensson's face. He looked so tranquil. Only the shell of the man had been left behind. In the quietude of the grove, she felt the gentle murmur of the Fountain around her, adding conviction to the deconeus's words. Yes, Alensson was ready for death. He had long considered his life a form of bondage. And now he was finally free.

A sliver of sunlight momentarily blinded her, and in that flash, she thought she saw a man and a woman walking away from the grove, hand in hand. There was a child as well, a little girl with dark curls, tugging at his other hand. Ankarette's throat swelled with emotion. She'd learned so much in the last few days. She'd learned a secret that she would take to her grave. It was a secret about a young woman from Donremy and her trust in a paupered lord. It was a story of betrayal. It was a story of conviction. It was a story of duty. And it melted her heart.

"Farewell, Gentle Duke," she whispered.

CHAPTER THIRTY-FIVE

The Shameful Treaty

The royal pavilion of Ceredigion was spacious and full of all the comforts of court. There were padded camp chairs, silken curtains, multiple changing screens, and a carpet that was long enough, unrolled, to fill the entire interior. Ankarette was concealed behind one of those changing screens. It had been two days since her return to Eredur's camp with the Deconeus of Ely. She had finally been able to rest, tend to her small injuries, and relate much of the sad tale of the Gentle Duke's life to the king. But there was a good deal she kept to herself.

Eredur was growing heavier than he had been during his prime. The rich meals and endless carousing were taking a toll on his health. Ankarette occasionally concocted potions that alleviated some of his symptoms, but no drug or tonic could counteract the effects of his poor choices.

The deconeus was also inside the tent, holding an unlit thurible by the chain in his hands. The metal orb swung from side to side as he watched the scene unfolding before him. Standing by the deconeus was the king's brother Dunsdworth, looking unusually satisfied with himself. There were others as well—Eredur's chancellor, Lord Hastings; as well as Lord Horwath of Dundrennan; Lord Rivers, the king's brother-in-law; and Lord Bryant, the king's stepson. But the argument unfolding in the pavilion was between the king and his youngest brother, Severn.

"I cannot believe you are heeding such reckless counsel, Brother!" the younger man spat out with a defiant and angry tone. "We came here to humble the Spider King. It is you who will be humbled."

Dunsdworth was always quick to stoke the flames of resentment with a barbed comment. "We are going to bleed dry Lewis's treasury, little Sev. That is hardly being humbled by him."

"If I wanted more of your ill-informed opinions," Severn whipped back, "I would have sought you out at an alehouse. You're more coherent when you're drunk."

There was a subtle ripple of Fountain magic as the insult was slung at Dunsdworth. Ankarette peered through the tiny gap of the changing screen, glancing from one person to the next. Who had caused the magic to react like that? The sensation ebbed like a retreating echo.

"Your words are as sharp as your daggers," Dunsdworth complained. "We're on the same side, lad!"

"Are we?" Severn challenged, turning his gaze back to the king. "If I heard Hastings correctly, you intend to offer a truce to the Spider King. Is that how we handle spiders, my lord? I thought we crushed them under our boots. Do you think Lewis will hold true to his oaths? He may promise you treasures from the Deep Fathoms, but you won't be able to reap your reward until you are *in* the Deep Fathoms. After all, the man intends to murder you on that bridge."

"Does that surprise you? What you are proposing," Hastings said with a testy voice, "is a protracted conflict in enemy territory and a small chance of success. Brugia has stranded us here with only Brythonica as an ally." He snorted with laughter. "And what can they *really* do but grow berries?"

Despite the fact that his opinion defied the consensus, Severn stood his ground. Ankarette did not like his acerbic wit and sarcasm, but she respected his personal courage. She knew Eredur treasured his advice more than all the others because it was always derived from logic and spoken in earnest. The two brothers were as different as the noonday sky and midnight, but their loyalty to each other had been tested and found to be true.

"No, Brythonica is not a help," Severn said dismissively. "We cannot count on them for strong support. Yes, it would have been *easier* to defeat Occitania with Brugia on our side. But we can still do this, Brother! It is not too late to call off the truce." He stepped forward, jerking his dagger loose in its scabbard and then slamming it down. His passionate and angry gaze did not waver from his brother's. "They have assembled on the bridge in that bizarre contraption of fences and gates because they *fear* you. They fear you as they feared defeat after Azinkeep. This is your chance to win back the crown of Occitania. Lewis is no soldier, and neither was his father. If you promise to marry Elyse to his son Chatriyon, if you end this conflict peacefully, you will be giving him an excuse to rise up against you later. It is cowardly, Brother. I thought it beneath you."

There were stifled gasps of outrage. Ankarette tilted her head to catch the king's expression. Severn's words had visibly struck him; there was molten anger in his eyes. Anyone would have been humiliated to receive such a public rebuke from a younger brother, and Eredur was a proud man.

"How dare you!" Hastings seethed. "You have gone too far, my lord duke of Glosstyr! The king will not—"

"Shut it, Will," the king said angrily, rising from his stuffed chair. A tall man, he towered over his brothers and everyone else in the room, except for Tunmore. "If anyone needs a rebuke, it's the rest of you. You all encouraged this peace because of the wealth it will bring you individually. The difference it will make to not just the royal coffers, but your own. At least Severn has the courage to speak the truth. Even if I don't care to *hear* it," he added with a surly tone.

The king scratched behind his ear, where Ankarette saw tufts of gray creeping through his dark hair like vines. He paced a moment, his lips pursed, his expression grim. "You have always been loyal to me, Brother. More loyal than some," he added with a glare at Dunsdworth. He was referring to a previous treachery that Ankarette had helped resolve.

"Loyalty binds me," Severn said firmly, his hand gripping the dagger hilt.

The king sauntered over to a small round wooden table held up by three rounded iron stays. Atop the table sat a chest with a curved handle. The king gazed down at the chest and grazed the top of it with his fingers. He glanced over at Tunmore, who stood imperiously to the side of the gathering, thurible chain still in hand, wisely saying nothing.

Eredur turned to face Severn. "While I value your counsel,

Brother, and I truly do, sometimes a king must make decisions that will be misinterpreted or even misjudged." He looked at his younger brother with intense eyes. "I *could* defeat the Spider King. The risks are great, but I have faced far worse! And with you at my side, Brothers, he would have no hope of defeating the might of Ceredigion. I have no doubt we'd be victorious. But at what cost? At what cost?" he added in an almost whisper. Then he shook his head. "Send word to my herald that we'll meet Lewis on the bridge. Announce us."

There was an audible gasp of delight and rapture from most of the other lords, including Dunsdworth, who cast a mocking glance at Severn. The Duke of Glosstyr stood there in his black garb, the badge of the white boar almost gleaming on his tunic. He stared at Eredur with smoldering anger, fists clenched.

"I'll not be joining you," Severn said angrily.

"So be it," Eredur said. "Do you want your portion of the reward?"

Severn shook his head. "I'll take none of the Spider King's treasure. You take my share, Brother. Spend it as you will." Then he whirled around and stormed out of the tent.

Eredur slowly shook his head in disappointment as he stared at the fluttering curtain of the tent.

"The man was weaned on spoiled milk, I daresay," said Lord Rivers. "I'll take his share if he doesn't want it."

"Don't you *dare* speak of my lady mother in such a way!" the king snapped, freezing everyone with his sudden anger. Then the king smiled, breaking the tension. "Only I can." A round of laughter graced his statement. Eredur knew how to charm when he wished to—there was no denying it. Only Duke Horwath didn't participate. He was as stern and solemn as ever.

Dunsdworth came up and clapped Eredur on the back. "Shall we go, Brother? I can't wait to see Lewis again."

"Go on, my lords," Eredur said. "I require a moment with the deconeus."

"Another confession?" Hastings said with a laugh. "Have you sinned so soon, my lord, that you seek the Fountain's blessing?"

Eredur narrowed his gaze at the other man, but said nothing. The lords quickly departed the spacious tent, some grabbing wafers and food from the half-eaten trays. Once their laughter and joviality started to fade into the distance, the king summoned Ankarette.

She stepped around the changing screen upon hearing her name.

The king was still staring at the chest. He rested his hand on it once more. The look he gave her was enigmatic. "Thank you, my dear," he said genuinely. "Your service may have gone unnoticed by everyone except the deconeus and myself, but it is no less valuable to me. You have brought me a gift that is worth more than the ransom King Lewis is attempting to bribe me with. This gift," he added, patting the chest. "Is worth more than a crown, though it cannot be used by any but the heirs to one. Do you know what it is?"

Ankarette shook her head. "I've not seen inside, my lord."

He nodded sagely. "It is unlike any treasure you've seen. It is a blessing from the Fountain to Ceredigion. It speaks of hope and peace." Tears suddenly moistened his eyes. "It whispers that King Andrew may yet return. From my seed." He shook his head in wonderment. "When I sent you to Pree to seek the Maid's sword, I didn't think that what you'd find instead would be even more important. We still don't know where her sword is. But I have a feeling the Fountain will reveal it in its own due time. And so we will wait." He looked at her with an expression that was almost imploring, as if he wanted her to understand something he wasn't permitted to reveal. "I am not surrendering my honor by agreeing to this truce," he said. "Believe that, Ankarette Tryneowy. Regardless of what my brother has said or what the world thinks. When this scene on the bridge is over, I want you to return to Kingfountain at once and explain to my wife what happened. Tell her the story you told me." He smirked. "She'll be pleased to hear it, I think."

"I will, my lord," Ankarette said with a small bow.

He gave her a kindly smile, one that showed the depths of his appreciation for her rare and useful talents. "It's time to begin the negotiations, per your strategy, Ankarette. Are you sure it is safe to go to the bridge?"

Ankarette smiled knowingly and said nothing.

♦　　♦　　♦

Everyone in the camps on both sides of the river had their eyes fixed on the ruler of Kingfountain as he approached Montreux Bridge on foot with the nobles of his realm, all save his youngest brother, who was brooding in his tent. The small group was trailed by the Deconeus of Ely, who gently swung a smoking thurible, invoking the power and blessing of the Fountain on the proceedings.

Ankarette, her braided hair concealed in a cowl, waited amidst the soldiers near the shore of the river. As the soldiers shuffled forward to get a better view, Ankarette and the six heavily armed Espion with her mingled in their midst. The soldiers were the king's guardsmen, but they were wearing the arrayment of common soldiers. A phalanx of pikemen formed a wall by the bridge, holding the crowd back.

The poisoner was close enough to hear the sound of boots as they tromped across the wooden slats of the bridge, held in place by stone girders. The bridge was not massive, probably only ten yards across, and—just as Alensson had forewarned her—two huge timber cages had been formed at either side to provide a physical barrier between the opponents. It was just as Alensson had forewarned. The illusion of safety.

The king wore his royal regalia and the hollow crown, and there was a sword belted to his girth. Beneath his robe, he wore his hauberk. Despite his age and a few bouts of ill health, he was still a formidable swordsman. The other lords looked oblivious to the danger they were facing, and Ankarette noticed the prideful smile on Dunsdworth's face as he innocently walked toward what would have been his doom.

The deconeus came in behind them, swinging the thurible more gently, and then stood at the end of the gate as it was closed behind them.

There were voices up on the bridge, and Ankarette wished she were close enough to hear them. But she knew Tunmore would give her a full account later. With a gesture from one of the Espion, the phalanx of soldiers parted slightly, letting Ankarette and her men pass. Everyone's attention was on the nobles assembled on the bridge, the King of Ceredigion and the King of Occitania meeting at last to arrange peace between their fractious lands.

The soldiers pivoted slightly, blocking the view as Ankarette and the Espion passed close to the edge of the river and started down the small embankment. She made a gesture and each of the Espion put a rag against his nose and mouth. She did the same.

They slipped beneath the bridge and moved amidst the reeds of the river. The Espion were equipped with long boots to endure the mud. One of them paused, examining the ground, then looked at her and nodded. Yes, he'd found boot prints in the mud revealing the trap laid for Eredur. A trap that was about to backfire.

The sound of muffled coughing came from the concealed wooden door at the base of the bridge. The men who had come to assassinate Eredur and his nobles were inside the hidden compartment. But Tunmore was standing on the trapdoor. And the poison from his thurible was sinking down into the hidden compartment with the incense smoke.

Ankarette motioned for the Espion to get ready.

The secret door shuddered open and men spilled out, their faces chalky and gray as they clawed at their throats, unable to breathe. Some fell face-first into the mud, twitching violently.

Another man came out, garbed all in black. Ankarette recognized him, looked into his panicked eyes as he struggled to breathe through his constricted throat. This was the black knight who had killed Alensson.

He staggered to his knees in the mud, gazing piteously up at the queen's poisoner. She gave him a knowing smile and watched him die.

CHAPTER THIRTY-SIX

The Heir of La Marche

Ankarette longed to be back in the poisoner's tower at King-fountain palace. It was atop a winding stairwell in the highest spire. After hearing the story of the Maid of Donremy, she wanted to stitch a replica of the Maid's banner, and while her deft fingers worked at needle and thread, she would ponder Alensson's story and glean from it lessons that would help teach her wisdom. But before she could enjoy that peace, she had to report back to her queen.

The Queen of Ceredigion was a beautiful woman with a past so rich and secretive that few truly knew it. She was an adept practitioner of politics and had long learned that the hand that rocks the cradle rules the world. As Ankarette walked down the secret Espion tunnels hidden within the bowels of the palace, she thought of how time and chance made kings and queens of the most unlikely of people. The queen was the daughter of the Duke of Deford's second wife. Some whispered that the queen was Fountain-blessed and had somehow used magic to seduce the king into loving her. It wasn't true, of course. But not all power belonged to those who were Fountain-blessed.

The queen had given her husband a brood of handsome children. She would be pleased to learn that their eldest child, the girl Elyse, was now destined to be a queen herself—the Queen of Occitania. The treaty with Lewis would make Eredur and his queen perhaps the wealthiest monarchs in all the kingdoms. And yes, Ankarette had heard many mutterings about the shameful treaty and how it had blighted Eredur's honor. But at least she knew the truth behind Eredur's choice.

At the end of the corridor, the ceiling and walls pinched together into a dead-end, marking the secret entrance to the royal couple's private bedchamber. She inspected the secret portal to make sure the queen was alone before she tapped on it and then triggered the release to open it.

"Ankarette!" the queen said with a delighted smile. She rose from her desk, where she had been answering correspondence. The two women embraced and the queen kissed her cheek. "Looks like you fought a rosebush, dearest," the queen said. "I was worried about you."

"You needn't worry," Ankarette said. "I am quite resourceful."

"You are indeed," the queen said, then took her by the arm and brought her to a wide bench where they could both sit. "I can tell you have news. I am eager to hear it! But you must tell me first. Did you have to kill the Duke of La Marche? I hope he didn't cause these injuries."

Ankarette shook her head. "No. He was kind and gentle, to be sure. These were incurred trying to help him escape. Unfortunately, he did not."

The queen looked saddened. "I've always pitied him for some reason. Lewis should have executed him much earlier for all the treasons he committed, but he was one of the last nobles who truly believed in the principles of Virtus. He died childless. He had no heir. Did you know that?"

"I did, my lady," Ankarette said. "You will be pleased to learn," she said, holding back a smile, "before the herald arrives, that a treaty of peace was signed by your husband and King Lewis yesterday. There will not be a war."

"Thank the Fountain!" the queen gushed in relief. "I'm sure Eredur is disappointed. He always loves a good duel to prove how strong he is. But to be honest, he is getting older. Our sons are so young; they need their father."

"I agree, my lady." Ankarette mentioned Severn's reservations and recounted his admonition and warning.

The queen's countenance darkened. "I fear that man," she whispered. After a moment, her eyes brightened and she said, "Tell me about the duke. I'd like to hear his story."

"I don't want to bore you with the details."

"You couldn't find a more willing listener, Ankarette. Please, tell me all." She clasped Ankarette's hands and looked into her eyes. They were dear friends and had been for many years. Ankarette did not like to deny the queen, and she would have heeded her even if duty hadn't demanded it. The solitude of the tower would have to be postponed.

And so Ankarette told her of her mission, but as she had done with Eredur, she held back some of the private details of Alensson's life. It was as if she sensed the Fountain *wanted* her to keep them secret.

When she finally finished, Ankarette patted her hand. "Well, my lady. I am weary from the journey. I will leave you to your letters."

"Yes, you may rest, but only for a little while," the queen said, rising from the bench. "Speaking of letters, one came recently from the Duchess of Westmarch. Her pregnancy isn't going very well."

"I didn't know she was pregnant again," Ankarette said.

"She is," the queen answered, returning to the table and searching for a letter amidst the heap. "Ah, here it is. Poor dear. She's had several stillborn children already."

The word struck Ankarette like a lightning bolt. She felt the Fountain's magic start to stir inside her, coming unbidden. Her pulse raced unnaturally with a sort of giddiness.

"Yes, m-my lady?" Ankarette stammered, suddenly distraught.

"The babe is due this month. I'd like you to go to Tatton Hall, Ankarette. You are one of the best midwives in Ceredigion."

"If you think so," the poisoner said demurely.

"You are too modest. I would like you to go offer some comfort to the duchess. It may be another boy, after all, though they have two already. Their oldest will make a fine heir, but you can never guess at the future. I think it would ease her mind greatly if you were there to help in the birthing. Whatever is wrong, Ankarette? You look a little pale suddenly."

"I'm just tired, my lady," the queen's poisoner said softly, thinking about the Maid's prophecy.

The heir of La Marche would soon be born.

And Ankarette needed to be there.

AUTHOR'S NOTE

While I was in college studying medieval history, I read about the trial of Joan of Arc. That began my fascination with this episode of history. I later read a biography about her while writing The Blight of Muirwood, and was inspired by one of the characters in her story to create the Earl of Dieyre. I've since read Helen Castor's excellent biography on Joan and watched her documentary about her as well as another excellent film done by BYUtv.

As I created the world of Kingfountain and wrote about its many Fountain-blessed individuals, I referenced the Maid of Donremy many times. This book is loosely based on the actual events of Joan of Arc's life, some of which were so amazing and curious that it felt like reading fiction. She did jump out of the tower after first being imprisoned and landed in a dry moat. She directed people to uncover a sword in the monastery of Fierbois. But my favorite character is the Gentle Duke, whom I didn't know about until reading Castor's version Gentle Dukeof the events. So while The Maid's War book is a work of fiction, many of the characters and details about the setting actually happened.

It was fun bringing Ankarette back as a character and

tying this story in to The Queen's Poisoner. I've also written this book to bridge the events between the first three books of the Kingfountain Series and the next three books. The story of Joan of Arc continues to inspire me, as it has for other authors and historians for centuries.

She is someone who helps us continue to believe in miracles.

ABOUT THE AUTHOR

Photograph © Mica Sloan

Jeff took an early retirement from his career at Intel in 2014 to write full-time and is now a Wall Street Journal bestselling author. He is, most importantly, a husband and father, a devout member of his church, and is occasionally spotted roaming hills with oak trees and granite boulders in California or in any number of the state's majestic redwood groves. He is also the founder of *Deep Magic: the E-zine of Clean Fantasy and Science Fiction* (www.deepmagic.co)

11032902R00176

Printed in Great Britain
by Amazon